PORTRAIT OF A SISTER

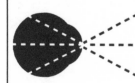

PORTRAIT OF A SISTER

LAURA BRADFORD

THORNDIKE PRESS
A part of Gale, a Cengage Company

Farmington Hills, Mich • San Francisco • New York • Waterville, Maine
Meriden, Conn • Mason, Ohio • Chicago

Copyright © 2018 by Laura Bradford.
Thorndike Press, a part of Gale, a Cengage Company.

ALL RIGHTS RESERVED
This book is a work of fiction. Names, characters, places, and incidents either are products of the author's imagination or are used fictitiously. Any resemblance to actual persons, living or dead, events, or locales is entirely coincidental.
Thorndike Press® Large Print Christian Fiction.
The text of this Large Print edition is unabridged.
Other aspects of the book may vary from the original edition.
Set in 16 pt. Plantin.

LIBRARY OF CONGRESS CIP DATA ON FILE.
CATALOGUING IN PUBLICATION FOR THIS BOOK
IS AVAILABLE FROM THE LIBRARY OF CONGRESS

ISBN-13: 978-1-4328-5302-0 (hardcover)

Published in 2018 by arrangement with Kensington Books, an imprint of Kensington Publishing Corp.

Printed in Mexico
1 2 3 4 5 6 7 22 21 20 19 18

To my readers, both old and new.
I'm glad you're here.

ACKNOWLEDGMENTS

Getting to tell Katie's tale was a true labor of love for me. Her story grew inside my heart until I couldn't ignore it anymore.

When I shared my idea with my agent, Jessica Faust, she, too, wanted to know more about Katie. Her belief in my story and my ability to tell it gave me the added boost I needed. So a huge thank-you goes out to Jessica for that.

I also want to thank my editor, Esi Sogah, who saw Katie's story both in its infancy and at completion and liked what she saw.

Dear Readers,

I've always held a fascination for the Amish and their way of life. Some of that, I suppose, stems from my love of the Laura Ingalls Wilder books when I was young. For grown-up me, the Amish live very much the way the Ingallses lived in the mid to late 1800s, yet they do it in a modern-day world. As a person who is curious by nature, that intrigues me. As a person who happens to be a writer, that same intrigue has a way of leading me in all sorts of different directions.

With each new book I write about the Amish, I spend days researching in the heart of Lancaster County's Amish country, learning everything I can about their lives. Usually, within a few hours, I have the seed I need for my next story. By the time I get back home, I have the makings of a plot fleshed out in my head.

9

Portrait of a Sister came about a little differently. In my Amish Mystery series, I have a police detective who was former Amish. He left after baptism, thereby losing all ties to his childhood family. While that background has given me great material to work with for that particular series, it's also a part of the Amish culture that's really tugged at my heartstrings and given me pause. With *Portrait of a Sister,* I gave myself permission to explore that pre/post-baptism decision through the eyes of twins; Hannah, who chose to leave before baptism, and Katie, who never considered leaving . . . Until now.

For Hannah, the choice was really just about geography and lifestyle.

For Katie, that same choice will mean cutting ties to everyone and everything she's ever known.

Hard to imagine, isn't it?

After you've read *Portrait of a Sister,* take a look at some of the book club questions I've included in the back. Many of them were things I found myself pondering as Katie took me along on her journey.

Happy reading!

Laura

CHAPTER 1

For the second time in her life, Katie Beiler prayed for God to change His mind, to make His will reflect hers. But the click of her parents' bedroom door, followed by her dat's sad eyes and pasty complexion, told her it wasn't to be.

"It is time, Katie."

Gathering the sides of her pale blue dress in her hands, she made herself part company with the wooden chair that had been both her post and her refuge over the past twenty-four hours and rise onto shaky legs. "I will get the children."

"No," he said, firmly.

Her answering gasp echoed against the walls of the hallway as she reached toward him, her fingers brushing against the suspenders she'd mended during the night. "She-she's gone? Already?"

"No, Katie. But God will welcome her soon. It is His will."

"His will is wrong!" she hissed through clenched teeth only to bow her head in shame just as quickly. "I-I'm sorry, Dat. I shouldn't have said that."

Bracing herself, she lifted her watery gaze from the toes of her black lace-up boots to the amber-flecked brown eyes that matched her own. For a moment, Dat said nothing, the shock on his face the only real indication he'd heard her at all. Eventually though, he spoke, grief winning out over anger. "She has asked to speak to you alone. Go now, child, before it is too late."

Before it is too late . . .

Her thoughts followed her father's heavy footfalls down the stairs and then skipped ahead to the five young faces she'd tried desperately to shield from reality the past few months. Two years her junior, Samuel would be devastated, of course, but he would cover his hurt working in the fields with Dat. Jakob, at fourteen, would take his cue from Samuel. Mary and Sadie would —

"Katie?"

The weakened rasp propelled her forward and through the partially open doorway, her heart both dreading and craving what was on the other side. More than anything, she wanted a miracle to happen, but short of that, she'd be a fool to waste away whatever

12

time they had left.

"I'm here, Mamm." She stopped just inside the door and willed her eyes to adjust to the darkened room. "Can I get you something? Another blanket, perhaps? A glass of water?"

"You can open the shade and let the sunlight in."

"Of course." Crossing the room, Katie gave the dark green shade a quick tug and then watched as it rose upward to provide an uninhibited view of the fields her dat and brothers worked each and every day. She allowed herself a moment to breathe in the answering sunlight before turning back to the nearly unrecognizable shell that was her mother. "Is that better?"

"Yah." Her mother patted the edge of the quilt-topped bed, her pale blue eyes studying Katie closely. "Come. Sit. There are things I want to say. Before it is too late."

"Shhh," Katie scolded. "Do not talk like that. Please."

"The dress I am to be buried in is in my chest. It is what I wore when I married your dat."

She stopped a few inches shy of the bed and cast her eyes down at the wood plank floor. "Mamm, please. I —"

"It is God's will, Katie."

13

It was on the tip of her tongue to lash out at those words the way she had in the hallway with Dat, but she refrained. To see the same shock on Mamm's face would be unimaginable.

"Katie, I need you to be strong for your brothers and sisters. They will need, you more than ever in the days and weeks ahead."

Sinking onto the bed, Katie covered her mother's cold hand with her own and gave it a gentle squeeze. She tried to speak, to offer the reassurance her mother needed, but the expanding lump in her throat made it impossible to speak.

"In another year or so, Annie will be three and Mary will be old enough to look after both her and Sadie on her own. When she is, you are to live your life, Katie. With Abram. He is a good man. Like your dat. It is my hope that your life together will make you smile again."

"I smile," Katie protested.

"Not as you once did."

She felt her mother's thumb encircling her hand and choked back a sob. "I have tried my best to keep this from the little ones. If I have failed, I am sorry . . . ."

"You have done beautifully these past few months, Katie. Dat has told me so. But your

14

smile dulled long before I got sick."

Slipping her arm back, Katie pushed off the bed and wandered over to the window. "I painted a new milk can last night while you slept. It is of the pond in summer, the way it was before the climbing tree fell down in that storm a few years ago." She rested her forehead against the glass pane and watched as her dat entered the fields to summon Samuel and Jakob for one final goodbye. "I will always remember the way you'd help boost me onto that first branch when I was no bigger than Sadie is now. I was so frightened that first time."

"That is because I boosted *you* first. When *Hannah* went first and reached down for your hand, you were not afraid."

Just like that, the tears she'd managed to keep to herself in her mother's presence began their descent down her cheeks. "I do not want you to go, Mamm. I-I need you . . ."

"You need only the Lord, Katie, you know that."

She bowed her head in shame. "You are right, Mamm. I know I should not be afraid."

But I am, she wanted to add. Horribly, desperately afraid . . .

"Do not forget what the apostle Paul said,

15

Katie. To fulfill the law of Christ, brethren must bear one another's burdens. There will be many hands ready to help you, Dat, and the children."

The children . . .

She lifted her gaze to the window again in time to see Dat heading back toward the house flanked by Samuel on one side and Jakob on the other. Their brimmed hats made it so she couldn't see her brothers' faces, but her mind could fill in the blanks.

Samuel would be stoic like their father — any emotion offset by his steadfast belief that Mamm's passing was God's will. He would mourn her, of course, but there would be work to be done.

Jakob would surely mimic Samuel, but she knew that in moments alone, while feeding the calves or milking the cows, the younger boy would grieve the woman he still looked to for hugs when he thought no one else was looking.

"I will hug Jakob for you," Katie whispered. "Until he does not need it anymore."

"Thank you, Katie."

She heard the faint sound of the screen door downstairs as it banged closed behind her father and brothers. If Dat had told Mary first, the thirteen-year-old would no doubt have Sadie and the baby ready and

16

waiting for the family's final moments together. If he hadn't, Katie could imagine her sister looking up from the chair in which she was giving Annie her morning bottle, wondering if she was late in preparing a meal. The absence of footsteps on the stairs told her it was the latter.

A noticeable change in her mother's breath made her turn and scurry back to the bed. "Mamm?"

"It is almost time, Katie."

She looked down at her mother, at the gaunt face and the dark shadows that encircled hesitant eyes. "Do not worry, Mamm. *Please.* I will take care of them all — Samuel, Jakob, Mary, Sadie, Annie, and Dat. I promise."

"That is not all that I worry about."

Swooping down to her knees, she gathered her mother's cold hands inside her own and tried to warm them with her breath. "There is nothing for you to worry about, Mamm."

"There is you, Katie."

She drew back. "Me?"

"Yah."

"But —"

"I want you to be . . . happy . . . again. The way you were when —"

A succession of footsteps on the staircase cut her mother's sentence short and brought

Katie back to her feet. She'd had her time with Mamm. To take more would be selfish. "The others are coming to say goodbye." Bending over, she held her lips to her mother's forehead while she worked to steady her own voice. "I love you, Mamm."

"I love you, Katie."

The footsteps on the other side of the door grew louder as they crested the top of the stairs and headed in their direction. Suddenly, it was as if she were being hoisted into that old climbing tree all over again. And just as she'd been when she was four, she was terrified — terrified at the notion of leaving her mother's arms behind.

"They're here, Mamm," she whispered. "I'll let them in."

Her mother's answering nod was slow and labored, but the sudden grip on Katie's arm was anything but. "Tell her, Katie. Tell . . . Hannah . . . I . . . love . . . her."

CHAPTER 2

She didn't need the sound of Sadie's bare feet running across the wooden floor, or Mary's audible inhale from somewhere over her left shoulder, to know Hannah had arrived. No, she could feel it just as surely as she could the fizz of the soapsuds on her hands.

Dropping the dish back into the sink, Katie backed away from the counter and slowly turned. Before she could blink, Hannah was across the room, pulling her in for a hug so tight she wasn't sure she'd ever breathe again.

"Oh, Katie, I-I can't believe this — I can't believe Mamm is . . . *gone.* I thought she was going to beat this. I really, really did."

Keenly aware of the two extra sets of ears in the room, Katie merely shook her head, her cheek brushing briefly against Hannah's tear-soaked counterpart.

"Was it . . ." Hannah's words traded

places with a hard swallow before returning cloaked in a tortured whisper. "Was it *awful,* Katie?"

"When it was time, Mamm just closed her eyes." It wasn't necessarily an all-inclusive portrayal, but it was close enough. Still, Katie sent up a silent prayer for forgiveness and then slowly stepped back, deliberately disengaging herself from the grief she was desperate to hold at bay. "Let me take a look at —"

The sentence fell away as she stared into the face that was both identical to and nothing like the one she glimpsed in the reflection of her bedroom window each morning. Yes, the shape of the eyes was still the same, as were the amber flecks that lightened their brown hue, but the lashes that bordered them were suddenly longer, thicker, and infinitely darker.

"Hannah," she said, dropping her voice to a near whisper so as not to be overheard by the younger girls. "You-you're wearing makeup."

"Just a little mascara is all. And some blush." Hannah touched her fingertips to her cheeks as a small, shaky smile momentarily chased the sadness from her pale pink lips. "It took a little getting used to, but I like it. It makes me feel . . . *improper.*"

"Hannah!"

"What? It does."

Unsure of what to say or even what to think, Katie followed her younger siblings' uncertain glances right back to Hannah and the dress she hadn't really noticed until that moment — a dress that followed the curves of her twin sister's body like a second pair of skin. She wanted to look away, to put the image into the same invisible box where she put all the English ways she didn't understand, but she couldn't. Not this time, anyway.

Hannah looked . . . *pretty.* In a grown-up, sophisticated sort of way. Like those faces that smiled out at Katie from the checkout aisle of the English grocery store. Only this time, instead of trying to imagine what she, herself, might look like if she wore those kinds of clothes or let her own soft brown hair flow across her shoulders in pretty waves, she knew.

"Katie?"

The sound of her name on her little sister's tongue pulled her from her fog and forced her back to the only world that mattered at that moment. "Yes, Mary?"

"I have gathered two buckets of potatoes. Do you think that will be enough?"

"I think that will be fine, Mary." Katie did

a quick mental count of the people she knew would come to Mamm's funeral while simultaneously trying to figure out the food they'd need to feed them. It was a daunting task on one hand, yet, at the same time, she welcomed the opportunity to focus on something other than the pain in her heart. "Would you and Sadie run next door to the Hochstetler's farm and check on the number of bread loaves Martha is making?"

"Yes, Katie."

Hannah crossed the kitchen, reaching for Sadie's small hand as she did. "Would you like me to go with you?"

Sadie's eyes, round and uncertain, moved between Mary and Hannah, with Mary finally breaking the silence via a slight shake of her kapp-covered head. "No. Thank you. We are fine."

Katie could feel Hannah's disappointment but, at the same time, she was glad for Mary's response. It would give her time alone with Hannah. "Now run along. It won't be long before Mamm's body is here and the buggies start arriving."

Mary's and Sadie's chins both dipped downward at Katie's words, but they remained stoic as they headed down the hallway. When the door banged closed in their wake, Hannah turned back to Katie and released an audible sigh. "It's like I'm a stranger to them," Hannah mumbled as she wiped a fresh set of tears from her cheeks. "Like they've forgotten I'm their sister."

Katie returned her focus to the sink and the dish that still needed to be rinsed and dried. "I don't think they've forgotten. It's just that you're so different now."

"*I'm* different?" Hannah echoed. "Look at *you.*"

"Me? I have not changed. I am still the same Katie I have always been." She gestured at her aproned dress. "I wear the same dresses, I do the same chores."

"Plus now you will do Mamm's, too."

Katie scrubbed at an invisible spot on the dish, the pity in her sister's voice heavy. "Only for a while."

"Oh?"

"Yah," she said over the answering squeak of the dish. "It won't be long before Annie is no longer a baby. When she isn't, Mary will take over."

"Then what?" Hannah prodded.

"Then I will be free to live my own life."

"Live your own life?" Hannah reached around Katie's shoulder and plucked the dish from her hand. "Would you please stop that? You're going to scrub a hole right through that plate if you don't."

She stared at her soapy hands and then shoved them into the water. "Yes. Live my own life. With Abram."

"Abram *Zook*?"

"Yah." Katie waited for Hannah to finish with the dishcloth and then stole it back to dry her hands. "We are to be married. When things have settled down for Dat and the children."

"Why didn't you tell me this in your last letter?" Hannah asked, her voice a veritable potpourri of accusation and hurt.

"I was . . . busy. Worried about Mamm."

Hannah grew silent, her eyes searching Katie with an unsettling intensity. Katie, in turn, focused on the part of the balled-up dishcloth she could see between her whitened knuckles.

"Are you really sure this is what you want?" Hannah hooked her index finger beneath Katie's chin and guided it back to start. "To marry Abram Zook?"

Inhaling deeply, Katie met and held her sister's gaze, the taste of the lie bitter on her tongue. "Yah."

Katie took one last look at the line of buggies stretched down the left side of the driveway and then slowly lowered the dark green shade to the windowsill. She'd been

24

so busy greeting mourners all afternoon and evening, she'd been able to ignore away the heaviness pressing down on her chest. But now, in her room, with Dat's orders for rest, it was crushing.

"Dat doesn't know what to make of me anymore, does he?"

"Dat has much to think about today." Katie filled her lungs with the breath she hadn't realized she was holding and then dropped onto her neatly made bed as it whooshed its way past her lips. "It has been a difficult day."

Wandering over to the waist-high dresser in the corner of the room, Hannah ran her fingertips around the edge of the porcelain bowl and pitcher it housed. "Do you think she thought about me?"

Katie looked up from the boot she'd just unlaced and studied her sister. All her life she'd seen English girls — their clothes, their shoes, their hair so different than her own. It was the way it was for them just as aproned dresses, white kapps, and lace-up boots were for her and her sisters. Did she wonder about their life on occasion? Sure. But it was as fleeting as the glimpse itself.

Hannah's choice had changed that.

"Did who think of you?" she finally asked, forcing her gaze off Hannah's strappy heeled shoes and back to her own scuffed boots.

"Mamm."

Katie snapped her head up at her sister's sudden and strangled sob. "Mamm?"

Tipping her own head back, Hannah stared up at the ceiling until her breath was steady enough to speak. "Before she passed . . ."

"Yah." Katie slid her feet out of her boots, tucked them under the bed, and then crossed to Hannah's side in her stocking-clad feet. "Mamm spoke of you."

A flash of hope skittered across Hannah's brown eyes before it disappeared behind thick lashes. "Don't tell me that if it's not true."

Katie drew back. "I do not lie. You know that."

"But you protect." Slowly, Hannah opened her eyes to meet Katie's. "You always have. Look at the way you care for Mary and Sadie and baby Annie. It is as if they are your own."

"That is what family does."

"Yes, but you have to protect yourself, too, Katie."

"Dat will look after us like he always has," she protested. "And when the time is right, Abram will look after me and the children

26

that *we* will have."

It was Hannah's turn to give the once over, only this time, as Katie watched her sister's gaze travel from her kapp to her stockings, she was aware of a wariness building inside her chest. All their life, they'd been able to communicate with one another without words; for the first time, she wished it wasn't so.

Words she could shush.

The look in Hannah's eyes, she couldn't.

"I'm talking about your heart and the things that matter to you," Hannah finally said. "Keeping them hidden under your mattress for fear of being shunned isn't right."

She stumbled backward into the table, rattling the wash basin in the process. "You-you looked under my mattress?" Katie stammered.

"You say that like this is something I've just discovered." Hannah coaxed Katie's hands from her cheeks and gently guided her back toward the bed. "Katie, I've known about your drawings for a long time. I just kept waiting for you to tell me about them on your own. Only you never did."

She let Hannah pat her onto the bed but the roar in her ears made it difficult to be sure of much else.

27

"You were always good at painting scenes on milk cans for Dat's stand in the fall, but the pencil sketches in your sketch pad are . . . wow. You're really good, Katie. I mean, really, *really* good. You should do something with that."

"*Do* something?" she repeated.

"Yes. With your talent. It's too good to hide away under a mattress."

She tried to clear the shame from her throat, but it refused to budge. "It is wrong, what I draw. You know that."

"*Wrong?*" The click of Hannah's heels looped around the bottom edge of the bed only to stop in line with Katie's pillow. With a knowing look in Katie's direction, she lifted the corner of the mattress, slid her hand into the space underneath it, and pulled out the sketch pad Katie had secretly purchased at an art store while on Rumspringa. Flipping the cover back, she turned the pad into Katie's sightline and gave it a gentle shake. "How is drawing a picture of Mary with her favorite barn cats *wrong?*"

Katie pitched her upper body to the side and tried to grab the pad from Hannah's hand, but Hannah pulled it just out of her reach. "Hannah, please. You know why it is wrong. 'Thou shalt not make unto thyself a graven image.'"

"It is a *memory,* Katie," Hannah protested. "There is nothing wrong with a memory."

"A memory is for here" — she tapped her temple with the tip of her index finger and then moved it to her chest — "and here."

Hannah lowered herself to the bed, pulling the pad onto her lap as she did. "Trust me, Katie, when you're missing someone as much as I miss you, a picture is a godsend."

"You miss me?" Katie echoed.

"Every day."

"You could come back! It is not too late to be baptized!"

"I miss you, Katie. I miss the family. But this isn't the right world for me. Not anymore anyway." Page by page, Hannah made her way through Katie's drawings, some stirring a smile, others a laugh. "I don't know how you did it, but you captured Luke Hochstetler perfectly . . . right down to the frog he was always trying to sneak into the schoolhouse."

"I see it in my head." Katie watched Hannah flip to the next page, the emotion in her sister's ensuing gasp necessitating a fresh round of blinking. "Is-is something wrong?"

"This one of Mamm in her bed, is-is this how she looked at the end?" Hannah whispered.

"Yah."

"Her cheeks are drawn, and-and her eyes are dull, but . . ." Hannah's words fell away, her gaze riveted on the sketch pad and the picture of their mother. When she finally spoke again, it was with a mixture of surprise and awe. "She looks almost *happy.*"

"She was speaking of you."

Hannah's eyes flew to Katie's. "Me?"

"Yah."

Slowly, Hannah lowered the pad to her lap, the tremble of her hands a perfect match to the one infusing its way through her voice. "What did she say?"

"She said she loved you." Just like that, the tears Katie had managed to keep at bay made their way down Hannah's cheeks, streaking it in —

"Hannah? What is wrong with your face?"

"My *face?*" Hannah repeated.

"Yah. It is turning black with your tears."

Tears turned to laughter as Hannah wiped at her cheeks. "It's just my mascara, Katie. Next time, I will remember to buy the waterproof kind." Sliding the sketch pad off her lap, Hannah stood, made her way over to the wall hooks on the opposite side of the room, and retrieved the small purse she'd arrived with earlier that morning. With a flick of her wrist, she opened the bag,

30

fished out a small round mirror, and promptly wiped even harder at her cheeks. "I am glad Travis cannot see me right now. He might not think I'm pretty anymore."

"Who is Travis?"

Hannah took one last look at herself in the mirror and then placed it back inside her purse. "Travis is my boyfriend. He's smart . . . and funny . . . and really, *really* hot."

"Soon it will be cold again, yah?"

"I suppose it —" Hannah's words morphed into a laugh that echoed off the walls of the room they'd once shared. "Oh you silly, silly girl, I don't mean *that* kind of hot. I mean the good-looking kind."

Propelled forward by an all too familiar warmth making its way across her cheeks, Katie narrowed her eyes on her sister. "Don't you do that, Hannah Beiler!"

Hannah jerked her head back as if she'd been slapped. "Do what?"

"Talk to me the way the English kids always did when they drove by in their cars!" Katie reached up and under the edge of her kapp, giving it a tug as she did. "You wore one of these, too, Hannah!"

Understanding traded places with shock before Hannah's hand returned to her purse for the thin brown object she promptly carried over to the bed. "I'm sorry, Katie. I didn't mean to hurt your feelings. Here. This is Travis. So you can see."

Katie took the small book from Hannah's outstretched hand and gazed down at the photograph housed beneath a clear plastic covering. Seconds turned to minutes as she studied everything about the man now looking back at her — the green eyes that sparkled with a laugh she could see but not hear, the dark blond hair that swooped to the side, the clean-shaven skin along his jawline, the muscled arms extending out from his short-sleeved shirt . . .

"*That* is what I mean by really hot," Hannah said, dropping onto the bed beside Katie.

Katie looked from the picture to Hannah and back again, her mind running in a million different directions. "Is-is he nice?" she finally asked.

"He is. And he is good to me." Hannah flipped the picture over to reveal a second photograph, this one of Travis sitting next to Hannah on a picnic blanket covered in rose petals. "He took me to the park that day as a surprise."

On some level she knew Hannah was still talking, but what, exactly, was being said, Katie wasn't sure. Her focus, her thoughts had shifted to the image of the veritable stranger sitting next to Travis — a stranger who just happened to share Katie's every feature.

"Katie?"

A few hours earlier, she'd been convinced Hannah's differences stopped with the makeup and fancy clothes. But she'd been wrong. They reached into Hannah's very being and —

"Katie? Are you okay? You look upset or something."

She looked down at her sister's fingers atop her forearm and did her best to steady her breathing before she spoke. When she was fairly certain her emotions were in check, she temporarily removed her kapp from her head and the pins from her hair. "It has been a long day. Tomorrow will be even longer. We need to do as Dat said and get our rest."

"I know." Hannah retrieved one of the pins from the top of Katie's bed and turned it over in her hands. "He really is a good man, Katie."

"Of course he is. He is Dat."

"I was talking about Travis."

Katie felt the prick of unshed tears gathering in the corners of her eyes and rushed to blink them away. It was one thing to mourn

Mamm. It was another thing to mourn someone who was alive and well and staring back at her, waiting. "Perhaps, one day, I will get to meet your Travis."

"He'll be here tomorrow. For Mamm's service."

"He-he's coming? *Here?*" Katie echoed, rising to her feet and making her way around the bed. "To Blue Ball?"

"He's coming here to the *house,* Katie."

To the house . . .

She swallowed hard. "So you told him you were *Amish?*"

"Of course." Hannah reached out, snatched the sketch pad from the top of the bed, and gave it a little shake. "*You're* the one hiding who you are, Katie, not me."

Chapter 3

All afternoon she'd watched them together, their respectful yet distinctly English attire standing out in the sea of kapped and hatted mourners finally making their way toward the road and the seemingly endless line of buggies. It had been a difficult day. The kind of day Katie was in no hurry to revisit again.

Pressure against her upper calf broke through her thoughts, stealing her attention away from Hannah and placing it, instead, on the pint-sized little girl at her feet — a little girl who would soon have no memory of their mamm's smile. Katie's heart ached at that truth as she reached down, lifted Annie into her arms, and buried her face against the toddler's freshly washed hair. "Hello, sweet Annie."

The little girl, in turn, popped her thumb in her mouth, sucked fiercely for a minute, and then let it fall to her chest as she looked at Katie. "Mamm."

Closing her eyes tightly against the sudden yet intense wave of pain that threatened her ability to function, Katie made herself breathe.

It is God's will . . .

It is God's will . . .

More than anything, she wanted to believe those words. But she didn't. Why would God want to take Mamm from them? From her?

"M-m-mamm . . ."

The quiver of uncertainty in Annie's little voice filtered through the pain and forced Katie to open her eyes. She needed to be strong. For Annie. For Sadie. For Mary. For everyone. She needed to keep her promise to Mamm.

"Oh, sweet Annie, Mamm is not here with us anymore. She-she is with . . . God now."

Annie's pale blue eyes, so like Mamm's, widened as if she were about to protest, but a kiss on her soft chubby cheek held it at bay.

"Let me take Annie. You need to eat."

Startled, Katie spun around, her body sagging with relief at the sight of their neighbor, Martha Hochstetler. "Oh, Martha . . . thank you for all that you did today. For the food, for helping me ready the girls, for helping to make sure everything was as it needed to be. I do not know what I would have done without you."

"Many hands make light work, Katie. Though, even with those hands, you still did not eat." Martha reached out, took Annie from Katie's arms, and then gestured toward a single plate of food on the top step of the front porch. "I shooed Isaiah King's youngest boy from that piece of chicken just so you could have it."

"I do not need that chicken." She looked toward the side of the farmhouse and then toward the open barn, but there was no sign of Jakob's hungry friend.

"Do not argue, Katie. You must keep up your strength. There is much on your shoulders now."

Even if it was polite to argue, she couldn't. Martha was right. The last thing Dat needed was for Katie to get sick. Still, a second glance at the plate of food failed to stir anything even resembling an appetite.

"I do not think I can eat right now," she whispered.

"Perhaps company will change that."

She followed Martha's eyes toward the side yard and the elderly English woman seated on one of two rocking chairs Martha's husband had brought over for the day.

Dressed all in black, the familiar face met her gaze with a beckoning hand. "Take the plate and sit with her for a while, Katie. Annie and I will see to the last of the cleanup, won't we, Annie?"

Annie removed her thumb from her mouth and nodded up at Martha.

"See?" Martha said, gesturing first toward Annie and then Katie's waiting plate. "It is all settled."

"Martha, I —"

"Go, child. Miss Lottie loved your mamm, too."

The pain was back. And this time, she let herself feel it as she swept her attention back toward Hannah and Travis, and whatever it was out in the field that was making them laugh.

Laugh?

Today?

Squaring her shoulders, Katie crossed to the step, retrieved the plate of food, and made her way over to the pair of rocking chairs and the woman now nodding at her with the faintest hint of a smile.

"Miss Lottie. I'm sorry I have not had much time to visit with you today." Katie lowered herself to the empty rocker and set the plate atop her aproned lap. When she was sure it would not fall, she met the woman's warm hazel eyes with what she hoped was a smile. "I-I'm touched that you came."

"There's nowhere else I'd want to be. Although, I wish it were for a very different occasion."

"It is God's will," Katie murmured.

She hated the way the words felt in her mouth, hated, even more, that she had to say them as if she believed them.

Lottie's rocker stilled just before her soft, wrinkly hand reached across the short divide to cover Katie's. "That may be so, Katie, but that doesn't mean it doesn't hurt or that you're not allowed to cry."

"I-I . . ." She stopped, swallowed, and started again, her voice heavy with the grief that was becoming harder and harder to keep under wraps. "I promised Mamm I would take care of the children . . . and Dat."

"And you are. You will." Lottie's hand patted Katie's softly and then retreated back to the armrest of her own rocker. "I bet you're glad to see Hannah even if it's only for a little while."

Katie turned in time to see Hannah and Travis disappear inside the farmhouse with Mary and Sadie in tow. She looked down at her food and then back up at Miss Lottie, her voice barely more than a raspy whisper. "She does not look like Hannah."

"Oh?"

"The Hannah I remember did not have such black eyelashes and such red cheeks. She wore the same clothes that I wear and did not hold hands with boys." She bit into a slice of bread in the hope it would somehow steady the tremor in her voice, but it didn't help. Instead, it simply confirmed her total lack of appetite. "I miss *that* Hannah."

"Inside, she is still the same Hannah you remember, Katie. Makeup and English clothes can't change that any more than a freshly scrubbed face and aproned dress can change who you are inside."

Blinking against the sudden stinging in her eyes, Katie stared down at the chicken leg and green beans she knew she shouldn't waste. "I miss her so much, Miss Lottie. I-I miss them *both* so much."

"Your mamm is still with you, Katie." Lottie placed her hand to her chest and closed her eyes for a brief moment. "In your heart and in your mind. Find comfort and strength in that."

Comfort.

And strength.

Comfort and —

"And as for Hannah, she is only a bus or

a train ride away."

Slowly, Katie lifted her eyes to Miss Lottie's, her lips quivering. "In a big city. With a job. And an apartment. And new friends. And" — her voice faltered — "Travis."

"You have Abram, don't you?"

She sucked in a breath. "H-how do you know about Abram?"

"Your mamm and I did not just sit and stare at one another when I came for a visit, dear." Then, with a slight wave of her hand, Lottie got them back on track. "You are still Hannah's sister, Katie. Nothing — not a city, or a job, or even a boyfriend — can change that."

Oh how she wanted to believe Miss Lottie was right. But the nagging sensation in her chest refused to acquiesce.

"We used to do everything together. She knew what I was thinking before *I* did sometimes. But now" — Katie stopped, inhaled sharply, and then sank against the back of her rocking chair — "it is like she is a-a . . . *stranger.*"

"Give it time, dear. I suspect that will change."

"But how?" she protested. "I do not live in her world and she does not live in mine. Soon, she will be just like all the English girls who stare at my kapp and dress."

"That will never happen, dear. At least not in the way you're implying."

"You sound so certain."

"Because I am." Lottie shifted forward in her rocker, stopping its gentle motion as she did. "One only has to see what I see to know how much Hannah loves you."

"See what you see?"

"Every time I spotted your sister in the crowd today, she was looking at you. With nothing but love in her eyes." Lottie bent forward, retrieved her cane from the ground beside her chair, and readied it for the support she needed in order to stand. "Which is why you should go inside now and soak up every minute you can with her before she heads back to the city."

"But I don't know what to say . . . or how to be around her anymore."

"Be yourself, Katie."

She looked down at her own simple dress and tried not to compare it to Hannah's formfitting one. "What happens if that is not enough?"

"It is."

Swiping at the pair of tears that made their way down her cheeks, Katie pushed off the chair, held out her hand, and carefully helped Miss Lottie to her feet. Once the woman was fully upright and steady, she pulled Katie in for a hug.

"Your mamm loved you, Katie. Loved you with her whole heart. More than anything, she wanted you to be honest and true."

Katie stumbled backward, her mouth gaped. "I did not lie to Mamm. Not ever."

Miss Lottie quieted Katie's protest with her finger and a gentle hush. "Being honest and true to yourself is every bit as important as being honest and true with everyone else, Katie."

Reluctantly, she accepted Travis's hand as she stepped from the buggy, a whispered "thank-you" the only response she could manage under the circumstances. Yes, he was nice, funny, even. But at that moment, all that mattered was the fact that Hannah was leaving. Again.

"Are you sure you cannot stay another day?" Katie pulled her hand from Travis's and used it, instead, to shield the last of the day's sun from her eyes as she stopped in front of her sister. "You could take a bus to the city *tomorrow*. Or even the day after."

Hannah tugged the strap of her pale blue zippered bag higher onto her shoulder, shaking her head as she did. "I'm sorry, Katie, but I have to go. Jack has a doctor's appointment in the morning that I have to take him to and Travis has a meeting with his boss."

"You are Jack's *nanny,* not his mamm. Can't *she* take him to his appointment as she should? And" — she cast a nervous eye at Travis before bringing her attention and her pleas back to her twin — "maybe Travis could go back now and you could follow in a few days. After we've had a bit more —"

"Attention, passengers. Attention, passengers. The Lancaster to New York City bus is now boarding on platform 6-B. The Lancaster to New York City bus is now boarding on platform 6-B."

Panicked, Katie reached out, grabbed hold of Hannah's hands, and squeezed. "Please, Hannah, stay for a few more days. I-I think it would help the little ones to have you around. They have been through so much."

Slipping her bag off her shoulder, Hannah handed it to Travis and smiled. "Can you take this?"

"Sure thing, gorgeous." Travis took the bag, balanced it with his own, and handed Hannah her ticket. Then, turning to Katie, he nodded, his green eyes sparkling. "It was great to finally meet you, Katie. I've heard

44

so much about you these past few months."

She knew she should say something. Or, at the very least, nod and smile in response, but she was at a loss. If Travis noticed though, he didn't let on. Instead, he gestured toward the waiting bus with his chin. "Maybe you could come visit us sometime." Then, without waiting for an answer, he shifted his attention back to Hannah. "I'll get us some seats while you say goodbye."

"Thanks, Travis."

And then he was gone, his back fading from sight as he stowed the pair of bags in the cargo hold and then headed onto the bus.

"He's right you know," Hannah said. "Once everything is settled here, you should visit us."

"Us?"

"Yes. Travis and me."

"Are you one person now?" Katie hissed.

Hannah reared back. "Katie!"

"From the moment he arrived yesterday morning, you have been with Travis." She heard the tremble of her voice but could do nothing to stop it. "But you are with Travis in the city. Did he really need to come here? To Mamm's funeral?"

"Yes!" Hannah snapped back. "He is my boyfriend. He came because I asked him to.

I *needed* him."

"You need only God!"

"Oh stop it, Katie. You're being childish."

"Childish? You think I'm being —"

"I don't want to fight with you, Katie," Hannah said as she reached out and tucked a piece of Katie's hair back beneath her kapp. "I really don't. I just want you to come visit me in the city. We'd have such fun."

"F-fun? *Fun?* How can you talk of fun, Hannah? Mamm is dead! Jakob, Samuel, Mary, Sadie, and Annie lost Mamm. *I* lost Mamm. And you-you left me behind to do this all alone!" Katie's hands shook with anger as she stared at Hannah and her black tears. "But you can do that, can't you? You've done it before. So go on, leave us again! Go have your fun!"

Hannah recoiled as if she'd been slapped. "Katie! Take that back!"

She opened her mouth to defend her words but, when Hannah pulled her in for a hug, only a strangled sob emerged.

"Oh, Katie. I miss her, too," Hannah said against Katie's ear. "So very, very much. But she will be forever in our hearts just as Miss Lottie said."

Katie stepped back, stunned. "You spoke with Miss Lottie?"

"Of course. She is one of the wisest people I've ever met." With a shaky hand, Hannah wiped her cheeks dry. "Miss Lottie helped me find peace with my decision to set out on my own."

"She did?"

"Yah — I mean, yes."

"Did Mamm know?" Katie asked. "That you two spoke?"

"I cannot say for sure. But even if she didn't, I'm sure she would have understood."

She stared at her sister. "*I* don't understand."

"That's because you don't talk to Miss Lottie the way we did."

"*We?*"

"Mamm had heart-to-heart talks with Miss Lottie, too."

Heart-to-heart talks?

Pressing her fingertips against her temples, Katie willed the pain she felt building in her head to stay away. She needed to focus. To make sense of what Hannah was saying. "Why would Mamm have needed such talks?"

"Mamm was human, Katie, just like everyone else. She had her own worries and fears, I'm sure. And more than that, she wanted the best for me," Hannah said as she gathered Katie's hands inside her own. "And she wanted the best for *you,* too."

"I —"

"Attention, passengers. Attention, passengers. Final boarding has begun for the Lancaster to New York City bus. All ticketed passengers should make their way to platform 6-B now. All ticketed passengers on the 6:45 Lancaster to New York City bus should make their way to platform 6-B now."

Hannah lurched forward, planted a kiss on Katie's forehead, and then stepped back, her hands still holding Katie's tightly. "I have to go, Katie. I am sorry you have to deal with all of this on your own, but Samuel and Jakob and Mary are older now, let them help. Do not try to do everything on your own. You are allowed to have a life, too, Katie, whether that life is to be spent with Abram here in Lancaster . . . or pursuing a very different life somewhere else. Remember that."

She tried to blink away the tears pooling in the corners of her eyes, but even with her best effort, one still escaped down her cheek. "It is not that simple and you know that, Hannah."

"Maybe, maybe not."

"There is no maybe about it," Katie protested. "Unlike you, I have been baptized. If I were to run off the way that you did, I would lose my whole family!"

Hannah's eyes narrowed in anger. "You say that as if Dat and the children are your only family. But I am still your family, too, Katie! My leaving didn't change that."

"How very lucky for you."

"That is not fair, Katie!"

"What is not fair? You did not see Mamm's sadness when you left. But *I* did. I saw it every time she looked at your spot at the table! I saw it every time Sadie would ask her about you! I saw it every time she would catch me crying! I saw it every time she would come into my room and try not to react to seeing your empty dress hook next to mine! You think I could have done that to her, too?"

Hannah drew in a noticeable breath. "I can't do this right now, Katie, I just can't. But I'm only a letter and *a bus ride* away. Remember that. Always."

"I —"

Releasing Katie's hands, Hannah motioned toward the bus. "I really have to go. Kiss the little ones for me every night, will you? And tell them I love them!"

"Of course."

Hannah took two steps and stopped. "Oh, and Katie? I'm sorry about . . . well, you'll see."

"Sorry about what?"

"That was probably the wrong choice of words. Because I'm not *sorry*, exactly. But if it helps, I left you one in return."

"Wait! I don't understand. You left me *what* in return?" she called as Hannah made her way toward the bus and the rather impatient looking driver standing beside the door. "I do not know what you are talking about."

Hannah stepped onto the bus, turned, and then popped her head outside the open doorway one last time. "You will, Katie. Soon. Very, very soon."

CHAPTER 4

The candlelight visible beneath her bedroom door disappeared as Dat extinguished the day with what had surely been a breath of resignation. He'd been stoic, of course, as he'd stood beside his wife's freshly dug grave and again back at the house as they greeted the hundred plus mourners who'd gathered for a meal afterward. But somewhere behind the expression he'd worn, Katie knew there had to be tremendous grief.

Mamm and Dat had been married for nearly twenty-two years. They'd fallen for one another in the same way many Amish couples did — while socializing at a neighboring district's hymn sing. From bits and pieces Mamm had shared over the years, they'd married the next winter and by the following fall, Hannah and Katie were born. Seven more children had followed with two — a boy, and later a girl — not making it

51

past a week old. Through it all, Mamm and Dat had been by each other's side.

Until now.

Slowly, Katie returned her focus to the ceiling above her bed and the image of Abram Zook now infringing on the outskirts of her thoughts. If she were to marry Abram, as Mamm said, would their daughter catch him looking at Katie the way she'd once caught Dat looking at Mamm?

Oh she remembered that moment like it was yesterday. She'd just finished cleaning the chicken coop and she'd gone inside to wash her hands. As she'd stepped into the kitchen, she'd caught sight of Dat standing at the back door, looking toward the stove with a hint of a smile on his lips. Certain she would see a cooling pie atop the stove or a plate of freshly made cookies sitting on the counter, she had been surprised to find only Mamm in his sight.

Now, her heart ached for Dat. For the loss he surely felt but would just as surely never show.

"Oh, Mamm," she whispered. "Why did you have to go?"

This time, she didn't wipe away the tears. She didn't have to. In her room, she was free — free to think, free to cry.

And free to draw . . .

Flipping onto her side, Katie reached around the edge of the mattress, slipped her fingers beneath it, and savored the quick thrill born on the answering feel of the artist's pad she'd purchased during Rumspringa nearly five years earlier. The thrill, of course, was quickly shoved to the side by an equally familiar rush of guilt — the same rush of guilt responsible for the handful of untouched pages calling to her now.

She tried to resist its pull, tried to focus, instead, on the next day's chores and the sleep they required, but it was no use. Tonight, more than ever, she needed the peace that was hers the moment her pencil touched down on the paper.

It was a feeling she didn't really understand, but that didn't make it less real. When she was alone with her memories and her pencil, it was like she was a different person. A person who wasn't defined by a kapp or a dress or a way of life.

When she was drawing, she was truly Katie.

Gently, she pulled out the large pad and placed it in her lap, the rapid beat of her heart as much about anticipation as the fear that one of her siblings — or, worse, Dat — would learn her secret. But for now, at that very moment, her secret was safe.

With careful fingers, she flipped back the cover and stared down at the picture of Mamm she'd drawn during Rumspringa. There had been many mistakes — a line beside the eyes that hadn't looked quite right, the curve of the chin that had been erased countless times, the shape of the nose that seemed off somehow, and Mamm's size in relation to the flowers she'd been planting in the garden. But for a first try, it hadn't been that bad.

She leaned closer, soaking up every detail of the woman she'd never known life without until now. Somehow, someway, Mamm had made everything look easy. Including her illness and death.

Katie swallowed against the lump she felt inching its way up her throat — a lump she knew would lead to even more of the tears Mamm hadn't wanted her to cry. Instead, she traced the high cheekbones with her finger while trying to block out the memory of the way they'd changed in the final weeks.

That Mamm — the sick Mamm — was temporary. The Mamm in her head and in the picture in front of her was Mamm as Katie would always remember her being. Happy. Content. And healthy.

After a while, Katie reluctantly turned the page, her need to breathe winning out over her need to remember. Yet the moment her gaze shifted to the picture of Samuel chasing a chicken, she knew Mamm was still there, still part of every memory she'd recorded with her pencil. No, Mamm wasn't standing beside Samuel, or even peering out from the kitchen window just over his left shoulder, but she was still there — there in Samuel's smile and in Mary's clap as the then almost ten-year-old looked on from the garden she was helping tend.

Katie secured the bottom corner of the page between her fingers and flipped it upward, her mind jumping to the sketch of Luke Hochstetler her eyes instantly registered as missing.

Bolting upright, Katie took in the sketch of Mary and Sadie walking across the pasture, hand in hand, and then lifted her gaze to the ragged edge that served as tangible proof that the sketch of Luke had, indeed, existed outside her head.

She willed herself to slow her breath and to think. But it was hard. Impossible, even. Instead, she flipped through the next few pages, the absence of another one — the one with Mary and the barn cats — morphing her confusion into fear.

Had Dat found her drawings? Had Jakob or Mary —

Desperate for an answer, she lifted the pad off her lap only to see a slip of paper flutter out, Hannah's familiar handwriting scrawled across it from top to bottom.

Dearest Katie,

Please do not be mad at me for taking your pictures. All I can say is that I needed to. I like my new life in the city, but that does not mean I don't miss all of you. If I could, I'd take all of these pictures with me. But I can't. While I will cherish the memories associated with the pictures I took, you need the rest to remember who you are.

Never let that Katie — the real Katie — go. Promise me that.

In the meantime, keep me close the way I will forever and always keep you close.

Your sister,
Hannah

PS Travis took this picture of me in Central Park. You would love it there.

"Picture? What picture . . ." The whispered words disappeared from her lips as a shake of the pad yielded her answer via a glossy photograph.

In it, Hannah smiled back at her from atop a stone bridge, massive buildings the likes of which Katie could only imagine serving as a backdrop. In Hannah's hands was a bouquet of wildflowers just like the ones she and Katie had loved to gather together for Mamm when they were not much older than Sadie . . .

This time, when the lump returned, Katie didn't try to distract it away. Instead, she rolled onto her stomach and prayed the pillow would block out her sobs.

Morning's first light was just starting to peek around the window shade when Katie opened her eyes. For a moment, she could almost pretend everything was normal. Dat's boots were moving toward the front door with Samuel's close on his heels. The smell of bacon frying on the stove was wafting up the stairs, beckoning to her stomach and —

"Mamm?" She tossed back the quilt Mamm had made the previous winter and cringed as her sketching pencil flew over the edge of the bed and skittered across the floor, the tip she'd sharpened several times throughout the night snapping against the sole of her waiting boots. She was reaching down to pick it up when the rattle of plates being placed around the table filtered through the gap beneath her closed door.

Confused, she glanced again at the window, the position of the sun confirming it was no more than six o'clock. Why was Mamm moving around so early . . .

The question trailed from her thoughts as reality snapped her from all final vestiges of sleep. Mamm was gone for good, the latest casualty of God's will — a will she must once again pretend to accept just as she had when Hannah had chosen an English life over her.

The telltale sound of the utensil drawer opening and closing broke through her thoughts, ushering in a far more likely image than the one that had forced her out from beneath her covers. Quickly, she removed the previous day's rumpled black dress from her body and replaced it, instead, with a fresh one hanging on the hook across from her bed. Then, with careful yet quick fingers, she removed her head covering, let down her hair, brushed it, and secured it in place once again, this time under the freshly washed kapp she'd looped around her bedpost.

Part of her wanted to let Mary finish breakfast on her own. But the other part of her, the one that had squeezed Mamm's hand and promised to look after Dat and the children, knew that would be wrong. Besides, the baby would be waking up soon and chores needed to be done.

Mamm's work, Mamm's *life* was now Katie's.

When her boots were laced and tied, she turned back to her bed and the sketch pad that hovered dangerously close to the edge. She didn't want to be angry at Hannah for taking her drawings, but she couldn't help it. They were her drawings, not Hannah's.

Hannah . . .

Her gaze immediately flocked to the photograph sticking out from under her pillow — a photograph she shouldn't have yet knew she'd never discard. Gripping the edges between her fingers, she pulled the picture into the middle of the bed and looked again at the image of Hannah and the bouquet of wildflowers. All Katie's life, the sight of her twin had been enough to give her whatever she'd needed. When she'd been sad, it had given her comfort. When she'd felt shy, it had given her courage. When she'd felt out of place, it had helped her belong.

But now, looking into the eyes laughing up at her from the center of Mamm's quilt, Katie was aware of only one emotion: deep and utter loneliness.

A knock at her bedroom door sent her scrambling for the sketch pad and Hannah's picture.

"Katie?"

Her heart skipped a beat as she imagined Sadie's round cheek pressed against the door, listening. Three days earlier, the image would have made Katie smile. Now, it struck fear in her heart. She'd always thought she'd been so careful with her drawings, limiting her work to quiet moments when no one else was around. Yet somehow, despite her best efforts, Hannah had discovered her secret — a secret she couldn't afford for anyone to know, especially Dat. He'd been through enough. To add the weight of her sins to that would be —

"Katie?" Sadie called again, the uncertainty in the four-year-old's voice evident even without the rasp and the follow-up sniffle. "Katie? Did you go to God like Mamm?"

Go to —

Pressing her hand against her answering sob, she squeezed her eyes closed. "No, sweet girl. I am here; I was just being a great big sleepyhead, that's all."

A second and third sniffle was followed by

60

a hiccup and then the sound of Katie's doorknob being turned.

"Wait! I-I'm . . . getting dressed." With her heart slamming inside her chest, Katie ran around the bed and shoved the sketch pad beneath her mattress. When she was confident it was out of sight, she grabbed up the photograph and note from Hannah, ran back to the opposite side of the bed, and tucked them into her boot in advance of her foot. "Okay, sweet girl, you can come in now."

CHAPTER 5

She hadn't thought it possible for her heart to be any heavier than it already was, but she'd been wrong. Imagining life without Mamm and living life without Mamm were two very different things.

Before she'd gotten sick, Mamm had been a steady presence in everyone's day. For Dat and the boys, she'd been the one to start and end their workday with a full stomach and a smile. Katie had helped, of course, but Mamm was Mamm. For Katie and her sisters, Mamm had been their model for how to live, how to function, how to be. No chore had been too big, no problem too daunting, no trouble she couldn't hush away with the reminder of God's wisdom.

Even during her final weeks, when she'd been confined to bed, Mamm had remained an ever present force, her sunny smile and encouraging words as much a given during the day as the fact that the sun would rise

62

in the morning and lower in the evening.

They'd known she was dying. They'd tried to ready themselves for the fulfillment of God's will, but in the end, if the sadness Katie felt emanating off her brothers as they moved about the fields was any indication, they'd failed.

Katie stood at the window, looking out at her dat and her brothers for a few more moments, the tightness in her throat making it difficult to breathe. They were carrying on outside just as Katie and her sisters were carrying on inside, yet somehow everything was different now.

"How are you holding up, dear?"

Startled, Katie turned toward the familiar voice. "Miss Lottie! I-I didn't hear you come in."

"Sadie let me in." The elderly English woman gestured toward the large wooden table in the center of the kitchen and, at Katie's nod, took a seat on the edge of the bench. "She was telling Annie about the different flowers when I came up the drive."

"And Mary?"

"She's hanging the wash."

Katie checked the clothes off her mental to-do list and crossed to the refrigerator. "Would you like a glass of iced tea, Miss Lottie?"

"I would love some, Katie." Reaching up, Lottie Jenkins removed her floppy straw hat from her head and set it beside her on the bench. "I take it Hannah and her young man got off okay, yesterday?"

"They did." She poured a glass of tea for Miss Lottie and a glass of water for herself and carried both to the table.

Miss Lottie took a sip and then studied Katie across the rim of her glass. "I bet that was hard, having her leave again."

"I asked her to stay on for a few days, but she didn't listen." Katie heard the bitterness in her tone and waited for the shame to follow, but it never came. "The little ones are having a hard time today. I have tried to smile and to make the chores fun as Mamm always did. But I am Katie, not Mamm, and I am not good at such things."

She felt Miss Lottie's hand on her arm, coaxing her to sit on the bench, but she was too keyed up to heed the woman's touch. "Hannah was always the one who could make the little ones giggle when I could not."

"And you're the one they go to when they need hugs, Katie." Miss Lottie took another sip of her drink and then pushed the glass into the center of the table, her large knowing eyes fixed on Katie. "Right now, if it's one or the other, they need hugs most."

"They should have both! The way they did with Mamm!" She regretted the anger in her voice, but before she could muster a worthy apology, she began to sob.

With little more than two swift moves — one to stand, the other to pull Katie close — Miss Lottie's shoulder helped block the sound from reaching the front window and the garden just beyond its open screen. Every time Katie thought she had herself under control, she'd begin sobbing again. Eventually, though, she was able to wipe her eyes and steady her breath enough to step away.

"Miss Lottie, I am so sorry. I didn't mean to yell at you. I-I am just Katie. I don't know how to do this without Mamm. She made it all look so easy. I am not strong like Mamm or courageous like Hannah. If I was behind them, I could do the things they did. But only because they did them first and told me I would be okay."

"Oh, child, your mamm was right, you do sell yourself short."

Katie stared at the woman, certain she must have misheard. "Mamm said that? About me?"

"She said you have a strength that is so unassuming even you do not see it. But it is a strength that is every bit as real as Hannah's." Reaching forward, the woman tucked a rebellious strand of hair back under Katie's kapp. "And it is a strength that will see you through the weeks and months ahead, dear one."

"I could never go off on my own and start a new life the way that Hannah did," Katie protested. "That takes courage I do not have."

"A famous writer once said, 'courage is grace under pressure.' I cannot think of someone more befitting of those words than you, Katie. You handled your mamm's illness with your head held high. And yesterday? At the service and then the meal? You honored your mother's life by looking after the wee ones and still seeing to it that everyone was greeted and fed and thanked just as she would have done. To do that while your own heart was heavy with sadness is the epitome of courage, young lady."

She felt her face warm at the praise and looked away. She wanted to believe Miss Lottie's words, to know that she was as courageous as her sister, but it didn't ring true. Clearing her throat, she wandered over to the window and its view of the fields in the distance. "Dat and the boys are carrying on as if it is just another day, but it's not.

Mamm is no longer here."

"I know it is the Amish way to carry on, to accept such a loss as God's will. But she was your mamm. It is okay to hurt."

"Mamm wanted me to take care of things, to look after the children and Dat. And I can do that. I can cook, I can clean, I can wash and mend clothes. But to smile the way that Mamm did? To be strong and brave the way Mamm was? I-I do not know if I can."

"Your mamm knew you could."

Katie spun around. "You cannot know that."

"I can. And I do."

Miss Lottie sat back down on the bench, removed her hat from atop her bag, and fished out a plain white envelope Katie recognized from Mamm's letter writing box. For as long as Katie could remember, she'd loved the sight of that box for it meant Mamm was going to write a letter to faraway family, taking care to include special hellos from Katie and her siblings. When the letter was written and Dat had taken it to the post office, Katie and Hannah would try to imagine when it would arrive at its destination and the joy it would bring.

Shaking the memory from her head, she pointed at the envelope. "That looks like

Mamm's."

"Because it is."

"She wrote you a letter?" Katie asked.

"She wrote *you* a letter, dear."

Katie drew back against the window. "But I was right here all the time. Why would she write me a letter?"

"For you to read when she was gone."

Slowly, she crept forward, her gaze returning to the envelope in Miss Lottie's hand. The sight of Mamm's careful handwriting stretched across the front stirred pain and excitement in equal measure. "What does it say?" she asked.

"Why don't you open it and find out?"

She started to take the envelope Miss Lottie held out but, at the last minute, she pulled her hand back and cocked her ear toward the front windows. "The young ones will be coming in soon to help prepare dinner. I do not want them to see me cry."

Miss Lottie gathered her hat and bag, stood, and made her way over to Katie. "Then read it before bed."

"I will." She took the envelope and held it to her chest. "Thank you, Miss Lottie."

Somehow, she'd made it through the rest of the day. She'd prepared supper, made polite conversation at the dinner table, cleaned

68

the pots and pans, put Annie to bed in her crib, read two stories to Sadie, and played a silly game with Mary and Jakob while Dat and Samuel talked about an upcoming horse auction.

On the surface, it had seemed like any other night. But it wasn't. Mamm's absence was ever present, manifesting itself in smiles that weren't as big as normal and laughter that seemed almost forced at times. And every once in a while, when she'd stolen a glance in Dat's direction, she knew he felt it, too.

She'd considered asking if he was okay, but she knew what his answer would be. Instead, she counted down the hours and then the minutes until she could disappear to her room and finally, mercifully, it came.

Sucking in a breath, Katie waited for the glow of Dat's candle to disappear beneath her door. She imagined him taking off his boots and draping his suspenders across the foot of his bed. She imagined him looking at the side of the bed Mamm had occupied just a little over forty-eight hours earlier. But when she started to imagine the look on his face now that he was alone, she made herself concentrate on nothing but the swath of light playing across the toes of her boots.

"Please, Dat," she whispered. "You have had a long day and you need your sleep . . ."

The light gave way to darkness save for that of the moon peeking around her window shade. Relief sagged her backward but not for long. Quietly, she made her way over to the bed, sat on its edge, and unlaced her boots. When she pulled off the left one, she reached inside, removed Hannah's note and picture from the area where her ankle had been, and set them on her pillow. Then, without waiting to remove her right foot, she reached inside her remaining boot and pulled out Mamm's letter.

For a moment, she just sat there, staring down at the letter that had consumed her thoughts over the past few hours. So many times during and after dinner she'd considered feigning a stomach ache just so she could read what Mamm had written, but she'd resisted. Part of that was because she didn't want to cloak her last communication with her mother in dishonesty. But an even bigger part was knowing she wanted to savor every word without distraction.

Now that the distractions were gone though, she was both eager and wary all at the same time. Yes, she wanted to know what Mamm had written, but once Katie read it, Mamm would truly be gone.

Katie ran her fingertips across her name and imagined when Mamm might have written it. While she was confined to bed? Before she'd become ill? How? When? Why?

Inhaling deeply, she turned the envelope over, worked her finger beneath the seal, and slipped out the simple white folded page it contained. With trembling fingers, she unfolded the paper and smoothed it across her lap.

Dear Katie,

If Miss Lottie has given you this letter, it is because God's will has made it so.

I know that my passing will mean a change in your life, but it will only be for a short time as we have already spoken about. Abram is a fine young man and I am sure that he will wait with understanding and patience.

When you are to marry, you will find a bolt of blue fabric in my chest. When you were not much older than Annie, you loved to look at the bright blue sky. You would look at me, point up, and then throw your head back and make this happy little sound. I never knew why you did that, but I knew that something about the sky made you smile.

I want you to smile like that again. And

I want you to smile the way you did when Hannah was close.

Make your wedding dress of this blue, Katie.

Smile the way you once did.

Smile with Abram.

It is God's will.

With love,

Mamm

She tried to catch the tear before it hit the paper, but she wasn't fast enough. Instead, she watched as the ink from her mother's pen darkened and spread with the moisture, the thump of her heart barely noticeable against the deafening silence in her head.

Why did Mamm think her smile had changed? It hadn't changed . . .

Clutching the letter to her chest, Katie pushed off the bed and, with the help of the moonlit windows she passed along the way, made her way down the stairs and into the kitchen. Her destination the home's lone mirror perched atop a counter.

The light was low, but it was enough to see herself, and for a second she actually pulled back, the differences between the face in front of her and the one she'd peered into at the bus station the day before startling.

All their life, Katie and Hannah had looked like clones — the same brown eyes, the same golden-brown hair, the same high cheekbones, the same heart-shaped curve to their lips, the same five foot four height, and the same petite build. They were so identical, in fact, that if not for the differences in their behavior and the scar on Hannah's chin from a nasty fall when they were young, one might think they were the same person.

Inside, Hannah had always been the one to try new things first, to speak to strangers first, to reach milestones first. But that was okay, because that's the way it was, the way it had always been.

Yet the face she saw peering back at her now looked nothing like Hannah anymore. Sure, they still shared the same eyes, but now Hannah's were flanked by long thick eyelashes the color of soot. And the golden-brown hair they both tucked under their kapps now hung down Hannah's back in soft, silky ringlets. The shape of Hannah's lips hadn't changed, yet with lipstick on them, they looked fuller, prettier, fancier . . .

Katie turned to the side and studied herself from the changed angle for a few moments before rising up on tiptoes in an effort to reach Hannah's heeled height.

Without really realizing what she was doing, she found herself tossing back her shoulders and trying to pick out the kind of curves Hannah's dress had displayed.

"Katie?"

Dropping her heels to the ground and her hand to her side, Katie turned toward the hallway and the eye-rubbing little girl blinking back at her. "Sadie, sweetie, what are you doing awake?"

"I heard a funny sound downstairs. But when I went to tell you, you were not in your bed."

Katie crossed the room and squatted down in front of the four-year-old, the moonlight streaming through the kitchen window enough to make out the sadness in the child's otherwise tired face. "I'm sorry if I woke you, Sadie. I . . ." She stopped, tried to come up with something she could say to explain why she was downstairs, and when she couldn't, closed her eyes just long enough to eke out an untruth. "I needed a glass of water."

Sadie stopped rubbing her eyes and pointed just over Katie's shoulder. "Why were you looking in that?"

She didn't need to look back to know Sadie was referencing the mirror. Instead, she reached out and tapped her little sister on the nose. "Because I was being silly, that's all."

"Hannah did that, too."

"Hannah did what?"

Sadie nodded. "When she was here. She did that, too."

"You mean looked in the mirror?"

Again Sadie nodded. Only this time, she turned to the side, tossed back her shoulders, and looked toward the mirror she was too little to see into. "She standed just like you."

Katie palmed her cheeks with her cool hands and waited for the heat she found there to lessen. She tried to think of something to say, but before she could settle on something to explain her actions, Sadie ran into her arms and began to cry.

"What's wrong, Sadie?" Katie asked as she kissed her sister's forehead and tried her best to stop the flow of the child's tears with her fingers.

"Please don't go away, Katie. Please. I do not want you to go, too."

She wiped the wetness against her dress and then rocked back into a sit, pulling Sadie onto her lap as she did. "*Go?* I'm not going anywhere, sweetie."

"B-b-but H-Hannah went . . . a-and M-Mamm went."

"Mamm is with God," she reminded around the lump building in her throat.

"Hannah is not with God. Hannah is in the city. With Travis." Sadie pushed her tear-soaked face against Katie's chest and hiccupped. "I do not want you to go there to live, too."

She heard the gasp as it left her mouth, the ludicrousness of her little sister's words almost too hard to comprehend in relation to herself. "*Me?* I-I would not go there to live. I belong . . . *here.* In Blue Ball. With you and Annie and Mary and Jakob and Samuel and Dat."

Sadie's answering yawn bought Katie a moment of silence, but it didn't last. "Do you promise?" Sadie asked around a second and far bigger yawn.

"Oh, sweetie, you're so sleepy. Let's get you back to bed, okay?" Katie scooted Sadie back just enough to be able to stand and then lifted the little girl into her arms for the trek back up the stairs.

Sadie looped her arm around Katie's neck but remained upright. "I miss Mamm."

"I know. I miss her, too."

Sadie buried her head in Katie's shoulder and yawned again. "You didn't promise, Katie," she said, her voice heavy with sleep.

"Shhh . . . We mustn't wake Annie."

This time when Sadie yawned, it was followed by a voice so sleepy it was only a matter of seconds before the little girl was out cold. "Please, Katie. Please say . . . you . . ."

Katie sneaked a sidelong glance at the now quiet four-year-old. Sure enough, the mouth that had been seeking reassurance less than a second earlier now hung open in sleep. Whispering a kiss across Sadie's forehead, Katie made her way up the stairs, the occasional creak of the floorboards beneath her feet a welcome distraction from a promise she'd deliberately avoided making for no apparent reason.

CHAPTER 6

Katie took a sip of water from her cup and flopped back against the trunk of the tree, spent. "I didn't know I could hit the ball so far."

"Nor did the other side." Ruth Zook dropped onto the ground next to Katie and giggled. "Did you hear the thump the ball made on Leroy Stoltzfus's head? It was so loud!"

"Ohhh, Ruth, do you think I hurt him?" Katie asked, tightening her grip on her cup and looking around for any sign of Ruth's neighbor.

"No. He was too busy making sure Martha Troyer saw him laughing about it to actually check for any bleeding."

Katie waved off the handful of odd looks brought on by her answering gasp and then turned back to Ruth. "Bleeding? Did I really hit him that hard?"

"Yah." Ruth broke her cookie down the

middle and held out half to Katie. "I know it is wrong to keep eating these, but they are so good, aren't they?"

Waving off the offer, Katie took a second, longer gulp of water. "You could eat *ten* cookies and it would not change anything."

Ruth nibbled her cookie half in silence before rotating her body on the ground to afford a better view of Katie. "I'm glad you came today. So is Abram."

She lowered the cup to her dress-clad lap and lifted her gaze to the late-afternoon sun. "Dat insisted."

And he had.

Every time she offered a reason she shouldn't go to the hymn sing with her peers, Dat had given a reason to the contrary, with the most convincing being the simple fact it was Sunday and she was to enjoy the day. Still, it was hard. Hard to be playing volleyball and singing as if everything was as it should be.

"It was a surprise to see Hannah."

Katie tightened her grip on her cup. "Why?"

"I didn't think she would come."

"Mamm went to be with God. Of course, Hannah would come."

Ruth finished the cookie and then wiped her hands against one another in an effort to rid them of any residual crumbs. "But she is of the English world now."

"That doesn't matter. She is still my sister. She is still Mamm and Dat's daughter." She heard the defensive tone in her voice and tried her best to rein it in. "Miss Lottie was there, too, Ruth, and *she* is English."

A round of laughter stole their collective attention for a moment and Katie was glad. But like everything else, it didn't last long.

"Hannah is so" — Ruth leaned forward across her lap and tugged at a piece of grass, stopping short of actually plucking it out of the ground — "different now."

"She is not different," Katie protested, the words hollow even to her own ears. "She is still Hannah."

Ruth made a face. "She wore such tight clothes and . . . *makeup.* And I saw her" — Ruth looked around them before lowering her voice to a whisper — "in the barn . . . back by one of the empty stalls."

"Perhaps she was looking for one of the barn cats. Fancy Feet was always her favorite, while Mr. Nosey was mine."

"She was not looking for barn cats, Katie."

Something about Ruth's tone drew her up short. "Oh?"

"She was kissing that man."

Katie knew the sudden warmth in her face

had nothing to do with the sun, but still, she raised her hand as a shield against its waning rays. "You mean Travis?"

"Yah."

"Travis is her boyfriend, Ruth."

"You and Abram do not do that."

Katie stole a peek at the makeshift volleyball court and immediately located Ruth's brother amid his same dressed counterparts. Roughly a good six inches taller than Katie, Abram moved with ease as he chased the ball, determined to keep it from hitting the ground even if he, himself, did time and time again. Each time he dove for the ball, he came back up laughing; the rich sound a welcome one.

Abram Zook was a handsome man. His bright blue eyes reminded Katie of a pretty summer sky. When he smiled at her, as he was at that moment, they shimmered like the top of the pond on a sunny day. His hair, unlike Travis's, was covered by a hat, but the ends that escaped the brim's base had a habit of curling around his ears whenever he sweat.

There was a quiet confidence about Abram that made her feel safe and at peace whenever he was near, and she liked that. Yet when she tried to imagine what it would be like to be enveloped in his arms with his lips on hers, she couldn't.

"Hannah can wear and do whatever she wants now," Katie reminded, turning back to Ruth. "She has chosen to be English just as I have chosen to be Amish."

"It was not a good choice."

"It was *her* choice, Ruth — one she made *before* baptism! So it is not wrong for Hannah to be English!" Aware of the emotion gathering behind her eyes, Katie blinked hard. She could feel the tears hovering, but it was the why behind them that she didn't understand. Hadn't she, too, just days earlier, thought all the same things Ruth was saying? And if she didn't agree with Abram's sister, did that mean she thought Hannah's decision to leave was good?

Katie took another, longer sip of water and forced herself to relax. Ruth was her friend and didn't mean any harm with her words. "I'm sorry, Ruth." She lowered the cup back down to her lap. "I didn't mean to raise my voice."

Ruth opened her mouth to respond but closed it as Abram joined them beneath the canopy of the maple tree.

"Would you like to play again, Katie?" He hooked his thumb over his shoulder toward the volleyball net he'd helped set up.

She looked out at the faces of her friends

— some she'd known since childhood, others she'd met through the weekly hymn sings — and then back up at Abram, the hope in his eyes as plain to see as his suspenders and brimmed hat.

Abram Zook was a good man. Two years her senior, he was hardworking and kind. A year earlier, when they'd met at this same home, Katie had found him funny and sweet. He'd known much about many things — like Dat. They'd played volleyball with everyone, yet between games, they had gravitated toward one another. Within a few weeks, he asked if he could drive her home in his wagon and Dat had agreed.

That first ride together had been such fun. They'd talked about the crops he was planting with his dat, the pies she and Hannah had helped Mamm make for the after-church meal, and the stars that seemed to dance in the sky above them as Abram drove her home.

It was on their third ride together that Abram told Katie of his love of woodworking. His enthusiasm for his craft had been so contagious she'd almost told him of her drawings, but she hadn't. She liked Abram very much and she didn't want to make him look at her differently.

"Katie?"

At the sound of her name, she tightened her focus on the man looking back at her, his bright blue eyes muted with concern. For her.

"Would you like me to drive you home, instead?" he asked, his voice hushed.

She knew she should say no in favor of another game of volleyball, but she couldn't. She'd smiled enough for a day without Mamm. "Yah."

"But you cannot go yet, Katie." Ruth gestured toward the food strewn tables just beyond the volleyball net. "There is more to eat and we must sing."

Abram extended his hand to Katie and, when she took it, helped her to her feet before addressing his sister. "Katie is ready to go and I will see her home."

"It is too early for stars," Abram said as he urged the horse forward and onto the narrow road that would lead them back to Blue Ball.

She braced her feet against the wagon floor as they cleared a series of ruts and then turned her attention to the unreadable face beside hers. "I'm sorry, Abram. I could stay longer if that is best."

"I did not say that to make you feel bad, Katie. I said that only because I am used to

84

seeing stars when I drive you home." He guided the horse closer to the edge of the road to allow a car to pass and then relaxed his grip on the reins. "How are you holding up?"

For a moment she was surprised by the question but only for as long as it took to remember who was doing the asking. Abram was different from many of the boys she'd known growing up. He was strong and sure like Dat, but he liked to talk more than most and he was a wonderful listener. Always.

"I miss her, Abram. The house is not the same without her."

"You are speaking of your mamm?"

She stared up at him. "Of course. Who else would I be speaking . . ." The words trailed from her mouth as the meaning behind his question took root. "Hannah has been gone for nearly a year, Abram."

"And you have missed her for nearly a year."

Unsure of what to say, she let her focus fan out over the farmhouses and fields to their left and their right while she searched for an answer she could give without crying. When she came up empty, she changed the subject enough to be able to speak. "She looked pretty the other day, didn't she?"

"Who?"

"Hannah."

He started to speak, stopped himself, and then took his eyes off the road just long enough to meet hers. "*You* are pretty, Katie."

"I am plain," she murmured. "In more ways than one."

They drove for a while in a silence peppered only by the occasional sound of an approaching car or the distant yet distinctive moo of a cow. It was the same way every Sunday night when they drove home together from a hymn sing. She considered asking him if the sameness of their world ever bothered him, but she knew what his answer would be. Abram had chosen the Amish way.

And so, too, had she.

"I don't know how Dat can do it," she finally said. "He and Mamm were together for so long."

"It is God's will, Katie. That is how your dat continues."

"Do you really believe that? That Mamm dying is God's will?" she whispered.

"You don't?"

"I-I don't know how it could be. Mamm left us too soon. Annie and Sadie are still so little and . . ." She sucked in a breath as the words she never meant to utter aloud circled around to her ears. "Oh, Abram. Can we pretend I didn't say that? I-I know Mamm's passing is God's will."

It was not the truth, but she was too tired for a lecture. She knew what the Amish believed. She, too, had been baptized.

Still, she braced herself for a response that never came. Instead, Abram pulled the horse to a stop and turned to Katie. "It is okay to be sad, Katie. You don't have to keep it inside when you are with me. I want you to tell me what is in your heart."

"There is much sadness," she whispered.

"I know." At the feel of his fingertips beneath her chin, she lifted her watery gaze from its resting spot atop her boots and fixed it, instead, on the face peering back at her. "I know we have spoken of getting married, and we will. None of this has changed that, Katie. Soon, Annie will be older and Mary can take over with both her and Sadie. When that happens, we will marry."

She felt his eyes probing hers, waiting for a yes or a smile or some sort of relieved agreement, but she felt none of those things. "I-I . . ."

He closed his hand over hers and squeezed. "Everything will be all right, Katie. Do not worry. This, too, is God's will."

CHAPTER 7

One by one, the days gave way to a week, two weeks, three weeks, and, finally, a month. And little by little, the smiles that had once been so easy to come by when Mamm was alive began to reappear, coaxed from their hiding places by life and time.

Now, when Samuel and Jakob came in from the fields, they told Katie of their work over a drink of cold water. Now, when Mary got frustrated over a stitch she couldn't get right, she asked Katie for help rather than dissolving into tears she was unable to hide. Now, when Sadie played with her dolls, she told them she was their Katie instead of their Mamm. And now, when Annie woke from her afternoon nap, she focused on Katie's face rather than looking past it for Mamm's.

It wasn't that they'd forgotten Mamm. One only had to listen to their prayers at night and see their pained expressions when they looked at Mamm's empty seat at the table to know that wasn't the case. They'd simply found a new routine in which to frame their days and, for that, Katie was grateful.

The days were busy with cleaning, sewing, mending, cooking, and gardening. In the evenings, after the dishes had been cleaned and put away, Katie loved to put Annie on one knee and Sadie on the other, and tell them silly stories about the barn cats. More than a few times, she'd been so engrossed in what she was saying she missed the moment Jakob and Mary had scooted their chairs closer so as not to miss out on the fun.

Bedtime, though, was still hard. Without the steady stream of chores to occupy her mind and hands, and the comradery of her dat and siblings to keep her mood light, there wasn't anything else to do but think. And think she did . . .

About Mamm.

About Dat.

About marriage.

About Abram.

About Hannah . . .

She'd looked at the photograph of Hannah so many times Katie had actually based a drawing on it in her sketchbook. The buildings in the background had taken some work to get just right. With the help of her eraser and a few sleepless nights, she'd finally done so. The bridge on which Hannah had stood presented a new set of challenges, but that, too, she'd gotten. All that was left now was adding Hannah and the bouquet of flowers in her hands . . .

"Katie! Katie! Come quick! Miss Lottie says you got one, too!"

Katie set the pie on the windowsill to cool and turned toward the hallway and the little girl happily bouncing up and down on feet that were in desperate need of soap and water. "Sadie Beiler, what have I told you about yelling like that in the house?"

The feet stopped bouncing. "That I might wake Annie from her nap?"

Katie grabbed the dishcloth from its holding spot around the oven handle and wiped her hands. "That's right. So why are you yelling?"

"Annie is outside," Sadie said amid a renewed round of bouncing. "Miss Lottie is reading Annie's now and she says you should come get yours."

"Get my what?" Katie shut off the oven, replaced the dish cloth, and then turned back to Sadie, waiting.

"Your letter!" Clamping a tiny hand over

her mouth, Sadie's eyes dropped to the ground. "I'm sorry I yelled again, Katie. But" — Sadie looked up again — "she sent me a sticker of a dog!"

"A sticker? How exciting!" Katie stepped toward her little sister only to stop as her thoughts finally caught up with her ears. "Wait. Who sent you a sticker?"

"Hannah!" And then Sadie was gone, her feet making soft padding sounds against the floor as she ran back outside and onto the front porch.

Katie followed to find Miss Lottie sitting on the top step of the porch with Annie on one thigh and a pile of letters on the other.

"Good afternoon, Miss Lottie, I didn't know you were here . . ."

The gray-haired woman handed Annie what appeared to be a cat sticker and then, when the toddler ran off to show Sadie, flashed a mischievous smile over her shoulder at Katie. "You were my next stop, dear."

Katie pushed open the screen door and stepped onto the porch, her gaze riveted on the trio of envelopes she could see from her vantage point. "Are those really letters from Hannah?"

"They are, indeed. Saw the mailman on my way up the drive not more than ten minutes ago." Miss Lottie picked up the remaining letters and gave them a little shake. "Mary is out by the clothesline reading hers, Jakob took his into the barn, and I read Annie's and Sadie's to them."

"Anything important?" she asked as her gaze strayed back toward the untouched pile on Miss Lottie's thigh.

"Just that she misses them and loves them and thought they'd each like a sticker."

A pair of happy squeals from the vicinity of the garden made Katie laugh. "I believe Hannah was right about that." Then, hooking her thumb toward the door, she turned her smile on Miss Lottie. "I just made an apple pie. Would you like a piece?"

"As much as I'd like to say yes, I shouldn't. I'm meeting a friend for dinner this evening and it wouldn't be polite to show up with a full stomach." Miss Lottie thumbed through the remaining letters in her hand and held the last one out to Katie. "Why don't you take a little time with Hannah, and I'll look after things here until you return. You've earned it."

Katie looked from the letter to Miss Lottie and back again; the pull to snatch the envelope and run much stronger than it should be. "I can't ask you to do that."

"You didn't. I'm offering."

The pull was getting stronger. But still, if

she did as her mind wanted, it would be rude. "Really, I can read it later, when the chores are done," she murmured. "Or . . . or later tonight, after everyone has gone to sleep."

"You could. But why should the wee ones have all the fun?"

"I'm older, I can —"

"Don't argue with your elders, child." Miss Lottie shoved the letter into Katie's hand and then jerked her chin toward the land east of the barn. "The pond would be a lovely place to spend a little time with your sister, don't you think?"

The second Katie came around the bend near Miller's Pond, the memories she'd been trying so hard to avoid rushed at her with such intensity she stumbled back a step or two. Suddenly, she was Sadie's age all over again and Mamm was leading the way with a sleeping Samuel in her arms. Hannah walked next to Katie, pointing out the trees she wanted to climb, the rocks she wanted to jump off, and the places she wanted to hide should Mamm agree to a game of hide and seek. And Katie, well, she shrank further into herself with every plan Hannah made, terrified that Hannah might not only do those things but also make

Katie do them, too.

She closed her eyes against the avalanche of memories that followed — memories that had Katie dipping her toes in the pond while Hannah swam to the other side, Katie sitting with folded hands in her lap while Hannah hopped on one foot along a fallen tree trunk, Hannah dangling upside down from a tree limb while Katie covered her eyes on the ground below, and on and on it went. Day after day. Year after year.

Hannah the brave.

Katie the scaredy —

The persistent buzzing of a bumblebee in the vicinity of her left ear broke through her pity party and prodded her forward, her mind's eye making short work of the many differences between the Miller's Pond of her youth and the Miller's Pond of today. To her left, along the north side of the pond, the grassy area that had long ago served as the perfect place to play leapfrog now boasted a series of picnic tables and park benches deemed a necessity by Blue Ball's ever increasing English population. Up ahead and to the right, where she'd spent many a summer day wading up to her knees with her younger siblings, a sign now stood warning visitors to swim at their own risk.

Tightening her grip on the letter, Katie

picked her way across a smattering of downed limbs bordering the southwestern edge of the pond. When she reached her destination, she lowered herself to the grass, settled her back against her favorite stump, and opened the letter.

Dearest Katie,
By now, I'm hoping you are no longer angry at me for taking those two drawings. I know I should have asked, but I also know you would have said no. Travis said that should have been reason enough not to take them, but I do not agree.

"You should," she murmured. "Because Travis is right."

I would like to be able to say I took them to hang on the wall in my apartment but that would not be true.

Katie sat up tall, her back parting company with the stump.

I took them because they are good, because they shouldn't be hidden in a book underneath your bed. You have talent, Katie. Real talent. And Mr. Rothman agrees.

"Mr. Rothman? Who is Mr. Roth —"

Mr. Rothman, the man I work for, owns a very big art gallery in New York City. It is this wonderful place covered with the kind of artwork that people pay money to see and to own.

The buzzing was back, only this time Katie didn't care whether she got stung or not. All that mattered at that moment was Hannah's letter and the break it gave Katie from her own reality for a little while.

I showed Mr. Rothman the pictures you drew and he says you have great talent. That your pictures will make much money one day.

You need to come here, Katie. You need to come here with your sketch pad and show Mr. Rothman all the pictures you have drawn. Show him the way you captured the joy on Sadie's face when Fancy Feet had kittens. Show him the fear on Mary's face when Jakob put that turtle in her lunch pail last year. Show him Annie's sweet laughter when that baby cow licked her little nose when they first met.

You need to show him, Katie. You need

to show him now.

It could change your life.

Your Sister,
Hannah

PS I did not tell Dat about your drawings. It might be best if you don't, either. For now, anyway.

PPS We are going to have so so so much fun!

She stared, unseeingly, at the final line of her sister's letter, her thoughts still fixed on the part about her drawings and Hannah's boss. Someone thought her drawings were good . . . Someone thought she had talent . . . Someone —

"*Stop it,* Hannah!" Closing her hand around the letter, she crushed it into a ball. "My life has changed enough because of you!"

CHAPTER 8

Katie could feel Dat watching her as she moved about the kitchen washing dishes, supervising Sadie's drying, and readying Annie's bottle for Mary. Twice, she'd stopped to ask if there was something she could do for him, but his answer both times had come via a shake of his head.

She tried not to worry, to accept his presence at the table as a sign he was taking a much-needed break after a long day in the fields with Samuel and Jakob, but she knew better. Dat always followed the evening meal with a final check of the barn. Always. Yet there he was, still seated at the table, quietly watching as she put the finishing touches on the day.

Had she forgotten a part of his meal?

Had she or one of her sisters missed a chore?

Had she said something during dinner he didn't like?

When the last dish was dried and put away and Annie was back on the ground with a full stomach, Dat shifted on the bench. "Mary, take Annie and Sadie into the front room. I must speak with Katie. Alone."

Mary's eyes widened with surprise, but she did as she was told. Still, as she passed, she pinned Katie with an unspoken question. Katie, in turn, offered the tiniest of shrugs and a hard swallow before turning back to Dat.

"Is something wrong?" she asked when Mary and the children had disappeared down the hallway and into the room used for church services two or three times a year.

Dat patted the section of table directly across from where he sat. "Sit, Katie. We must talk."

"Did I do something wrong? Was something not right with dinner? Did I say something unkind?"

Again, he patted the table. And again, he asked her to sit.

Katie sat.

"Lottie said you got a letter from Hannah."

She wasn't sure what she was expecting, but that wasn't it. Yet the second he ended the suspense, she found herself right back at the pond with Hannah's letter clutched

99

in her hands. Only this time, instead of being alone with the enormity of her sister's words, she was at a table, across from Dat . . .

"H-Hannah sent letters to-to everyone — Jakob, Samuel, Mary, Sadie, and even little Annie." Katie stopped, quieted the shakiness in her hands and voice, and then continued, her gaze stopping just shy of Dat's eyes. "She-she sent one to you, too, Dat. Did Miss Lottie give it to you?"

Dat captured her gaze with his and held it firmly. "Yah. But it is your letter I would like to speak of."

She wanted to look away, to busy herself with some chore she might have left undone, but Dat was waiting. Katie released her lip from between her teeth and found what she hoped was a carefree smile. "Hannah spoke of Fancy Feet . . . and the time that baby calf licked Annie's nose and startled her!"

"Did she speak of the city?"

An uneasiness she couldn't explain began at the base of her neck and traveled down to her fingers and toes. *The city?* she echoed. "No, not really. She mentioned her boss once but that was it."

Which was true.

To a point.

"Hannah would like a visit."

100

And just like that, the unease was gone, replaced, instead, by the kind of joy she hadn't felt in weeks. "Hannah is coming here? To Blue Ball?" Then, as their new reality reared its head, she leaned forward. "She will come alone this time, yah? Just Hannah?"

"No, Katie. Hannah would like you to visit her. In the city."

She stared at her dat, waiting for him to smile, to tell her he was joking, but he didn't. Instead, he splayed his hands atop the table and waited for her to speak.

"I can't go to the city," she protested. "I'm needed here, with the children."

"Mary can look after things for a short time, Katie. Soon, when you are married to Abram, she will take over."

Her mouth grew dry, making it difficult to speak. "But that's not until winter, Dat. There is much time until then."

"Winter will be here before you know it."

She couldn't believe Dat was speaking like this, that he actually seemed to be considering Hannah's request. It made no sense. "Dat, I can't go to the city. I belong here. With you and the children."

"It would not be forever, Katie. It would just be for a few days. Maybe a week."

Her head was beginning to spin in a way

her hands could not stop. None of this made sense. Not Hannah's request, not Dat's reaction, none of it. "You-you want me to go?"

"At first, I did not. But Lottie said I should think about it, that —"

She dropped her hands back down so hard the napkin holder in the center of the table jumped a little. "Miss Lottie knows about this?"

"Hannah sent her a letter, too, asking Lottie to speak with me on her behalf."

It was too much to process. Too much to even try. Still, every time she considered getting up from the table, she found that she couldn't. "If you didn't want me to go at first, what changed? What did Miss Lottie say to *make* you change?"

"She did not *make* me change, Katie. She made me *think*."

"I do not understand."

"Hannah is still family. She is still your sister. And like your mamm, I, too, want to see you smile again."

"I smile, Dat!" she protested.

He leaned forward, his gaze intent on hers. "When, Katie? When do you smile?"

"I-I smiled today . . . when Sadie got so excited about the dog sticker Hannah sent. And I smiled when Annie saw her cat

102

sticker!" Desperate to make her point, she continued the verbal tour of her day, making sure to hit on the moments that had lessened the heaviness in her heart. "I smiled tonight at dinner when Jakob spoke of the frog hopping behind you on the tractor this afternoon. And-and I smiled when Samuel said my apple pie tasted just like Mamm's!"

His hand closed over hers for the briefest of moments. "It is just a visit, Katie. That is all. Enjoy it; enjoy your time with Hannah."

She wasn't sure how long she'd been standing there at the window, looking out over the moonlit fields. A glance at the darkened gap beneath her door told her it had been long enough for Dat to blow out his candle, but beyond that, she could only guess.

In fact, if it wasn't for the telltale pinch of the boots she needed to replace, she might actually think she was dreaming. But her boots *were* pinching . . . And she *was* standing at the window in the same clothes she'd been wearing when Dat told her she should go to the big city to see Hannah.

Her — Katie.

In New York City.

The background roar that had filled her head through much of her conversation with

Dat returned. All her life, she'd only known one place — Blue Ball. Sure, she'd accompanied Dat and Mamm into neighboring towns on occasion for weddings and funerals, but everything had still looked the same. Farms stretched as far as one could see, dats and brothers tended crops, and mamms and sisters hung the wash and picked vegetables from gardens.

She didn't need to go to New York City to know it would be different. Hannah's letters and stories told Katie that. And so, too, did Hannah's —

Turning quickly, Katie made her way around the bed, her thoughts jumping to the buildings her pencil had finally captured — buildings that rose up from the earth like glistening giants. When she reached the right spot, she slid her hand between the mattress and the wooden base Dat had made. Sure enough, the roar in her ears gave way to the same accelerated thump in her chest she felt every time she pulled out her sketch pad.

She knew it was wrong.

Knew keeping a secret from Dat was wrong.

Knew drawing graven images was wrong.

But still, she did it, the pull to record life on paper winning out over her shame, time and time again. Sure, she'd been close to throwing it away on occasion. Several times she'd even gone so far as to wrap it in one of Annie's baby blankets and sneak it into the buggy when a trip to town was planned. But every time she had, every time she'd actually envisioned throwing it into one of the many garbage cans lined up in the alleyway behind the English stores, the courage everyone around her always seemed to have eluded her once again.

Lowering herself onto the edge of her bed, she flipped through her drawings until she came to the one she'd yet to complete. Then, bending over, she pulled out the photograph Hannah had given her and set it on her lap beside the sketch; her eyes moving between both before she'd fully removed her hand from page-turning duties.

She was pleased with the buildings. It had taken some doing to get the angles and the sizes just right, but after many tries, she'd succeeded. The bridge had been trickier, but finally, as the first sign of daylight had made its way around her shade on the third of three sleepless nights, she'd managed to get the curves and the ornamentation just so . . .

Swinging her focus back to the photograph, Katie studied the face that smiled back at her — a face that, while identical to hers, portrayed something very different. It was that difference that had made her wait to draw Hannah.

But now, looking between the sketch and the photograph, she knew it was time. The skyscrapers and bridge were all the proof she needed that she could draw what she didn't understand. So really, why should this new Hannah be any different?

Her mind made up, Katie closed her fingers around her pencil and began to draw.

CHAPTER 9

Katie stared down at the half dozen neatly folded dresses on the left side and the half dozen neatly folded aproned fronts on the right. In the center were socks, a smattering of hair pins and clothing pins, and an extra kapp should she soil the one currently on her head.

She'd seen these same clothes hanging from the hooks on her wall countless times, yet somehow, in Miss Lottie's suitcase, they looked different. Like they belonged to someone else . . .

"It's almost as if Hannah were here and getting ready to leave us again."

Katie whirled around to find Mary standing just inside the bedroom doorway, her pale blue eyes, so like Mamm's, staring back at her. "Like Hannah? How do you figure that?"

"Your clothes. In that suitcase Miss Lottie lent you." Mary took a few more steps into the room but stopped well short of Katie's position beside the bed. "Hannah's clothes are the only clothes I've seen folded like that."

"Hannah's clothes are English. Mine are not."

Mary's gaze lifted to Katie's for several beats before dropping to the floor and then shifting back toward the door. "Everyone is hoping you'll come downstairs for a bit before Abram arrives so we can give you a proper" — she stopped and swallowed — "goodbye."

"Mary? If you are uncertain about me leaving, I will stay."

"Dat says it is good."

"I don't know why he says that or why he thinks that." Katie let the last pin fall from her hand into the suitcase and then turned and perched on the edge of her freshly made bed. "It is good for me to be here . . . with you and the other children . . . doing as Mamm wanted. *That*'s what is good. Not riding in a bus into the big city where I don't belong."

"But you will be with Hannah and that is good. Unless . . ." Shaking her head, Mary hooked her thumb over her shoulder and stepped back through the open doorway. "We will be downstairs. Waiting."

And then she was gone, leaving Katie alone with Miss Lottie's suitcase and an ever growing sense of dread. She knew she wasn't to question Dat, knew he was only trying to do what was best for her, but leaving wasn't best. She belonged right where she was, doing what she always —

The clip-clop of an approaching buggy wafted through the open window, propelling her off the bed and back to her suitcase for one final check of its contents.

"Hurry, Katie! Hurry!"

Breathing in the courage she knew she needed but was having a hard time finding, Katie grabbed hold of the zipper pull and worked it around the bag, stopping suddenly as she reached the halfway point. With one ear cocked toward the hallway for the first sign of footsteps, she reversed the direction of her hand until she was looking down, once again, into the neatly packed bag. Only this time, instead of looking at her clothes, she tried to gage whether the bag was wide enough for —

She dropped her hand to her side and made haste around the bed. When she reached the correct spot, she slipped her hand beneath the mattress, retrieved her sketch pad from its hiding place, and made her way back to the suitcase. A quick reorganization of its contents yielded a place just big enough to house the pad before Sadie appeared in the doorway.

"Abram is here, Katie. Dat says it is time for you to go."

"I am ready, sweet girl." Katie zipped the bag closed and hoisted it off the bed and onto the floor. "Lead the way."

Sadie marched ahead, the excitement over Abram coming to call guiding her little feet back down the staircase and into the kitchen. At the base of the stairs, Abram smiled, took the suitcase from Katie's hands, and carried it out to his buggy while Katie remained behind. With the girls.

She spied Annie peeking out at her from behind Dat's chair and squatted down beside her. "Don't do any growing while I'm gone, okay?"

Annie's eyes widened with uncertainty across the top of her sucking thumb, but she said nothing.

Swallowing hard, Katie turned her attention to Mary, next. "If you need anything while Dat and the boys are in the fields, you can always go next door. To Martha's."

"I don't want to be a bother," Mary protested.

"It is not a bother. Martha knows I am going and she made sure to tell me you are to come straight to her if you have any questions." Katie lifted Annie into her arms and looked at Mary across the baby's head. "But you will do fine. I know it."

"Thank you, Katie."

Using her tiny hand to shield her mouth from Katie's view, Sadie slid off the bench seat and moved closer to Mary, her hand doing little to block the volume of her words. "Can we give Katie her surprise now?"

"Surprise? What surprise?" Katie echoed.

Sadie dropped her hand to her side and looked up at Mary. "I tried to say it quiet. I really did."

Rolling her eyes, Mary pulled a tan-colored book from behind her back and swapped it for Annie.

"What is this?" Katie asked as she looked from the book to her sister and back again.

"It is a place to write what you do and what you see . . . so you can share it with us when you are back."

Slowly, she opened the book, the lined pages untouched. "Oh Mary, this is lovely. Thank you!"

"And here is a pen from me and Annie!" Sadie pulled a small wrapped package out from behind her back and handed it to Katie. Sure enough, it was a pen . . .

"You knew I'd need a pen to write with, didn't you, sweet girl?" At Sadie's excited nod, Katie pulled the book and the pen against her chest, inhaled the courage she wanted to portray, and then spread wide her free arm for the hug she both needed and feared all at the same time.

Sadie, in turn, flew against her and began to sob. "P-please, Katie . . . do not go."

"Sadie!"

Katie met Mary's eyes over the top of Sadie's head and quietly shook off the older girl's angst. Then, turning her attention back to the distraught child in her arms, she waited until the tears slowed enough to be heard. "Sweet girl, I'm only going for a few days. In fact, it'll be so quick, I'll be back before you even really notice I'm gone."

"What if y-you ch-change your m-mind?" Sadie wailed.

She tried to shush the tears away, but when that didn't happen, she met Mary's eyes once again. "What am I missing?"

"It is nothing to worry about."

"It is something *Sadie* is worried about . . ." Katie reminded.

Mary tightened her hold on the thumb-sucking toddler and took a step closer to Katie and Sadie. "She's afraid you will stay in the city forever. Like Hannah."

"Stay in the . . ." Katie stopped, whispered her lips across the top of Sadie's head and then slowly extricated the child from her arm. "Sadie, I'm not staying in the city. I'm just visiting, that's all."

Sadie hiccupped. "What happens if you change your mind?"

"Not a thing. Because I won't." She brushed the tears from the little girl's cheeks and replaced them with kisses. "Blue Ball is my home, sweet girl. It is where you and Annie and Mary and Jakob and Samuel and Dat are."

Sadie waited until the kisses were over and then stared at Katie. "*Hannah* didn't come back."

"Katie is not Hannah, Sadie." Mary set Annie down on the ground and then motioned toward the front room and the door just beyond. "Katie, Dat does not want you to miss the bus. He told me so."

Mary was right. Time was ticking. Abram had taken time from work in his father's fields to deliver her to the bus station. To delay any further would be unfair.

Still, she couldn't ignore Sadie's continued sniffles and tear-induced hiccups. They had a special bond, the two of them — a bond that began within hours of Sadie's birth.

113

Mamm had placed it on Katie's presence during the child's delivery, but she'd been present at Annie's as well. And while she adored Annie to the ends of the earth, her relationship with Sadie was different. She'd tried to put it into words for Abram after a hymn sing one day, but it wasn't until she was alone in her room afterward that the true reason had reared its head with startling clarity.

Sadie looked at Katie as if she was courageous and strong — all the things Katie dreamed about being, but wasn't . . .

"P-please d-don't g-go, Katie."

Pulling the little girl close once again, she channeled the strength Sadie needed in that moment and hoped it sounded more real than it felt on her tongue. "It's just a visit, Sadie. I promise. By this time next week, I'll be right back here . . . in this kitchen . . . with all of you. And I'll have lots of stories to share with you from my special journal."

She didn't need to turn away from the window to know she was being scrutinized by the woman in the next seat. It was a feeling you got used to when living in an area frequented by tourists wanting to get an up-close look at people who lived as Katie lived. Instead, she focused on Abram as the bus

114

pulled away from the curb; his smile widening as she returned his wave in kind.

"I take it you two are newlyweds, yes?"

Startled away from the view, Katie turned. "No. Abram and I are not married."

"Ahhhh. Then the lack of a beard makes even more sense now." The woman Katie guessed to be about Mamm's age reached into a bag at her feet and offered an apple to Katie. When Katie declined, she shrugged and took a bite herself. "I'm Gabby, by the way. Which, you'll soon see, is a fitting name. Or so I'm told."

She sensed she was supposed to laugh, but the best she could do was smile in return. "I'm Katie."

"I take it you'll be changing buses in the city and heading upstate? To one of them Amish communities way up north?"

"No. I'm going to the city. To visit my sister."

Gabby drew back. "Your sister?"

"She is English now." She hated the way the words sounded, hated the pain they stirred every time she said them, but to deny them would be akin to lying.

"And you can still talk to her?"

"Hannah was not baptized."

"Ahhh. And was that your brother? In the buggy back there?"

"No, that is —" She sat up tall as another look outside the window turned up no sign of Abram or his buggy. "Where did he go? He was right there a minute ago."

"A minute and a mile ago, sweetheart." Gabby wiggled what was left of her rapidly shrinking apple and then pointed at the bag on the floor. "You sure you don't want one? I've got three."

Even if she was hungry, which she wasn't, she doubted she could get anything past the growing lump in her throat. More than anything, she wanted to run up to the driver and beg him to turn around, to take her back to the station and Abram. But she couldn't, especially if she didn't want to disappoint Dat.

Still, the thought of making small talk when all she really wanted to do was cry was more than she could handle. So after a silent prayer for forgiveness, she faked a succession of yawns, murmured something about being tired, and let her eyes drift closed.

Soon, the motion of the bus eventually made it so she really did sleep — a dream-filled sleep that included Mamm's voice, Sadie's cries, Katie's sketch pad, and Hannah's insistence that she had talent. But when Dat entered her dream in tandem

116

with her sketch pad, she woke up with a start.

It took a moment to remember where she was, but one look out the window at the passing cars and unfamiliar landscape delivered her reality in short order. Glancing to her right, she was grateful to see that Gabby, too, had fallen asleep. Not having to talk gave her time to think and feel, even if she wasn't sure what to think or feel about anything at that moment.

Was she excited to see Hannah? Maybe. A little. Before Hannah's choice, they could talk for hours about the silliest of things — the barn cats, the garden, the English people they'd glimpsed that day, the last hymn sing, who was courting who, and so on.

She wanted to believe nothing had changed; that they could still talk about everything and nothing all at the same time. But they lived in different worlds now. Yes, they could listen to one another's stories, but they no longer knew the same things. Maybe after a few days in Hannah's world, Katie could picture some of the things her sister wrote about in letters, but in the end, what difference did it really make?

Hannah had chosen her life.

And in turn, she'd chosen Katie's, too.

117

CHAPTER 10

"Wake up, Katie, we're here."

Pulling her head from its resting spot between the corner of her seat and the window she thought she'd been looking through, Katie looked over at her seatmate to find the woman pointing her back to the window. "We're here."

"Here?" Her confusion was short-lived as she peered out at a sea of people that went on as far as Katie could see — people scurrying left and right in front of buildings that stood taller than she could see from her seat. "I-I must have drifted off to sleep again."

"There's no 'must have' about it. You were out cold. I actually thought about waking you as we were approaching the tunnel, but —"

She sensed Gabby was still talking but she couldn't focus enough to nod, let alone respond. In her mind, thanks to Hannah's

118

picture, she'd visualized a few tall buildings, some trees, and maybe the kind of crowds they saw in and around Blue Ball during the summer tourist season.

How wrong she'd been. How horribly, stupidly wrong.

Every building as far as she could see was tall — reaching so high into the sky she had to press her face against the window to find the tops of the ones closest to the bus. Any greenery came from a person's clothing as they scurried across the street, or into a building, or down a set of stairs, or around one of a half dozen corners Katie could see from her seat.

"Where are they all going?"

She hadn't realized she'd spoken aloud until Gabby's voice pulled her attention back inside the bus. "Where is *who* going?"

"Them." Katie pointed out her window.

"Ahhh . . . welcome to New York City, young lady. Or perhaps, in your case, I should say, welcome to a completely new and different world." Gabby stood, hiked her bag onto her shoulder, and stepped into the aisle. "Your sister is coming for you, yes? Because I don't want to leave you alone in this city looking like" — she gestured first toward Katie's kapp, and then lower to Katie's aproned dress — *"that."*

Her stomach tightened at the woman's words. "Hannah is to be here. Dat said so."

"Good." Gabby filed in between the man who'd been seated in front of them and a woman who'd been in the row behind them. "Anyway, it was very nice to meet you, Katie. I hope you enjoy my hometown even half as much as I enjoy yours."

The woman took two steps toward the door and then stopped to glance back at Katie one more time, her brows furrowed. "If you're waiting for your bag, it'll be on the ground, next to the door, when you step outside."

"Thank you. I-I just need a moment to catch my breath."

"Sometimes it's better just to jump right in, Katie."

And then Gabby and her bag of apples was gone, leaving Katie alone with her parting words and the overwhelming loneliness they stoked to the surface. She knew she was supposed to get up. That she, like everyone else, was supposed to get her suitcase and be on her way. But at that moment, all she really wanted to do was stay seated until it was time for her visit with Hannah to be —

Hannah.

Jumping to her feet, Katie made her way

to the front of the bus and the stairs that led down to the driver and the single unclaimed suitcase at his feet.

"This yours, miss?" he asked, pointing down. "Because it's the last one, like you."

"Yah, it is mine! It has all of my things!" She wrapped her fingers around the handle and pulled it close — her mind's eye sifting through the contents in rapid succession . . .

Her kapps.

Her dresses.

Her sketch pad and pencils.

Her new writing book and pen.

She knew it was wrong to feel such a pull toward worldly possessions, but at that moment those same possessions were the only thing that made her feel as if Blue Ball hadn't disappeared completely.

"Through that door, miss."

Startled, she looked back up at the driver to find him pointing her through a large doorway to the crowd beyond. She tightened her hold on Miss Lottie's bag, looked around, and tried to clear her throat of the odd sensation that was making it difficult to breathe. "Dat said Hannah is to be here to meet me, but I do not see her yet."

"All waiting happens out there." Again, he directed her attention back toward the open doorway and a room that looked like it was in need of a good scrubbing. "But be careful. People here are different."

"They *look* very different . . ." she whispered.

"I'm not talking about their clothes, miss. I'm talking about the stuff you can't see. Trust me when I tell you that there are people out there who prey on girls like yourself. So keep your eyes open, and if you don't find your sister, or you need any sort of help, find a policeman."

Katie drew back. "I do not talk to the police. It is not the Amish way."

The driver turned, closed the luggage door beneath the windows, and then wiped his hands down the front of his pants. "That's right, you're a pacifist. I've read about that. That might work where you're from, but *here*? In *New York City*? You might want to rethink that practice for your own well-being and safety." He gestured toward the room on the other side of the door. "Anyway, I'll be boarding soon for my next run, so I really need to hit the head and grab a bite to eat."

"You are to hit your head?" Katie echoed.

He stared at her for a moment before a slow, knowing smile ignited across his narrow face. "Hit *the* head. It's an expression. It means to go to the bathroom."

"Oh." At a loss for what else to say, she followed him into the waiting area and then watched as he made haste toward a set of stairs that appeared to be moving. Sure enough, the driver stepped on, stood still, and rode all the way to the top. Just beyond him she could see food signs with bright neon lights, a smattering of tables and chairs, and an even bigger sea of people.

A flurry of activity off to her side pulled her focus back to her immediate surroundings in time to see a trio of girls pointing at her and her clothes. Swallowing, she turned her head only to spot yet another grouping of people eyeing her in much the same way baby Annie did a new-to-her bug. . . .

"Katie, right?"

Surprised by the sound of her name, Katie glanced over her shoulder to find an English man about the same age as Abram smiling back at her. She took a moment to drink in the green eyes gazing back at her and then shifted in her spot behind Miss Lottie's bag. "You must be looking for another Katie, an English —"

"No, you're her. Although, if I'd passed you on the street and you were wearing different clothes, I'd think you were Hannah."

She pulled her fingers from the bag's handle but not in time to cover her gasp

123

completely. "You know my sister? You know *Hannah*?"

"I sure do. She's dating my friend, Travis." He held out his hand but let it drop back to his side when the gesture went unreturned. "Anyway, I'm Eric — Eric Morgan. And since you're probably not enjoying the smell of this place any more than I am, why don't we get going."

"But I don't know you, and Hannah is to come and get me. Dat said."

"Dat?"

"My father."

"Oh. Right. I think I've heard Hannah say that word a few times." He pointed at Katie's bag and, at her nod, lifted it up and onto his shoulder. "Anyway, Hannah couldn't get away from work as planned, so she asked Travis to get you. *Travis* is hung up somewhere uptown and so he called me and asked if *I* would get you. And since my job at the moment is designing websites for people, I was able to put that aside for a while to come get you."

"But I don't know you."

"You know your sister, yes?"

"Yah."

"And you've met Travis, yes?

She nodded.

"Well, I'm sure you know they wouldn't

124

send someone to get you that wasn't okay."

"But Hannah —"

He raked a hand through his mop of dark brown hair and then hooked his thumb toward the moving stairs. "C'mon. You'll be fine. I'll have you at Hannah's place in ten minutes — fifteen if, for some reason, cabs are a little limited when we get out of here. But since we're between showtimes, I'm thinking they'll be pretty easy to find."

She wanted to protest, wanted to pull her bag back off his arm and wait until Hannah could come, but she didn't want to stay in that dank and dirty room any longer than necessary. Instead, she followed him and her suitcase across the room and onto the same moving stairs she'd seen the bus driver take.

At the top, she stumbled forward, slamming into Eric's back. He, too, lurched forward, but managed to keep himself upright while simultaneously grabbing hold of her arm until she was steady again. "I-I'm so sorry. I didn't mean to bump into you like that."

For a moment he said nothing, his eyes darting between Katie and the stairs before coming to rest solely on hers. "Have you ever been on one of those before?"

She looked back at the moving staircase

and the parade of people it delivered up to the restaurants and down to the buses. "We don't have moving stairs in Blue Ball. We move our own feet."

The answering smile he flashed in her direction carved a single hole in each of his cheeks. "That's actually an escalator. And yeah, if you're not paying attention, the transition back to stationary ground can be a little jarring."

"Yah."

Eric motioned toward a set of doors on the far side of the restaurants and then held the same hand in her direction. "It's easy to get lost in a crowd when you're not sure where you're going, so hold on tight, and I'll get you through this mess and outside in no time."

"I will be fine if I just follow." She tucked her hand behind her back and, when he shrugged and began walking, trailed him in zigzag fashion through the crowd of varying shapes, sizes, and colors.

Some people barely looked their way, intent on their own destinations. Others would stop and stare at her as she raced to keep up with Eric. Once, a long whistle from a group of men seated against a wall to her left had Eric doubling back and remaining by her side the rest of the way.

Her excitement over finally reaching the outer door was short-lived thanks to the cacophony of sights and sounds that practically rooted her to the sidewalk the second they stepped outside. Everywhere she looked, she saw people . . . and buildings . . . and picture signs . . . and cars. Laughter mingled with shouts and car horns competed with sirens. People pushed past her with shopping bags and food, cameras and maps.

In return, all she could do was stare.

"Katie? Are you okay?"

She wanted to answer, she really did. But every time her brain tried to focus, she saw or heard something that made her mouth gape all over again.

Eventually, Eric gave up and swept her limited attention span toward the road and the cars and buses that zipped past. "Don't move, I'm going to try and get us a cab."

He took a few steps forward, lifted a finger into the air, and then waved her over as a yellow car sped to a stop not more than a foot from where she stood. "C'mon. Let's get you out of here and —"

"Is it like this by Hannah's?" she asked.

"What do you mean?"

She tried again, this time using her hands to indicate the busyness around them. "Is it like this everywhere in the city?"

Understanding dawned in his eyes as he relaxed his hold on the taxi's back door. "No. We're in the Times Square area at the moment. It doesn't get much busier than this, thankfully. Up where Hannah is, is pretty peaceful."

She looked from Eric, to the back seat of the taxi, and back again, her need for air and semi-open spaces simply too overpowering to ignore. "Could we just *walk* to Hannah's instead?"

His brows inched upward. "You want to walk *thirty blocks*?"

"Yah."

He looked back at the taxi, shrugged, and then relinquished control of its back door to another would-be passenger. "Okay, I guess we're walking."

CHAPTER 11

Even without the occasional laughter, Katie could feel Eric's amusement every time she stopped to stare at something — a building that seemed to reach all the way to the clouds, a person sporting pink or purple hair, a store window with English clothes being showcased by headless bodies, dogs sitting next to people with signs asking for money . . . She tried to keep walking, she really did, but the images she'd dreamt up for Hannah's new town paled in comparison to the reality that was New York City.

"I'm sorry I keep stopping," she said as she hurried to catch up with Hannah's friend for the umpteenth time since leaving the bus terminal. "There are just so many things to look at."

Switching Miss Lottie's bag to his opposite arm, he smiled down at her. "I've got nothing pressing to get to, so it's no problem. Besides, it's kind of fun watching your

129

reaction to things I barely even notice any-more."

This time it was his words rather than their surroundings that stopped her feet. "You don't notice purple hair?" she asked. "Or that there are no trees?"

"We have trees."

"Where?" she asked, scanning the streets to her left and right. "I don't see trees."

"There aren't any here, exactly, but we have trees. Trust me on this." He nudged his chin toward the other side of the street and a half dozen or so people walking by. "As for purple hair, no, I don't really notice that kind of stuff anymore. But I *did* notice that thing you wear on your head the second I spotted you at the bus terminal."

"It is not a *thing,* it is a kapp."

Slowly, Eric made his way around Katie, stopping briefly to point at the back of her head. "It's almost heart-shaped here in the back."

"Yah. That is the way prayer coverings are for Lancaster Amish."

"Do you have to wear it all the time?"

She turned so they were facing each other once again. " 'But every woman that pray-eth or prophesieth with her head uncovered dishonoureth her head; for it is one and the same thing as if she were shaven. For if the woman be not covered, let her also be shorn: but if it be a shame for a woman to be shorn or shaven, let her be covered.' "

"Oh, okay, so it's a biblical thing . . ." Eric's gaze traveled back down to her eyes. "Well, now I know, so thank you for that. Maybe next time I see someone wearing one, it won't stand out as much now. Kinda like the purple hair I see at least a couple of times a day."

She studied him for a few seconds and then pointed upward. "You don't notice these buildings?"

"Not really, no."

"But they are so . . . *big.*"

"To me, they're normal. Like I imagine a farmhouse is to you."

"If you came to Blue Ball, you wouldn't stop to stare at farmhouses."

"Don't be so sure. This is different to you. That would be different to me." He looked around at passersby and then back at Katie. "Besides, you have farm animals, don't you?"

"Yah."

With the help of his chin, he guided her back in the desired direction and walked beside her as they crossed the next block, heading uptown. "My parents took me to a petting farm once when I was a kid. I don't remember a lot of things from those years, but I remember that clear as day. Especially getting to feed a pair of goats with a baby bottle. When the milk was all gone, one of 'em tried to eat my shirt."

"My brother Samuel once lost a school paper to the Hochstetler's goat. The teacher made him redo it." At the next block, Katie stopped, lifted her nose upward, and inhaled. "What is that smell?"

"I don't smell any — wait. Okay, yeah, that's Big Ned's." Eric pointed to a yellow awning with red lettering halfway down the street. "Best pizza around, if you ask me."

"That smell is pizza?"

"*New York* pizza, yeah." Then, hooking his thumb across his shoulder, he took a step in that direction. "Want to stop and try some?"

Propping her hands on her hips, she narrowed her focus on Eric's handsome face. "I've had pizza before, you know."

"This is your first time in the city, right?"

"Yah."

"Then you haven't had pizza like this before. Which is my way of saying I'd be a pretty lousy tour guide if I didn't take you to Big Ned's for a slice." He took another few steps and then stopped when it became apparent Katie wasn't following. "C'mon, it's already taken us an hour longer than it should have to get to this point, so what's another twenty or thirty minutes?"

A sudden rush of warmth in her cheeks forced her eyes down to the sidewalk. "I am so sorry; I didn't mean to be so slow when I asked to walk. It is just that everything is so big, so different."

"Hey . . ." He closed the gap between them with three quick steps. "That wasn't me complaining, Katie. I've actually enjoyed this walk more than I have in a long time, which is why I'm trying to stretch it out even further."

"Stretch it out?"

"Yeah, by suggesting we stop for a slice of pizza." His smile was back, along with a stomach gurgle even Katie could hear. "That and the fact all this talk about Big Ned's has made me pretty hungry."

"If you are sure . . ."

"Oh *we're*" — Eric pointed down at his stomach — "sure, trust me."

She followed him down to the yellow awning and through the door marked Big Ned's. The restaurant was small, maybe five or six tables, but one step inside confirmed Eric's belief as to the origins of the smell that had stopped Katie in her tracks.

"Mmmm, you were right. It was pizza that I smelled out there."

133

"See? Now, just wait . . . . That smell has got nothing on the taste."

Five minutes later, she was in complete agreement with the man watching her first bite from across the small window-side table. "Wow. I have never had pizza like this. It-it . . . I don't know. It is just good."

"Welcome to New York, Katie Beiler."

"Here we are . . ."

For the first time in more than an hour, Katie felt her smile fade. A glance at the building that now claimed Eric's attention snuffed it out completely. "Wait. Hannah lives *here*? In-in *this* building?"

"Yup. Working for the Rothmans definitely comes with its share of perks. Like free rent and a doorman, for starters." Eric waved to a uniformed man stationed on the other side of the door and then slipped Miss Lottie's bag off his shoulder as the man approached. "Miss Beiler is here to see Miss Beiler in 412."

The man who introduced himself as Martin and wore the shiniest gold buttons Katie had ever seen gave her a once-over before looking back at Eric. "You'd swear they were twins, wouldn't you, Mr. Morgan?"

"That's because they *are* twins, Martin." Then, reaching out, Eric guided Katie to a spot just outside Martin's earshot. "Hey, thanks for showing me New York today, Katie. I honestly can't remember the last time I've had this much fun."

Katie drew back. "But *you* showed New York to *me.*"

"That's a matter of perspective, I think. Anyway, it was great to meet you, Katie. *Really* great, in fact."

Suddenly, the unease she'd felt at the bus terminal was back. This time, though, the source of that unease was a little harder to pinpoint. Sure, being there, in New York City, was still daunting, but the past few hours with Eric had managed to soften that somehow. Until now, anyway . . .

"If Hannah is irked that it took me so long to get you here, just tell her I got lost." Then, before she could wrap her head around what he was saying, he pulled her in for a hug that was over before she'd fully blinked. "Okay, I've taken enough of your time. Go inside and see your sister. Your visit is all she's been talking about for weeks."

He took a few steps toward the road and then stopped, his eyes and his smile finding her again. "Maybe we'll get to see each other again before you head back home. To Blue Ball."

And then he was gone, his occasional glance over his shoulder in her direction necessitating another wave or another smile until he was no longer in sight.

"Miss Beiler?"

At the sound of her name, she forced her attention off the sidewalk and back onto the man with the shiny buttons. "I'm sorry . . . yes, I'm ready now," she whispered.

She followed him through the glass-paneled door and over to a nearby desk where he stopped to check a list and pick up a cream-colored telephone. "I know Miss Beiler is expecting you, but I need to let her know you've arrived and that I'm sending you up. In the meantime, take the elevator to —"

"Elevator?"

Nodding, he pointed toward a silver door on the other side of an interior hallway. "Take it up to the fourth floor and then turn right. Miss Beiler's apartment is the sixth door down on the left. I'll have your bag brought up to you in a few minutes."

"No, I can take it." She retrieved the bag from its brief resting spot beside the man's desk, hoisted it onto her shoulder, and headed over to the shiny silver door, her heart pounding. When she reached it, she hunted around for a knob only to give up as the door slid open and an elderly man with a small black and white dog stepped out.

"Just step in and press the button with the number four on it."

She looked back at Martin and, at his nod, stepped into the box to find a series of circles with numbers on them. The four turned orange at her touch, and she watched Martin disappear from view as the door slid closed between them.

Less than ten seconds later, the door slid open again to reveal a carpeted hallway and a series of doors lining both sides. Katie took a moment to catch her breath and to straighten her kapp atop her head, but before she was completely done, the sixth door on the left opened and Hannah stepped out. "*Katie! Katie!* You're *here*! You're really, *really* here."

"Yah."

Hannah ran down the hallway and threw her arms around Katie. "I've thought about having you here so many times, but now that you actually are, I feel like I'm dreaming!"

"But you are not asleep. You are standing in a hallway hugging me." Closing her eyes for a moment, Katie breathed in the strangely familiar potpourri of smells that clung to Hannah's hair and clothes — smells that reminded her of Mamm and flowers and . . . *baking*? "You-you smell like dough."

Hannah released her hold on Katie and stepped back, laughing. "That is because Jack and I made homemade sugar cookies today after his nap, and I made sure to bring one home for you."

"That was nice, thank you."

Hannah plucked Miss Lottie's bag from Katie's hands and led her through the open door. "I thought for sure you were going to be here when I got back from work and" — Hannah stopped, spread her free arm wide, and grinned — "welcome to my new home, Katie. It's pretty incredible, isn't it?"

Slowly, tentatively, Katie made her way into Hannah's apartment, her mind registering everything within eyesight — the white couch and red pillows, the television atop a nearby stand, the bookshelves lining the walls with a smattering of books and framed photographs of Travis on a bridge, Travis in a car, Travis eating a pretzel, and Travis . . . *kissing the air*?

She swung her attention to the left and noted a small table with two chairs and a shiny napkin holder on top. Beyond that, in a room not much bigger than one of the horse stalls in Dat's barn, was a kitchen with white cabinets and black sparkly counter-tops.

"Pretty fancy, isn't it?" Hannah draped her arm across Katie's shoulder and squealed. "It's just like that magazine we saw at the store that time, remember? The one with the big house and all the pretty rooms we dreamed about living in one day?"

"I did not dream of such things — *you* did," Katie corrected.

"Relax, Katie, Dat is not here. You do not have to pretend when you are with me."

Katie wiggled out from Hannah's hold and turned so her back was flush to the wall. "I'm not pretending, Hannah. I wasn't the one who dreamed of an English life. That was all you. All the time."

"Oh *please,* Katie. You looked at those pictures every bit as much as I did and don't you dare tell me you didn't!"

"Of course I looked. How could I not? You would put the magazine on my lap at night and point to every page. You'd point at pillows, and kitchens, and bedrooms as if they were the most wonderful things you'd ever seen."

"Because they were! Don't you remember the way the pillows on the chairs would match the curtains and the placemats and the dishcloths? Everything was so pretty and fancy and not anything like our plain house."

"That is because we are *plain people,* Hannah!" she challenged.

"I'm not plain." Hannah rose up on pink-polished toes and slowly turned to show off the white jeans and powder-blue top she wore. "Not anymore, anyway."

"But *I* am." She felt the answering tears gathering in the corners of her eyes and did her best to blink them away before Hannah officially completed her turn. "I like our home the way that it is. It has many memories and much laughter. This, here, is so" — she stopped, swallowed, and looked around — "quiet."

"That is only because Travis is at work. When he is not, he comes to visit and we laugh. Sometimes he brings Eric, too, and . . ." Hannah sucked in the rest of her sentence along with her breath. "*What?* Why are you turning red like that, Katie?"

Katie rubbed at her face. "I'm not red."

"Yes you are." Hannah pointed Katie toward a wall-mounted mirror and then headed into the kitchen, herself. "So what would you like to drink? Lemonade, soda, tea, water, *beer . . .*"

"Hannah!"

"What? Dat won't know."

"But *I* know." Katie waited for the strange patch of red to recede from her cheeks and then took a seat at the small table just outside the kitchen. "I do not drink beer and neither should you."

Hannah waved her off and then extracted a glass from a nearby cabinet. "Well, I do, and I wouldn't write it off just yet if I were you. Things are different here in New York City."

"You should not be different." Katie accepted the glass of water from her sister and took a small sip, the water cold against her throat. "You should still be Hannah."

"And I am. Just a newer, better version . . . with a better place to live and cooler clothes to wear."

She considered a variety of responses but opted, instead, to change the subject completely. "Dat said you would be waiting for my bus, but you weren't."

"Jack was invited for a playdate at the last minute and I had to take him. Had I known your bus was going to get in late, though, I probably could have met you."

"I didn't get in late," she said across the rim of her water glass.

"Then how did I beat you here?" Hannah crossed to the refrigerator and yanked it open. "It's only a ten-minute cab ride."

"We walked."

Hannah grabbed a can of soda from the top shelf, glancing back at Katie as she did. "From the bus terminal?"

"Yah." Katie traced her finger around the edge of her water glass and then dropped it back down to her aproned dress. "We stopped for pizza."

"And?"

"It was very good."

"And Eric?" Hannah asked as she carried her still unopened can back to the chair across from Katie's.

"He is very nice. Funny, too. He liked to try to guess what other people would order before they even got to the counter, and he was right three times in a row!" Katie's laugh stopped only as another memory floated in. "And I think the only reason he didn't get the one before that right is because I took my first bite of pizza and he could not concentrate with my moaning."

Lowering her voice to a whisper, Katie leaned against the edge of the table and locked gazes with her twin. "I didn't know pizza could be so good, Hannah!"

Hannah's eyes crackled with the mischief of old, and she pushed her drink out of the way to match Katie's lean. "Wow, I don't think I've ever seen you smile like that."

"What do you mean?" Katie asked as she lifted her hands to her face and felt around. "What is wrong with my smile?"

"Nothing. It's just that your smile and your laugh just now looked so different."

"Don't be silly, Hannah. A smile is a smile and a laugh is a laugh. I have done both many times."

"Not like that, you haven't." Hannah grabbed her soda can off the table and popped it open. "But I get it, Katie, I really do. That is exactly how I felt when I met Travis."

She stared at her sister. "What are you talking about?"

"Your smile a few seconds ago? That had absolutely nothing to do with pizza."

"It was *good* pizza, Hannah!"

Hannah's laugh sounded funny against the now-opened can. "I'm sure it was. But it is not why you smiled like you did."

"How do you —"

Hannah held up her hands. "That smile had nothing to do with pizza and everything to do with the person you were eating it with."

"What are you saying?" Katie reached for her glass and held it against her face. "And why is it so very *hot* in here. Are you baking

143

something in the oven that I can't smell?"

"Nothing is in the oven and it's not hot in here. You're just blushing because I caught you. *Again.*"

"What do you mean you caught me again?"

"First, I caught you with the whole sketch pad thing. Now, it's this thing with Eric."

She sputtered her sip of water across the table and then lunged for a napkin to wipe her chin. "There is no *thing* with Eric!"

"We may not share a room any longer, Katie Beiler, but that doesn't mean we're not still twins. I know you better than anyone else, and you know me better than anyone else. That's just the way it is and the way it's always been."

Katie pushed back her chair and stood, the shake in her legs manifesting itself in her voice. "I don't know what you're talking about."

"I'm talking about the way you were smiling and laughing when you were talking about Eric."

"I didn't smile and laugh because of Eric. I smiled and I laughed because I had fun. There were many new things to see on our walk."

"Your walk *with Eric,*" Hannah insisted as she, too, stood. Only instead of remaining by the table as Katie did, Hannah crossed to Miss Lottie's suitcase, wrapped her hand around the handle, and pulled it through an open doorway on the opposite side of the room. "But don't worry, your secret is safe with me."

Katie followed, her head spinning. "There is no secret, Hannah. I am to marry Abram, remember?"

"But you haven't yet." At the foot of a bed covered in a baby-pink blanket, Hannah released her hold on the bag and gestured toward a white dresser located to the left of the window. "This is your room while you are here. You can put your clothes in the drawers and everything else in the closet over there —"

"We aren't sharing a room?"

"No, why would we? There are two bedrooms. One for me and one for you."

"But we talk when we are in bed," Katie said. "It is what we have always done."

Hannah waved her off and then hoisted the bag onto the bed. "That is because our bedroom was the only place we knew we could be alone — just us. But here, everything is just us. No pesky brothers listening in, no little sisters asking to play games, no Dat to overhear what we do not want him to overhear, and no Mamm to . . ."

Dropping onto the edge of the bed, Hannah released her hold on the bag's zipper and reached for Katie's hand. "Oh, Katie, I am sorry. I promised myself I wouldn't say her name this week so you could try to forget for a little while."

"I don't want to forget Mamm. Not ever."

"I'm not saying you should *forget* Mamm. I'm saying you should forget everything else — your responsibilities for the children, your chores around the house, having to draw at night so Dat doesn't find out . . . you know, that kind of stuff."

Hannah reclaimed her hand to reach inside Miss Lottie's bag for Katie's things. "I know you had to bring this stuff for Dat's benefit, but" — she pulled out the stack of dresses and kapps — "if you want to borrow some of my clothes while you're here, that's okay. I have some pretty cool things now thanks to my job with the Rothmans."

"I can't wear your clothes!"

Hannah stood, crossed to the dresser, and yanked open the second drawer. "Of course you can, silly. No one is here to know otherwise."

"But *I* would know," Katie hissed. "And I know I can't wear such clothes."

Shrugging, Hannah placed the items into the otherwise empty drawer and crossed back to the bed and the open suitcase. "Okay, okay, I won't push and I won't bring it up again. But just know that if you change your mind and want to look more like me, all you have to do is say so."

"I will not change my mind." Katie pushed Hannah's hand from atop the bag and reached inside for the pile of underwear and stockings. "It doesn't matter if I am in Blue Ball or in your New York City. I am still —"

"Oh my gosh, Katie! You brought it! You brought your sketch pad!"

Before Katie could stop her, Hannah pulled out the pad, sunk onto the edge of the bed, and flipped back the cover; a peaceful sigh passed through her lips as she looked down at the first picture. "Oh, Katie. You have such a gift, you really do. I just wish you could see that."

"What I see is something I should not be doing."

"That's crazy talk, Katie. This right here?" Hannah tapped her finger on the picture of baby Annie and the nose-licking calf and then turned the page. "This is talent, Katie. God-given talent. Don't you think you should be allowed to do it for that reason alone?"

It was a point she'd never really thought about before. But still, to draw faces as she did was wrong. She knew this.

Turning, Katie made her way over to the dresser, pulled open the top drawer, and placed her underwear and stockings inside. When all was where it should be, she stepped in front of the window and its view of yet another tall building against a backdrop of even taller buildings. "It is so different here," she whispered over Hannah's continued page turning.

"That's why I like it. *Because* it's different. It's — oh, Katie!" The sounds emanating from the vicinity of the bed ceased. "This is the picture I left for you! The one Travis took of me on the bridge! You drew it!"

Katie closed her eyes but said nothing.

"You got it all exactly right — the buildings, the bridge, the people in the background, the water in the foreground, the . . ."

Katie waited for the rest of the sentence, and when it didn't come, she turned back to find her sister leaning over the sketch pad for a closer look. "Is something wrong?"

"This picture." Hannah looked up at Katie. "You captured everything in the photograph I left for you except one thing."

"Oh?" Katie crossed to the bed, pushed the suitcase back, and sat down next to

Hannah so she, too, could see her most recent drawing. "Did I forget a flower or a cloud?"

"It isn't what you forgot, Katie. It is what you drew."

Katie felt her shoulders sag. "It is the buildings, isn't it? I tried for a long time to get them just right but —"

"The buildings are perfect, Katie."

"Is it the bridge?" Sighing, she pointed to the eraser marks at the spot where the bridge and land met. "I tried to get the curve just right, but it was a little tricky in that —"

"The bridge is great, too."

"Then what did I draw wrong?" Katie asked.

Hannah set her own finger down on the person standing in the center of the bridge with the bouquet of wildflowers in her hand. "This is supposed to be me."

"It *is* you."

"No, it's *you,* Katie. See?" Hannah tapped the sketched face they shared and then pointed to her own chin. "You didn't include my scar from that fall when we were not much bigger than Sadie is now."

"I must have forgotten," Katie protested. "I am not an artist, Hannah. I do not draw those kinds of details."

"Of course you do." Hannah turned back to an earlier page and a picture of her and Jakob brushing Dat's buggy horse. "You have my scar in this one. And" — she turned back a few more pages to the one of her leaving Blue Ball for her life in New York — "in this one, too. See?"

Katie took advantage of a hard swallow to gather her thoughts enough to respond and then hoped the rasp in her voice wasn't as audible as she feared. "I was tired the night I drew you in, that's all."

"I don't believe that, Katie." Hannah met and held Katie's gaze for a few beats before breaking out the same mischievous smile that had always sent Katie running in the opposite direction when they were children. "And I don't believe it was a mistake."

"Of course it was a mistake!" she protested.

"You're too good to forget something like that."

"But it's not there, so I *did* forget, Hannah!"

"If you hadn't included my scar in all these" — Hannah flipped through to the earlier pictures again — "*other* pictures, I might be able to agree. But, since you did, I think you left off the scar because you weren't drawing me at all."

"Who else would I be drawing?"

"You!"

Katie felt her stomach beginning to churn. "That's silly. Why would I draw me on a bridge in New York City? I do not live here, remember?"

"That doesn't mean you don't wish that you did, or that you won't choose to by the time your visit is over . . ."

For a few moments, Katie said nothing. She simply stared down at the picture as Hannah's words circulated in her head.

Was Hannah right? Had she drawn herself on that bridge because —

No.

Grabbing the sketch pad off Hannah's lap, Katie stuffed it back inside Miss Lottie's bag and zipped it closed.

"Katie! Stop! What are you doing?"

"You think I will *choose* to live here?" Katie shouted. "*Choose?* I have *no* choices, Hannah — none! You made sure of that, didn't you?"

Hannah's eyes narrowed. "How did *I* make sure *you* didn't have choices?"

"Someone had to do the things you didn't do!"

"Such as?"

"Are you really asking me that, Hannah?"

"I asked it, didn't I?"

Katie stormed out of the room, her feet propelled by an anger she knew she shouldn't have. But without the anger, she knew there would be tears — tears she refused to shed for fear they'd never stop. "I have to stay!"

"Why?"

"Because I know what leaving does! I saw it on Mamm's face at the end, I hear it in Dat's voice when he speaks of you, and I see it every time your letters come in the mailbox for the children! Your choice *hurt* them, Hannah! And unlike *you,* I don't want to hurt people just so I can live in some stupid magazine!"

CHAPTER 12

Even without opening her eyes to the morning sun seeping through the fancy window coverings, Katie knew she was far from Blue Ball. At home, it was a toss-up as to whether Samuel's rooster, the newest calf in the barn, or Dat's footsteps on the stairs would serve as the sound that roused her from sleep. Here, morning ushered in a whole new host of noises she tried to identify from the safety of her bed . . .

Car doors slamming shut?

A horn blaring?

A person shouting?

The refrigerator opening?

Silverware being tossed onto the table?

Hannah's angry murmuring?

Katie closed her eyes against the memory of the argument that had ended the first night of their visit. She knew she'd been harsh in her responses, but Hannah had gotten under her last nerve. And since Hannah was always after her to speak her mind, well, she'd spoken it. Loud and clear.

If Mamm were alive, she'd have been shocked by Katie's outburst. If Dat had been in the apartment when Katie unleashed her anger the way she had, he'd have shunned her until she asked for forgiveness. But Mamm wasn't alive, and Dat wasn't there, and . . . well, Hannah had it coming.

"I know you're awake in there and that's fine. I don't care to see you right now, either." Hannah's voice, clipped and slightly hoarse, made its way past the closed door. "I left a loaf of bread on the table for toast, and there are strawberries and apples in the fridge. I'd tell you to clean up after yourself, but since you're so perfect all the time, I don't need to say that, do I?"

The headboard smacked against the wall as Katie shot up, ready to respond, but kept it to herself as Hannah continued. "I'm heading over to the Rothmans' to look after Jack and should be home around four. Maybe when I get back, you'll be ready to stop feeling sorry for yourself and we can actually have some fun."

Katie tossed back the covers, hurled her feet over the side of the bed and onto the floor, and stood, the previous night's anger bubbling to the surface. "Feeling sorry for myself —"

The click of a door in the distance stole the rest of her words and she reversed course from the door to the window. Pushing the blinds off to the side, she shoved her forehead against the glass and strained to make out the sidewalk directly below. Sure enough, within a matter of a few short minutes, Hannah emerged from the building and began walking in the direction of the sun.

For a few moments, Katie just stood there, watching her twin from the back, noting the stylish sneakers, the cute shorts that showed far too much skin, and the way Hannah's light brown hair swooshed against her back as she walked. It was as if Katie was looking at a stranger rather than someone who'd been a part of her life since the very beginning.

She felt the tears building and squeezed them away with a familiar yet no less potent anger. For months she'd been told Mamm's sickness and subsequent death were God's will. She knew such words were supposed to lessen the hurt, but they didn't. If anything, all it really did was make her angry. At God.

But with Hannah, it wasn't God's will that

had made her turn her back on everyone. That had been *Hannah's* will — *Hannah* had chosen to pick up and move out, to hurt Mamm and Dat and the children, to make it so Katie —

She backed away from the window, biting down on her lip as she did. "I'm *glad* I don't have to spend the day with you, Hannah Beiler!"

Squaring her shoulders, Katie marched over to the bedroom door, yanked it open, and froze.

She was alone. In New York City. For the next — Katie scanned her surroundings until she spied a clock mounted on the wall above the kitchen table — *eight hours.*

At home, she'd pass the time gardening, doing the wash, mending clothes, cleaning, and cooking. Yet here, in Hannah's apartment, there was no garden to tend, no clothesline to fill, no sewing machine to use, and nothing to clean that Katie could see. There was only breakfast to eat and eight hours in which to eat it.

Swallowing, she made herself step forward toward the loaf of bread Hannah had left out; her gaze moving between it and the toaster plugged into the wall atop the kitchen counter. A note attached to the bread pulled her in that direction.

For the next week, you are connected to the outside world with electricity. That's the way it is here. Dat knows this, and Dat said you could come.

Put the bread in the toaster just like you've seen Miss Lottie do, and press the button. It's easy.

Hannah
(I am not selfish)

"Writing it does not make it so," Katie murmured before turning her attention to the top section of the note once again.

For the next week, you are connected to the outside world with electricity. That's the way it is here. Dat knows this, and Dat said you could come.

Dat *had* told her to come . . .

She opened the loaf of bread and extracted a slice, only to drop it as a telephone, mounted to the wall between the table and the kitchen, began to ring.

One ring . . .

Two rings . . .

Not sure what else to do, Katie picked it up and held it to her ear. "Hello?"

"Hey, Hannah. How'd it go last night?"

"This is Katie." She stole a glance at

herself holding the phone via the side of the toaster. "Hannah is not here . . . she is at work."

"Oh hey there, Katie! It's Eric." A beat of silence that rivaled only the sound of her heart slamming inside her chest gave way to the male voice in her ear once again. "You know, from yesterday."

"I remember." And it was true, she did. She just wasn't sure why her face felt so hot and her phone-holding hand suddenly felt so slippery.

"So how was your first night in the city with Hannah? Did you do anything fun?"

"We . . . talked."

"Good. Good. I know Hannah has been so excited for you to get here."

She stepped away from the toaster and, instead, leaned against the counter as snippets of the screaming match that had constituted her conversation with Hannah replayed itself in Katie's thoughts.

"Katie? Are you still there?"

"Yah. I-I mean, yes."

"When will Hannah be back?"

Katie's shoulders slumped as, once again, she took in the clock. "Four o'clock."

"And what are you going to do in the meantime?"

It was a good question. "I don't know."

"Want to hang out with me in the park?" he asked.

"The park?"

"Yeah. That way you can see with your own two eyes that we have trees and even some grass, too."

She practically ran back to the toaster, this time looking past the phone to the rest of her — her disheveled hair, her rumpled bedclothes, her reddening cheeks . . . "I don't know. I really should just stay here and wait until Hannah gets home."

"No, you really shouldn't. Besides, I'll have you back long before she is, I promise."

He was waiting as she stepped out of Hannah's building and onto the sidewalk; his smile was a welcoming sight against a backdrop that made her feel completely out of place. And while one only had to look at his English jeans and short-sleeved shirt next to her pale blue dress with its aproned front to know she was out of place with him, too, at least he was something a little familiar.

"Ready to see our version of country?" he asked by way of a greeting.

"Yah — I mean, yes."

"Good. Let's go." He pointed in the opposite direction from which Hannah had set off for her nanny job, and when Katie acquiesced, he fell into step beside her. "And you don't have to do that, you know."

Katie stopped. So, too, did Eric. "Do what?"

"Change the way you talk. If you want to say yah, say yah." She felt the instant heat in her cheeks and was grateful when he got them walking again with little more than a nod in the desired direction. "So what were you thinking so hard about when you were looking out Hannah's window a few minutes ago?"

This time, when she stopped, it was more of a lengthy pause. "How do you know I was looking out Hannah's window?"

"It's a window, Katie," he said, not unkindly. "I saw you when I looked up. I tried to wave so I wouldn't have to call, but your attention was on something else."

"It is so . . . so *different* here." She hadn't meant to share the thought aloud, but in a rush it just came out. Then, anxious not to seem as if she were judging, she tried her best to fill in the answering silence. "At home in Blue Ball, people don't really walk past my window. Especially in the morning when there is so much work to be done. But if I do see someone walking along the side of the road, they walk a little slower.

And they look around more."

"Look around more?"

"Yah. At home, there are neighbors to wave at, cows to say silly things to, wildflowers to stop and pick for . . ."

She let the rest of the sentence go in favor of a hard swallow. If Eric noticed, he didn't let on. Instead, he swept his gaze from the building on the left to the building on the right as they continued walking.

"I guess maybe the people you were noticing have seen all of this a bazillion times so there's not really a reason to look around, you know?"

She nodded as if she understood, but she didn't. Not really. Every single spring there were calves born in the fields, and she still looked. Every day, Dat and the boys worked in the fields, and she still waved to them at least a half dozen times a day. Every afternoon, Fancy Feet moved herself around the yard according to the sun's rays, and she still laughed.

"That's why yesterday afternoon was so special."

Confused, she stopped again. "But yesterday afternoon you were with me."

His smile widened to include his eyes. "Exactly."

"But I don't understand. There is nothing" — she dropped her gaze down to her boots — "special about me. I am just Katie. I am . . . Amish."

"Which is what I expected I would find when I walked into the terminal yesterday." He guided her forward and then, at the end of the sidewalk, he pointed across the street. "So? What do you think? Not bad, eh?"

She made herself abandon the odd conversation long enough to humor him, and when she looked in the direction indicated, she felt her mouth gape. For there, just beyond the line of cars slowing to a stop for the traffic light, were trees. Lots and lots of trees. In fact, from where they stood, trees were all she saw in the distance. "Those are . . . *trees.*"

His rich, deep laughter tickled her ears a split second before his hand found hers and tugged her across the street. "You wanted trees, I give you *trees*! *Big* trees, *little* trees, and *everything-in-between* trees."

She ran with him across the street, her own laughter mixing with his as they slipped through an opening in the black wrought iron fence and came to a stop. In front of her, as far as her eyes wanted to see at that moment, was grass . . . and trees . . . and the first sense of peace and absolute calm she'd felt in twenty-four hours. No, it wasn't

Blue Ball, but it was closer.

"Oh, Eric, it is . . ." She drank in her surroundings a second time and then, when her breath had steadied enough to allow something more than a raspy whisper, added in the only thing that fit at that moment. "It is *beautiful.*"

An odd expression skittered across his face as he, too, stood perfectly still. "It is, isn't it?"

They stood there for a while with Eric seemingly lost in thoughts Katie didn't or couldn't know. But that was okay. For at that exact moment, all that really mattered was the feel of the sun on her neck, the gentle breeze that lapped at her cheeks, and the warmth of his skin as —

She pulled her hand from his, tucked a piece of flyaway hair back in place beneath her kapp, and took a step backward in the direction from which they'd just come, a sadness not unlike the one that had accompanied her away from Blue Ball settling across her heart. "Thank you for showing me this. It . . . helps."

"You're homesick, aren't you?"

"Very much."

He looked from their surroundings to her, and back again only to widen the gap between them as he stepped farther into the park. "Tell me about it — about Blue Ball, about growing up with Hannah, and your life there now."

"I took enough of your time yesterday with all my silliness. I don't want to do that again today."

"Your silliness?" he echoed. "Are you kidding me? When I was with you, I was not one of those people you saw from the window this morning — the ones who walk but don't look. You made me look at the buildings and actually notice the architecture. Heck, I even waved to someone I didn't know . . . *Twice!* Granted, they looked at me like I was nuts, but it was different. Fun."

She gave into the laugh born on his words. "I'm pretty sure *everyone* looked at me that way yesterday. But you get used to it."

"People might have done a double take on the clothes a time or two, but really, that's one of the things I like about living here. Everyone gets to just be."

"I don't understand."

He darted his gaze around trees and up a nearby hilly mound before looking back at Katie. "Take a look at the guy on top of that hill — the one reading the book under the tree."

"I read under a tree at home, too. Only

it's by the pond." Katie took a half step to the right, bobbed her head around Eric, and visually located the man in question, her mouth gaping for the second time. "His hair is . . . *blue.*"

"That it is."

"But hair is not to be blue and it is not to be purple like we saw yesterday."

"He disagrees. And so, too, do the purple-haired people." Slowly, Eric began to turn, stopping midway in what appeared to be a circle. "Now check out that woman pushing the stroller where that pathway branches to the left and right."

Katie shifted her position until she, too, could see the woman. "What is that shiny thing in her nose?"

"An earring."

"In her *nose*?"

"Yup. And do you see that couple getting ready to pass her right now?"

"Yah."

"Do you see them pointing at her? Or stopping to stare?"

She watched the elderly couple nod at the woman, wiggle their fingers at the baby, and then keep moving. "No."

"Well, that's a plus side to what you saw outside your window earlier. People are busy, yes, but they also just don't care.

Which, translated, means no one will notice your kapp unless you keep messing with it."

Dropping her hands, Katie met Eric's eyes once again. "You remembered to call it a kapp."

"Because you took the time to explain it to me and I listened. So, come on, tell me more about Amish life."

"I don't want Hannah to worry."

He pulled a phone from the back pocket of his jeans, hit a button, and then turned it so she could see the screen. "It's not even eleven yet. We've got five hours before Hannah is back home."

Pulling the phone close, he pressed a few more buttons before placing it back in his pocket. "And so she doesn't worry if she tries to call, I just sent her a text letting her know I'm with you and we're going for a walk. So let's walk."

Not sure of what else to do, she followed him across the grass and over to the path. When they reached it, he stopped, considered both directions, and then led her toward the right and a canopy of trees not unlike one she'd seen on Mamm's kitchen calendar the previous year. At the time, she could only imagine what it would be like to walk down such a path so unlike any she'd ever seen.

"Every year, Mamm would hang a new picture calendar on the wall in the kitchen. Each page showed something pretty — a meadow of flowers, a waterfall down a mountainside, river water falling over rocks, and a path that looked just like" — she stopped fiddling with the sides of her dress and held out her hands — "*this*. I remember changing to another seat many times that month just so I could see that picture and imagine what it would be like to be inside it."

His footsteps slowed beside her as he cleared his throat once, twice. "Hannah told me about your mom, and I'm really sorry. I know how hard that is."

Like clockwork, the constant ache that was Mamm's death took everything that was good about the day and turned it a drab gray. She gathered her breath the way she'd taught herself to do the past few weeks, and then released it through her lips along with the expected "it is God's will" response.

"Yeah, I know. That's what people told me, too. But all that did was make me hate God for a really long time."

Katie's answering gasp sent a squirrel running in the opposite direction. "Eric! You are not to speak like that about God!"

Veering off the edge of the path, Eric

backed his way up against the trunk of a nearby tree. "I don't feel that way *now,* but back then? When all the other kids had moms except me? You bet I was angry."

"Your mom passed, too?"

"Yup. When I was eight. Died in a car accident on her way to the grocery store to buy cake mix for the church bake sale." He ran his hand down the front of his face and then released his own labored breath. "Haven't eaten a piece of cake since."

"What was your mother like?" Katie asked.

Eric bent his left leg at the knee and rested his foot against the trunk of the tree, a small smile playing at the corners of his mouth. "She was funny . . . and smart . . . and she always made a big deal out of holidays and birthdays for my dad and me." Then, pushing off the tree enough to reach into his back pocket, he pulled out his wallet and beckoned Katie to come closer. When she did, he pulled out a picture of a dark-haired woman standing beside an equally dark-haired man and behind a young, but still recognizable, Eric. "My dad has the more formal version of this picture in a frame on the mantel at home, but I liked this one because the photographer caught the three of us laughing about something goofy Mom had said. I can't remember what it was, but I can remember the way her laugh sounded and the way it made me feel."

"I miss everything about Mamm," Katie whispered. "I miss her smile . . . I miss her kind words . . . I miss the feel of her hand on my shoulder and her voice in my ear when I couldn't do things like Hannah." Now that the words were flowing, they wouldn't stop. "Everyone says it was God's will, but how could it be His will to take her from Dat and the children? And from me?"

"I don't think it was. I think it just happened." Eric closed his wallet and slipped it back into his pocket. "So? How about you? Do you have a picture of your mom?"

Casting her eyes downward, she toed at a pebble. "No. The Amish do not take pictures."

"But you just talked about the calendar picture that looks like" — he motioned toward the canopy of trees just beyond where she stood — "this, didn't you?"

"That is a place, not a person."

"And there's a difference?" he asked.

"The Bible says, 'Thou shalt not make unto thyself a graven image.' "

He dropped his foot back to the ground and stepped away from the tree, disbelief

169

holding court on his face. "So you don't have any pictures of your mom at all? Wow. That really stinks."

At a loss for how to respond, Katie made her way back onto the path with Eric close on her heels. "Hey-hey, Katie . . . I'm sorry if that just got a little heavy. It wasn't my intent."

"It is not you or anything that you said. I think of Mamm every day and it always makes me sad."

"Then it sounds like you've had your sad for the day. We both have. So let's find some happy now, okay?"

She looked up to find him smiling down at her. "Where?"

"Patience, patience."

Laughter chased away the last of the sadness for Katie. "Mamm used to say those very words to Hannah all the time when we were little."

"Why Hannah?"

"Because she didn't like to wait for anything."

"Ahhhh, yes. That certainly sounds like the Hannah *I* know, too." His deep, rich laugh tickled her ears and warmed her cheeks from the inside out. "But today is about you, not Hannah. So stop right there and close your eyes."

"But if I close my eyes, I will not see what you want me to see."

"It'll only be for a minute, I promise. And I'll have your hand so you don't bump into anything."

"But I —"

"Close them, Katie."

She closed them.

She took the five steps he requested.

And she tried not to dwell on the feel of his fingers suddenly entwined with hers.

"Okay, you can open them now."

Parting her lashes, she peeked out to find a pond with an assortment of toy sailboats floating around in the center. People walked around the pond, talking, while others sat along its edge, basking in the late-morning sun or laughing with nearby companions. A handful of ducks swam beside the boats, voicing their displeasure at any and all sudden changes in direction.

"Oh, Eric, Sadie would *love* this." She clapped her hands together beneath her chin and stared at the scene in front of them, trying her best to memorize it all. "She's always trying to make boats out of leaves and twigs! At first, she tried to use rocks, but that didn't work very well. She'd get them all ready for their voyage, push them away from the shore, and watch them

171

sink to the bottom. That's when she moved on to leaves and twigs. And once? Last summer? One of them actually made it all the way across to the other side! She squealed so loud and so long I'm quite sure the Hochstetlers *and* the Millers heard her clear out in the middle of their fields. And truth be told, I wouldn't be a bit surprised if the Fishers heard her, too."

"Who's Sadie?"

"My little sister. She's four."

"Sounds like she keeps you busy."

"Yah. But happy, too." Katie bobbed her chin toward the lake, and at his nod, made her way down the hill for a closer look. "Do you come here often?"

"To the park?" At her nod, he shrugged. "I walk through it mostly. Less people to maneuver around when I'm trying to get across town to my favorite writing spot."

"Writing spot?" she echoed.

"I write songs. Or, at least, I try to. And there's this cool little coffee shop on the other side of the park that I like to go to when I need a change of scenery." He stopped at the water's edge, looked around the lake, and, at the answering shrug from an elderly man on the opposite side, liberated a toy sailboat from a snarl of leaves and set it back on course. "That's my dream

172

— to hear a song that I've written being played on the radio."

"Perhaps it will happen one day."

"Maybe. But even if it doesn't, it's still something I do that makes me happy . . . like talking about your little sister did for you a few minutes ago."

"If you knew Sadie, you would understand."

"Funny kid?" he asked as they continued around the lake, stopping from time to time so Katie could point out a particular duck or sailboat.

"Mamm used to say Sadie is like me because she misses nothing. But she's also adventurous in a way I never really — *look*!" Katie pointed toward a man and a young girl seated on stools beneath a tree, facing one another. The man looked between the girl and a big white board while the girl stood perfectly still. "What are they doing?"

"Who?" Eric followed the path forged by Katie's answering finger. "Oh, okay, so that's a sidewalk artist, for lack of a better word. There's dozens of them scattered around the park on any given day."

"What do they draw?"

"People — mostly tourists, and mostly caricatures. Something people roll up and put in their suitcase to remember their trip to the city, I guess."

She knew he was still talking, even registered a little of what he was saying, but her focus was on the man looking between the girl on the stool and a large sketch pad. The concentration on his face called her to come closer and she obliged. Eric, too, changed course, moving in beside her as she stopped in view of the man's easel.

"Why is he making her face look like that?" she whispered. "Her lips are not that big."

"That's what he does. He finds a feature or two and overemphasizes it."

Fascinated, Katie moved a little closer. "I wish he would just draw her as she is."

"I'm guessing that would take longer."

"Yah. But it would be *better.*" She leaned closer to Eric to ensure the man could not hear. "See her cheekbones? If he turned his pencil to the side a bit more like *this*" — she held a pretend pencil between her fingers and moved it back and forth quickly — "he would get more depth."

"You say that like you know. Are you an artist?"

"No, I am Amish."

He looked at her from beneath raised eyebrows. "And those are mutually exclusive because . . . wait, I know this! It's because he's drawing her face, isn't it?"

"Yah."

She watched as the man finished the picture, showed it to the girl, and, at her squeal of appreciation, handed it to her in exchange for a ten-dollar bill. There was no denying the girl's happiness or the way it stirred something deep inside Katie.

"I draw at night," she whispered. "When Dat and the children are sleeping. I-I know it is wrong, that I could be shunned if they found out, but still, I draw."

"Why?"

Katie looked down at her feet, the answer she knew she shouldn't utter the same one she could no longer hold back. "Because I think it is *my* dream."

CHAPTER 13

She'd tried the couch in the living room, the table near the kitchen, and the armchair closest to the big window, but in the end, just like at home, Katie opted to prop herself against the headboard of the bed with the sketch pad balanced across her crisscrossed legs. The lighting was different on account of the late-afternoon hour, but the most liberating change was knowing she could draw without listening for evidence of Dat's footfalls in the hall or an early rising Sadie trying to get a peek underneath the door.

Here, she could bask in a freedom she didn't really know yet found infinitely appealing. Here, she could wander around the room, trying to recall details of her day without worrying whether others knew she was awake or not. And here, she didn't have to draw by moonlight only to cringe at the results come morning.

In fact, if she was honest with herself, the picture taking shape beneath her pencil was some of the best work she'd ever done. Somehow, someway, she'd managed to re-create the lake and the ducks and the sailboats so clearly it was as if she were standing in the park, looking at it in real time, rather than calling on her mind's eye to fill in the blanks. Even Eric's hands as he repositioned the boat in the water looked good, though she'd had to redo the pile of leaves he'd pulled from the vessel a half dozen times to make them look natural.

The only aspect still weighing on her was whether she'd made the right decision to start the picture at his hands so that, when she was done, the only part of Eric seen beyond them was the side of his face . . .

His strong jawline . . .

The way his dark brown hair stopped just shy of his ear . . .

The edge of his dimpled smile . . .

A distant click from the direction of the living room broke through her thoughts, bolting her upright in time to identify the next sound as footsteps. The answering thump of her heart had her launching forward, gathering her pencils and sketch pad in a mad grab, and then freezing in place as the reality of her current surroundings reared its head in tandem with the familiar voice now moving toward her room.

"Katie? Are you here?"

"Yah. I'm in my room."

She willed her heart rate to slow, opened her fist to let the pencils drop back onto the bed, and then looked up as her sister appeared in the doorway, curiosity lighting the eyes that were a mirror image of her own. "I am *drawing*," she whispered.

"I can see that." Laughing, Hannah closed the gap between the door and the bed, sinking down onto the edge of the mattress closest to the hastily closed sketch pad. "But just so you know, you don't have to whisper that here. You also can skip the whole scurrying to hide everything part, too. Your secret is safe with me."

"I did not scurry."

Hannah dipped her chin almost to the base of her neck and studied Katie the way Miss Lottie studied them on occasion. "Please, Katie . . . I heard enough to know you were scared." Then, before Katie could say anything else, Hannah gestured toward the sketch pad. "So? Can I see what you added today? I promise I won't say another word about my scar."

"I started a new picture. One from this morning."

"This morning?" Hannah echoed as she looked around the guest room Katie had made sure to neaten before settling down to draw. "You mean you drew this room?"

"No. I drew the lake at the park. The one with the boats on it."

Hannah drew back so fast she almost toppled off the bed. "You went to the park? Alone?" And then, as she recovered enough to really take in Katie's words, a smile replaced the surprise. "See? I knew you'd come out of your shell here."

"I wasn't alone."

A second round of surprise pushed Hannah's overly tweezed and darker than normal eyebrows halfway to her hairline. "I don't understand."

"I went with Eric. He sent you a text, remember?"

The surprise remained for about as long as it took for regret to register in Katie's brain.

Uh-oh.

"Ooooh, that's right . . . Do tell." Hannah clapped her hands in glee. "And leave nothing out."

"It was not like that, Hannah! He called to talk to you and I told him you were working until four o'clock. He asked what I was going to do and when I said nothing, he suggested we go for a walk in the park. That's all."

"And?"

"And what?"

"Did you have fun?"

She tried to answer via a noncommittal shrug, but her own smile, born on the memory of her time with Eric, refused to be denied. "I did. Eric is very nice."

"What did you do?"

"We walked. And we talked. He talked about his childhood and the songs he writes. I told him about Blue Ball and Sadie and" — Katie looked down at the sketch pad — "my drawings."

Hannah opened her mouth as if she was going to ask more, but in the end, she simply pointed at the pad. "So? Do I get to see what you're working on?"

"I suppose." She flipped back the cover and then stopped, her gaze seeking and finding Hannah's. "I'm sorry I got so angry last night. It was not right to yell at you the way that I did."

"You were angry. You're allowed."

"I shouldn't say such things to you."

Leaning forward, Hannah brought her lips close to Katie's ear. "Psst . . . you're *human,* Katie. That means you're *allowed* to get angry. You're also allowed to cry and stamp

180

your feet and ask for help when you need it."

"But —"

"It's *okay,* Katie. I get it." Then, pulling back, Hannah pointed at the sketch pad again. "Now, show me. Please."

Katie gave up and paged through her drawings until she came to the one of the park. "It's not done yet. I still have to add the side of Eric's face. But this is it so far." Nibbling her lower lip inward, she spun the pad so it was right side up for Hannah and then waited.

"Oh, Katie . . ." Hannah lifted the pad off the bed, her eyes moving from the ducks and boats in the background to the boat in Eric's hands. After a few moments of silence, she looked back up at Katie. "This is amazing — *you* are amazing! I-I don't understand how you learned to draw like this when no one was looking. I mean this is *talent,* Katie, *real talent.*"

A sudden infusion of heat in her cheeks propelled Katie off the bed and over to the room's back window. Down below, on the ground level, was a small garden area bordered by the buildings on either side of Hannah's, as well as the backside of another. Scattered around the garden were benches. An hour earlier, the benches had been inhabited by school children doing home-work or chatting on phones. Now, save for one lone elderly man reading a paper, there was no other sign of life. "It was back before Rumspringa when I started to think about it. I was painting a scene on a milk can for Dat's stand. It was of that fence along the north side of Hochstetler's farm. For some reason, instead of seeing the fence I was trying to paint, I kept thinking about Luke and the frog. No matter how hard I tried, I could not put that memory aside. It was as if my mind could see nothing else that day. So, when we were on Rumspringa, I bought a sketch pad and practiced until I could draw that memory."

"That's my point. When and where did you practice when I was still living at home? And why did you keep it from *me* of all people?"

The first part of Hannah's question was easy to answer and so she started there, the man on the bench down in the courtyard quickly bowing to another, equally vivid im-age. "Remember those days when I would walk Mary and Jakob home from school?"

"Okay . . ."

"That is when I would draw."

"But you weren't gone long enough to walk them all the way home *and* draw."

182

"That's because I didn't walk them *all* the way home."

"I don't understand. You just said —"

"I met them on that path between the road and the pond . . . the one that we always took home from school when we were their age, too."

"But that isn't even halfway!"

"They were old enough to walk the whole way by themselves, but they were always happy when they came around the trees and saw me waiting for them."

"And you would draw there while you were waiting?"

"Yah." Katie watched the elderly man fold his paper atop his lap, struggle to his feet with the help of a walker, and then head toward the building's back door, disappearing from her sight completely. "You know that old shed on the Hochstetler's land that is not far from the pond? The one with the door that does not close as it should? That is where I kept my sketch pad — underneath an old horse blanket on the top shelf."

"You didn't have that much time."

"Most days, I had twenty minutes before I had to hide it under the blanket again." She felt her mouth stretching wide with the memory. "The picture you took from the pad? The one of Luke and the frog? That

183

took me from the start of the school year until nearly December to finish. It got so cold those last few weeks that I had to erase many times because of shaking fingers."

"But there are a lot of pictures in here," Hannah protested. "If it took you more than three months to draw *one,* how did you draw so many?"

"Once you left, I could draw inside . . . at night . . . after Dat and Mamm went to sleep. Sometimes, I would draw for hours."

"Okay, but why didn't you draw in our room from the start? Did you really think I would tell?"

"No. I knew you wouldn't tell."

"Then why didn't you tell me? Why did I have to find it under your bed when I visited in the fall?"

Eight hours earlier, she couldn't have answered that question. But now, thanks to her time with Eric, she knew the why. Slowly, she made herself turn away from the window and venture back toward the bed and Hannah; her need to answer rivaled only by the fear of sharing what had been a surprising admission even to herself. "I didn't *want* to tell you. I wanted my drawings to be *mine. I* wanted to learn something you couldn't do and I wanted to be good at it. I-I wanted to be . . . *Katie.*"

Hannah scrunched her face. "Who else did you think you were?"

"What I've always been, Hannah — *your* twin."

"*My twin?* Hey, that's not true! Mamm loved you, Katie, you know that!"

Sinking onto the bed, Katie reached for her sketch pad with one hand and waved away Hannah's protests with the other. "I know that. She showed me that every day."

"Okay good. And this other stuff? About wanting to be good at something? What about the children? You've always been better with them than I was. And that was even *before* Mamm passed. Now, you do everything for them."

"I am simply doing things as Mamm did them."

"So. And what about Dat? He trusts you in a way I'm not sure he ever trusted me."

"But whenever we would meet people for the first time, Mamm and Dat would always say 'this is Hannah's sister, Katie.' And at school, I was always Hannah's sister, too. I was never just Katie."

"Okay, but that held true whenever something went wrong, too. If a barn door was left open or Fancy Feet was found in the house, they came looking for me."

"Because it always *was* you." Katie ran

185

her hand across the picture of the lake, lingering her fingers in the place where the side of Eric's face would soon be. "But the drawings in this book? They are something I've done all on my own — not because I'm Hannah's twin or Hannah showed me how, but because *I* put my mind to it and *I* found a way. Just me. By myself — me, *Katie.* I need that, Hannah. I need that for me."

CHAPTER 14

She waited for Hannah to finish petting the third dog of the morning and then fast-walked to catch up with her as she resumed the kind of pace Katie had always equated with a brewing storm. This time, though, they weren't rushing to close windows or secure the horses in the barn before the black clouds unleashed their wrath, they were swerving around people and running across city streets for a start time that was still twenty minutes away.

"You said the Rothmans are close — just ten blocks. We have gone seven. Why are we running?" Katie asked between increasingly labored breaths.

Hannah reached into the small bag tethered to her neck and shoulder and pulled out her phone. A quick glance at the screen yielded a shrug. "I'm sorry, Katie. It is the way real New Yorkers walk."

"We've passed many people."

"If they weren't tourists, then they aren't trying to get somewhere like we are." Still, Hannah slowed enough that Katie's boots no longer smacked against the concrete. "I wish you would've worn the jeans and top I handed you when you came out of the bathroom. They'd have been a lot more comfortable than" — Hannah flicked her hand at Katie's aproned dress and stockings — *"that."*

Katie felt a resurgence of the anger she'd apologized for the previous night and worked to keep it in check. "I don't know why you keep saying that, Hannah. I am Amish. This is the way Amish dress — the way you once dressed, too."

"A lifetime ago, maybe."

Katie stopped in the middle of the sidewalk and waited for Hannah to do the same. When she did, Katie closed the gap between them in an effort to keep her anger from being heard by passersby. "It has been one year, Hannah. *One year.* Was life in Blue Ball with Mamm, Dat, the children, and me so truly awful you must now pretend it didn't happen?"

"No, of course not, silly." Hannah swept her arms outward, splaying her hands as she did. "But this here? It feels so right to me that it's hard to picture myself anywhere else."

"You do not remember chasing the barn cats with me? Or laughing until our sides ached when Eli Fisher's suspender snapped off in the middle of class that one day? Or sitting on the front porch listening to stories of Mamm's childhood? Or . . . or waiting for the first taste of Mamm's apple pie?"

Hannah dropped her hands to her side and swallowed. Hard. "Of course I remember those things. How could I not?"

"Then you haven't forgotten what it is like to be Amish." Katie held Hannah's gaze for a few silent beats and then gestured in the direction they'd been going. "We should go. So you're not late."

Resuming their previous pace, they made their way down the remaining half block to the crosswalk. When the pedestrian light changed to white, Katie repositioned her sketch pad beneath her arm and fell into step beside Hannah one more time. "I don't know why you wanted me to bring my drawings if you want me to get to know Jack."

"Because Jack takes a nap after lunch every day and that will give you time to finish the picture of the park that you didn't get to finish yesterday."

Katie slowed her steps even more. "I could help you do the lunch dishes or fold laundry."

"The Rothmans have a cleaning lady who does that. My job is to care for Jack." Crossing her arm in front of Katie, Hannah pointed to the next street. "We're almost there. The Rothmans live in a beautiful brownstone that is three whole floors."

"*Three* floors?"

"The top floor is where Mr. and Mrs. Rothman sleep. It's this grand room that is bigger than your room, the boys' room, and the girls' room all put together. And Mrs. Rothman's closet? It is bigger than Dat's whole room and it's filled with beautiful clothes from fancy stores."

At the corner, they turned right, the excitement in Hannah's voice continuing to build. "The second floor is where Jack sleeps. His room is a zoo theme and, well, I can't wait for you to see it. He has a stuffed giraffe that is as tall as the ceiling and a stuffed sea lion that he can sit on while we're reading books! He even has a table in one corner where he can play with colored dough and paint if he wants to. His room is the biggest on that floor but there are three others as well — all bigger than yours."

"Our — I mean, *my* room is plenty big,

Hannah, you know that."

"Maybe. But just wait, you'll see how much better the Rothmans' place is, how much better *everything* about their life is." Hannah tucked her hand through Katie's arm and fairly dragged her to a stop in front of a staircase. It led to a dark brown door Katie recognized as the same kind of wood Dat had used to make Mamm's chest. "We're here!"

Katie took in the door, the wide front window that bowed outward, and the handful of flowering plants she could see through the glass as they began their ascent. "Are you sure it is okay that I'm here?"

"I'm positive. Mr. Rothman is anxious to meet you."

She stopped, mid-step, and eyed Hannah closely. "*He* is anxious to meet *me*? Why?"

The question hung in the air for a few seconds as Hannah's gaze traveled the remaining steps, her cheeks noticeably flushed. "Because . . . because he's heard me talk about you many times, that's all."

"Is there something you're not telling me?" Katie prodded.

"Don't be silly, Katie. What would I not be telling you about my employer?" Hannah continued them up the stairs and through the front door as if she, too, lived

191

inside. "Jack, I'm here! Find your hiding place!"

A flurry of footsteps somewhere in their general vicinity built to a crescendo only to cease mere seconds before a muffled voice emerged from the end of the hallway. "I'm hiding! Find me, Hannah! Find me, find me!"

Hannah slipped her arm out from under the strap of her bag and then pulled it off her neck, grinning at Katie as she did. "He's hiding under the piano bench in the hearth room."

"How do you know that?"

"Because he hides in exactly the same place every single morning." Hannah placed her bag on a glass-topped table to their right and pointed for Katie to do the same with the sketch pad. "I keep waiting for him to find another place, but he doesn't."

"Sadie did that when she was three, too, remember? Only *her* hiding place was under Mamm's sewing chair." The memory, while painful in some ways, was welcome, too, and Katie allowed herself the smile it stirred. "Now, she hides in all sorts of places — *good ones* that are hard to find."

"Playing with the little ones was more your thing. Besides, I left when Sadie was three. So the only spot I ever saw her in was under the sewing chair."

"Find me, Hannah! Find me, *find me!*"

A woman, dressed in a jacket and skirt the color of warm chocolate, came down a winding staircase to their left with a shiny, darker brown bag in one hand and a pair of sparkly gold earrings in the other. "Good morning, Hannah."

"Good morning, Mrs. Rothman." Hannah grabbed Katie by the arm and pulled her close. "This is my sister — Katie."

The woman's large green eyes traveled the entire length of Katie — from the top of her kapp to the tips of her black lace-up boots before returning, finally, to her face. "Hello, Katie."

"Hello, Mrs. Rothman. Hannah has told me a lot about your son and —"

Waving the rest of her sentence away, the woman crossed to the same door they'd entered only seconds earlier and opened it wide. "After shopping and lunch, I'll be seeing a matinee on Broadway with a friend, Hannah. So I'll be home after Mr. Rothman this evening."

And then she was gone, the door clicking closed behind her as Katie recovered her own jaw well enough to speak. "She didn't say goodbye to Jack?"

Hannah shrugged. "She leads a busy life."

"She's *shopping*," Katie protested.

"You haven't seen the stores here. They're not like they are at home. They're much busier and —"

"Find me, Hannah! Find me, find me!"

Katie grabbed hold of her sister's shoulders and gave her a gentle shove in the direction of the now slightly less muffled voice. "Go find him so I can meet him."

Slowly, and with deliberate yet tentative steps, Hannah walked from room to room on the first floor with Katie close on her heels. "Can you believe this place?" Hannah whispered as they made their way from a fancy room with floor-to-ceiling bookshelves and leather couches, to the biggest kitchen Katie had ever seen. Two more rooms followed, including one with a table large enough to accommodate sixteen people.

"How many people live here?" Katie whispered.

"Three. Mr. Rothman, Mrs. Rothman, and Jack." When they reached the final room, Hannah winked at Katie. "Okay, Jack, you've really stumped me this time, buddy. I've looked everywhere and I just can't find you."

A giggle pulled Katie's attention toward the piano on the other side of the cavernous room, and sure enough, a little boy with blond hair peeked out from beneath a bench.

"Wait." Hannah winked at Katie. "Did you hear that? It sounded like a gig—"

"Who's that yady?"

Hannah shielded her mouth from Jack's view with her hand and moved closer to Katie. "Jack has problems saying his l's, but he's seeing a speech therapist and that should start helping soon."

"Who's that yady?" Jack repeated.

"Hmmm . . . Do you hear someone talking, oh sister of mine?"

Jack sucked in an audible breath. "That's your sister?"

Hannah crossed to a couch, pretended to look beneath a few cushions and behind a pillow or two, and then froze. "I hear someone breathing, don't you, Katie?"

"Her name's *Katie*?" Jack asked; his voice no longer muffled.

Clapping her hands together, Hannah ran over to the piano bench, pointing. "There you are! Wow, Jack, I didn't think I'd ever find you."

"I'm right here." Jack crawled out of his hiding place and inched his way toward Katie. "I like your dress, Hannah's sister. It's very pretty."

"And I like your shirt, Jack, it's my most

195

favorite color." Katie squatted down to the child's eye level, the urge to pull him in for a hug the way she would Sadie, almost overpowering.

Jack looked down at his pale blue shirt and then back up at Katie, his eyes wide. "How do you know my name is Jack?"

"Because my sister talks about you all the time, that's how."

"She does?" Jack looked from Katie to Hannah and back again. "You look just like Hannah."

"That's because we're twins."

"Twins? What does twins mean?"

"It means we look exactly alike."

Jack leaned closer to Katie, pointing at her chin as he did. "You don't have the same mark as Hannah." Then, straightening up, he spread his little hands out. "Hannah fell out of a tree when she was yittle yike me."

"I know. I was there," Katie said, grinning.

He sucked in a second, louder burst of air. "You were *there*?"

"Yah — I mean, yes. I was there."

"Did you fall, too?"

"No."

Jack moved his little feet in place. "I'm glad." Then, pointing from his shirt to Katie, he added, "You and me . . . we have the same color. 'Cept mine is a shirt because

I'm a boy, and yours is a dress 'cause you're a girl. But we both have blue."

"You're right, we do."

He ran in place a second time only to stop and turn to Hannah. "Can Katie read to me? Please?"

Hannah met Katie's eyes across the top of Jack's head and, at Katie's emphatic nod, shrugged. "Of course. We'll show her all your favorites and let her pick which one she wants to read."

"I want her to read all of them to me!"

"All of them?" Hannah echoed. "I don't know, Jack, that's a lot of books —"

"You can sit on my sea yion with me, Katie!"

"Whoa. Slow down a minute, kiddo." Again, Hannah's gaze lifted just enough to meet Katie's. "Are you okay with this? Because if you're not, I could put on the television and let him watch one of his shows."

Katie stood, her heart melting as Jack wrapped his fingers around her index finger and tugged her toward the hallway. "I'm pretty sure you don't need me to answer that, do you?"

Hannah was waiting when Katie stepped into the hallway, pulling Jack's door closed in her wake.

"So he's asleep?" Hannah whispered.

"His eyes were drooping before I was even halfway through the story of when we found Fancy Feet," Katie whispered back. "I think his full tummy from lunch, and all those books we read this morning, tuckered him out."

Hannah motioned Katie to follow her down the stairs and into the hearth room. Though, this time, instead of playing hide and seek, Hannah dropped onto a cushioned chair next to the fireplace and pointed Katie toward its mate on the other side of the thick rug. "Jack sure loved you."

"He is completely adorable." She felt her smile growing as she remembered the way he kissed her cheek after every book she read and then insisted on making her peanut butter sandwich when it was time for lunch. "I can see why you love your job so much. Though, for all your talk, it's really no different than what I do."

"What I do here is *nothing* like what you do, Katie." Hannah nestled into her chair, sweeping her hand around the room as she did. "I mean, first off, look at this place. It's gorgeous. And unlike you, I don't have to scrub floors or wash clothes. I don't have to hang things on a clothesline and then run outside three hours later to pluck them down before the rain comes. I'm not here from the moment I open my eyes until they fall closed at the end of the night — I get to have a life with a boyfriend and friends, too."

Katie's smile faded. "I have Abram!"

"Who you see one evening a week . . . at a hymn sing with twenty other people. Besides, for all your talk about wanting your own thing, why are you so content to simply lead Mamm's life? Don't you want to do your own thing? Live your own life? Be your own person, like me?"

"Perhaps you are trying to lead *Mrs. Rothman's* life by caring for her child when she doesn't?" Pushing off the chair, Katie wandered over to the corner and the handful of pictures displayed across the stone mantel. "Because that is how it sounds."

"This job is just temporary . . . So I can make enough money to do what I really want to do."

Removing her hand from a framed photograph of Jack on a swing, Katie turned back to Hannah. "What do you want to do?"

"I want to learn how to do hair the way they do in the fancy salons Mrs. Rothman goes to. I mean, I'm trying to teach myself some things" — Hannah touched her long curls — "but I want to learn how to do all

199

sorts of things. Like the stuff I used to show you on the cover of the magazines at the store, remember?"

"I remember." It was emblazoned in her brain as the starting point for losing her sister. Sure, she'd noticed the magazines while waiting to pay for something Mamm needed at the store, but as curious as she'd been about the English faces she saw, Hannah could speak of nothing else all the way back to the house.

The hairstyles . . .

The clothes . . .

The makeup . . .

And if there had been time to actually open some of the magazines while they'd waited to pay, Hannah would add in talk about the boys, the houses, the swimming pools, and sometimes even the naughty things she'd managed to read.

Katie had always tried to change the subject. But no matter how many crops she'd pointed to, or farm animals she'd made a funny observation about, Hannah would find a way to bring the conversation back to English ways.

"Hannah? Jack? Are you here?"

Hannah's eyes widened a split second before she rocketed onto her feet. "That's Mr. Rothman," she whispered, sliding her focus between Katie and the mantel clock. "He is early! Come on, let's go!"

She followed behind her sister as they made their way up the hallway to the front entryway. Sure enough, the tall dark-haired man Katie had spied in a few of the photographs with Jack was flipping through a stack of envelopes next to her sketch pad. When he heard them, he looked up, surprise filtering across his face as his focus came to rest on Katie.

"If not for the vast difference in clothing at the moment, I'd think I was seeing double. But since I'm clearly not, you must be Katie." He stepped forward, offering his hand to Katie as he did. When she returned his shake, he smiled. "I'm Doug, Doug Rothman. Welcome to New York City."

Then, moving his attention to Hannah, he gestured toward the staircase. "I take it he's sleeping?"

"He is. He played hard with Katie this morning and it tuckered him out."

Mr. Rothman smiled again at Katie and then pointed to the sketch pad lying beside the envelopes he'd abandoned in favor of talking to them. "Is this yours, Katie?"

She looked to Hannah for direction and, at her sister's nod, found her voice. "Yah."

"May I look?" he asked.

201

Again, she looked at Hannah, and again, Hannah nodded. "They are nothing special, just a few pictures I have drawn . . ."

He lifted the pad off the table and flipped the cover back, a quiet whistle escaping his lips as his eyes settled on the picture of a healthy Mamm. "Who is this?"

She opened her mouth to answer but it was Hannah's voice she heard. "That was our mother. Before she got sick. If you flip ahead five or six pages, you'll see her as she was at the end — *see*?"

He leaned close as Hannah's hand retreated to her side. He studied it for a few moments and then lifted his gaze to Katie's. "In this drawing, I can see your mother's strength and her fears, but I can also sense a peace . . . like she knew everything would be okay."

"She *was* at peace. Because she accepted what was happening to her as God's will," Katie whispered.

Clearing her throat, Hannah reached across the pad and turned back through the handful of pictures her boss had missed, stopping on the one of Samuel chasing the chicken with a delighted Mary looking on from the garden.

Mr. Rothman's eyes darted back and forth between the children. "Here, you give us a sense that it is imperative the boy catches the chicken, yet, because of the inclusion of the girl and her pure amusement, you also let us feel as if everything will be okay in the end."

"He *did* catch the chicken . . ."

Laughing, he changed the page to the drawing of Mary and Sadie walking hand in hand across the pasture. "Oh, Katie, this is absolutely stunning. Do you work from photographs or models?"

"The Amish don't take photographs," Hannah interjected. "Katie draws these from her memory. By candlelight."

Katie could only nod along with her sister's words, her focus torn between her drawing and Mr. Rothman's expression as he continued to study it with rapt concentration.

"You manage to capture the beauty in life's simpler moments — the moments so many of us tend to overlook *because* of that same simplicity. Yet while doing so, you also manage to grip us with the same human emotion we see on the faces of your subjects — joy, fear, peace, determination . . . The kind of emotions we all face in life regardless of where and how we live. And it is in doing that, you make it so we feel as if we're there — on the fringes of whatever it is you've drawn. As if we, too, are seeing it in real time."

Katie pressed her hands to her cheeks in an attempt to cool them. "I don't know what to say. I-I do not try to do such things. I just draw my memories — things I don't want to forget."

"And by doing so, you've given me pause and made me want to see my own life in a different way — to slow down and see the beauty that is a child's laughter or a mother's peace or two siblings setting off together." With a reluctance she could physically feel, Mr. Rothman closed the sketch pad and handed it to her. "I would love to exhibit the rest of your pictures at the gallery. I think your work would really resonate with people."

"I don't understand."

"Well, as you already know, I own a gallery here in the city. The front room is for the main exhibit. It's that exhibit that brings the reviewers and the art critics and those wanting to enjoy art. Pencil sketches such as these, are not exhibited there. But a few years ago, I opened a smaller room where I like to exhibit little-known artists I think have something to show the world, regardless of the method used. It's in that room where I'd like to add" — he tapped Katie's sketch pad — "the rest of these."

"You-you like my drawings that much?"

"I do. Though, if I may, can I ask if you've ever given thought to using charcoals or watercolors? Because *those* mediums could land you the top spot in a gallery showing one day."

She had thought about charcoals and paint. Many times. But neither would lend themselves to being stuffed under a mattress with no shred of evidence left behind . . .

"No."

"It was just a question. Not a judgment. Anyway, may I add the rest of these to our exhibit?"

"I-I don't know what to say. I'm not supposed to draw such pictures at all."

Mr. Rothman nodded. "I know, Hannah has shared that with me. But you have both the eye and the talent to really go places, Katie. Your work is very reminiscent of an artist named Norman Rockwell. People were drawn to his work because of the memories and feelings it evoked. Your work does something similar while adding the kind of innocence so many of us crave in a world that's forever changing.

"It's why I'm confident people will love your work. With just a few pictures you have managed to teach me not only about the Amish, but also life in general."

Hannah flapped her hands quickly before bringing them together, almost prayer-like, beneath her chin. "See? What did I tell you, Katie? Your drawings are amazing."

Inhaling slowly, Katie replayed Mr. Rothman's words over in her head. Never in her wildest dreams could she have imagined a moment like this. It was scary, and exciting, and it needed to end.

She needed to end it.

Now.

"I thank you for your kind words, Mr. Rothman, I-I really do. I will remember them for many years to come, I am sure. But" — she pulled the sketch pad to her chest and released her breath — "I can't share these with you or your gallery. I'm sorry."

CHAPTER 15

Katie was grateful for the sun's position in the sky as they made their way down the brownstone's front steps to the sidewalk below. Without it, Eric wouldn't be worrying about locating his sunglasses. And without that momentary preoccupation, he might have noticed the death glare she gave Hannah on the way out of the Rothmans' front door.

"I'm sorry my sister asked you to do this. I begged her not to, but she didn't listen." She tried to shove the piece of hair Hannah had tugged out of her kapp back into place, but it was no use. She was simply too angry. "Hannah forgets that we are the very same age. If she really had to take Jack to something with his parents tonight, all she needed to do was tell me how to get back to her apartment, and I would have been fine."

Eric slipped his glasses into place and

stopped, mid-step. "Hey, I'm glad she called. Really. Gave me an excuse to get some air."

"You did not need to get stuck with me to get air." She continued past him, her feet powered as much by anger as anything else. "But that is Hannah . . . always trying to run my life. When we were little, if I didn't want to climb, she would refuse to come down from the tree until I came up. It didn't matter if I wanted to play quietly on the grass, or if I was in the middle of a conversation with Mamm. If Hannah wanted me to climb, she made it so I had to climb. And later, when —"

"Whoa, whoa, whoa." He closed the growing gap between them with several long strides and guided her to a stop just shy of the corner. "First up, I don't consider myself being stuck with you. I'm here because I want to be. Period. Second, I don't think Hannah is trying to run your life by wanting someone to walk you back to her apartment. You've only been in the city for what? A little over forty-eight hours? This place can be daunting after *five* days, let alone *two*. And that's not even factoring in the part about you being Amish and never having been here before."

"Amish does not mean dumb," she protested.

He drew back almost as if he'd been slapped. "I didn't say it did. I just meant —"

"Hannah forgets she was Amish, too. Sometimes, she even looks at me the way the English girls always do . . . like we are odd. But we're — I mean, *I'm* not."

Now that she was going, she couldn't stop, the words tumbling from her mouth with a vengeance. "I can walk down a street just like she can . . . I can choose not to use the electric lamp in her guest bedroom if the light from the window is enough to change my clothes by . . . I can tell Mr. Rothman no about" — she smacked the edge of the sketch pad protruding out from beneath her opposite arm — "my drawings if I want to."

"Wait. Your drawings are in there?"

"Yah."

"Can I see them?"

Something about the earnestness in his voice caught her by surprise, draining the anger from her body. "Why? They are just pictures."

"You drew them, yes?"

She nodded.

"And you said they make you happy, right?"

Again, she nodded.

"Have you eaten yet? Because I know a great place between here and Hannah's where we can stop for dinner." The same smile that had been on his face when he first arrived at the Rothmans' returned, bringing with it the same answering flutter inside her chest. "And maybe while we're waiting for our food I can see your work . . ."

"I'm not hungry."

His smile slipped a little but not for long. "Then I'll just walk you back to Hannah's, and on the way there, you can tell me what's got you so worked up."

"I'm not worked up."

"Yes, you are. So how about you just get it out so you can be done with —"

"Mr. Rothman looked at my pictures." She hadn't meant to blurt it out like that, but it just kind of happened.

"And?"

"He-he said they are good. That I have" — she glanced up at the sky as they walked — "talent."

A single clap brought her attention back down to street level and the man walking beside her. "Katie! That's incredible!"

"It was very nice of him to say such things."

Eric's steps slowed, necessitating the same

from Katie. "*Nice* of him? Are you kidding me? Rothman saying you have artistic talent would be like the president of a major recording label telling me my songs are good. I mean, that's *huge* — *super* huge, actually."

When she said nothing, he bobbed his head until her gaze mingled with his. "This guy owns a big-time art gallery not too far from here, Katie. Do you know what it could mean if he decided to show your stuff there?"

"I said no."

"Excuse me?"

"I said he could not show them."

He stumbled backward a step. "Wait. You're telling me he offered to show your stuff? Now? Already?"

"Yah. But I said no."

"But that's your dream!"

"But drawing what I draw is wrong."

"Wrong? How can it be wrong?"

"It is as I told you yesterday. The Bible says, 'Thou shalt not make unto thyself a graven image.' "

"But I thought that was just about photographs."

"My drawings are like photographs. They are graven images."

Fisting his hand in front of his mouth, he

211

exhaled, hard. "But it's your *dream,* Katie."

"It's a dream I can't have."

"So leave. Like Hannah did."

"It's not that simple," she whispered.

"Why not?"

"Because I've been baptized and Hannah wasn't."

"And there's a difference?"

She didn't mean to laugh, but it was either that or bow to the tears she'd been fighting off and on since declining Mr. Rothman's offer. "Hannah can still talk with Dat and the children. She can visit when she wants. She can come for holidays if she wants. She can come when there are weddings and when there are funerals, too. In between, she can keep in touch with letters and send the little ones stickers if she wants."

"Okay . . ."

"But if I left, I would lose them all — Dat, Samuel, Jakob, Mary, baby Annie, and" — her voice broke — "Sadie. I couldn't write to them, I couldn't visit them, I couldn't speak to them. I couldn't be part of their lives in any way."

"Ever?"

She swallowed against the lump climbing up her throat. "Ever."

"And if you stay but let him show your work? Then what?"

"I would be shunned. My family and my community could not speak to me until I repented."

"Okay, so what you're saying is that if you ask for forgiveness things would go back to normal?"

"Yah."

"So why don't you do that?"

"Because I just can't. I can't allow Mr. Rothman to show my pictures in his gallery. To do so would be wrong, and to make it right I would have to walk away from the only life I know."

She made herself look away, to focus on something, anything that would buy her time while she steadied her breath and blinked away the tears. For a moment, that something was a woman getting into the back of a yellow car. Then, when the car was gone, it was an elderly man crossing at the next light with a walker.

Every time she thought she was ready to resume their conversation though, the telltale prick of tears resurrected itself in her eyes. Finally, after taking in so many different things she couldn't remember them all, she glanced back at Eric to find him leaning against the front of a building, studying her in return.

"Is something wrong?" she whispered.

He started to speak, stopped, and then, after a few seconds, continued, the alluring rasp of his voice paling against the punch of his words. "A different life doesn't mean the wrong life, Katie. Remember that."

"I-I don't understand."

"I think you need to figure out what makes *you* happy. Because in the end, when all is said and done, it's really your life to live."

Twenty minutes later, Eric's words were still echoing in her head as she fought with the lock on Hannah's door. At home, in Blue Ball, no one questioned her life. It was as it was supposed to be. But here, in New York —

The answering click to what had to be her fifth attempt at opening the door stole her thoughts long enough to get inside and shut herself away from a day she wished had never happened. Tossing her sketch pad onto the couch, Katie marched into the kitchen, yanked open a cabinet, helped herself to a box of crackers she'd spied while pulling together breakfast earlier that morning, and tried to ignore the mental images of the dinner she could have had with Eric if she hadn't been so angry at Hannah.

Yet even as she sunk down next to her

sketch pad with the cracker box in tow, she knew the anger she'd carried for the first part of their walk home went beyond Hannah to something deeper, something more befitting the general malaise now weighing her down.

She tried to push it off on her grumbling stomach, but six crackers in, she knew that wasn't the case. It wasn't the busy morning with Jack, either. She'd loved every moment she'd spent with the little boy. It wasn't the fact that Eric had been summoned to walk her home, either, although that had certainly given her something to blame . . .

Releasing the breath she hadn't realized she was holding, Katie set down the cracker box and pulled her sketch pad onto her lap. Slowly, page by page, she went through her drawings, stopping on occasion to study a shading choice, or a detail she'd felt the need to include — the tilt of a head, the lift of a chin, the glint of mischievousness, the joy of an innocent . . .

"You have both the eye and the talent to really go places, Katie."

She ran her hand across Mary's young face, the youngster's joy over Samuel's inability to catch a chicken bringing an unexpected misting to Katie's eyes. So much of her pictures were about reliving special moments and documenting them in a way they could never be forgotten even if she was the only one who could ever see them ...

"You've given me pause and made me want to see my own life in a different way — to slow down and see the beauty that is a child's laughter or a mother's peace or two siblings setting off together."

Every time she started a new picture, she told herself it would be the last, that it was wrong. That *she* was wrong. But by the time she made the final mark on each new picture, she knew she couldn't stop. It was as if the uncertainty she felt in her day-to-day life slipped away the moment she picked up her pencils and began to draw, leaving behind a different Katie than everyone else saw. Including herself.

"A different life doesn't mean the wrong life, Katie. Remember that."

Was Eric right? Could she really be that Katie all the time?

Turning to the last picture in her pad, she took in the lake, the toy boats, the mother duck and her two ducklings, and the spot where she, herself, had stood while quietly contemplating the life Hannah had now. Regular Katie didn't belong in a world made up of dreamers like Eric. It wasn't the

Amish way. But what if she wasn't regular Katie? What if she was the Katie she was when she was drawing?

She liked that Katie . . .

She wanted to be that Katie . . .

She —

"Do not worry, Mamm. Please. I will take care of them all — Samuel, Jakob, Mary, Sadie, Annie, and Dat. I promise."

Bowing her head nearly to her chest, Katie gave in to the tears she could no longer hold back.

217

CHAPTER 16

Katie was sitting on the windowsill the next evening, looking out at the buildings and the people, when Hannah breezed in the front door and tossed her purse across the room and onto the couch.

"You've got a total of ten minutes to freshen up before we need to head out of here, so let's get a move on." Hannah clapped her hands. "Quick. Quick. Quick."

Slowly, Katie dropped her feet to the floor and stood. "What's going on?"

"It's a surprise — something I think will wipe that sourpuss off your face once and for all."

"There is no sourpuss."

"No?" Hannah closed the gap between them with three quick strides and then led Katie over to the mirror next to the door. "You still say there's no sourpuss?"

Katie wiggled out from under Hannah's hands but remained in front of the mirror, the sad eyes looking back at her making it difficult to argue. "It has been a long day of doing nothing," she protested.

"I told you that you could come with me to work this morning, remember? But you insisted you wanted time alone. So if you've been bored that's on you, Katie."

She knew Hannah was talking, but really, all she could truly concentrate on at that moment was the face peering at her from just beyond her own shoulder — a face that was both the same and completely different than her own. Yes, the basics were still the same — the brown eyes they shared with Dat, the soft brown hair they got from Mamm, and the high cheekbones that were somehow a combination of the two. But even those givens were suddenly not so given anymore, thanks to Hannah's makeup, kapp-free head, and the way the amber flecks in her eyes seemed to dance with her smile.

"You look so . . . so *happy*, Hannah."

"That's because I am."

"Does makeup and fancy hair really do that?" Katie asked.

Hannah's laugh filled the space between them a split second before she closed it with an arm around Katie's shoulder and neck. "It certainly doesn't hurt." Then, resting her chin on Katie's shoulder, their gazes met in the mirror. "But really, Katie, the thing that makes me look like this is about being where I'm supposed to be. Here. In New York City."

"With Travis?"

"That certainly helps, but it's more than that, Katie. It's getting to be *me*. It's taking a dance class one evening a week. It's getting to go to shows with Travis and Eric. It's getting to be neat if I want to be neat, or sloppy if I want to be sloppy. It's getting to sleep in on my day off if I want to, or stay out late with friends if I have nowhere to be the next morning. It's getting to decorate this place in a way that makes me happy. It's getting to listen to a radio and sing the same kind of songs that other people my age are singing. It's wearing dresses and shoes that make me feel pretty. It's walking down the road holding hands with Travis because I like the way his hand feels around mine. It's stopping in the middle of the sidewalk and kissing him. It's meeting people who are different than me and getting to hang out with them. It's getting a paycheck from Mr. Rothman and getting to deposit it in an account with my name on it, knowing that one day, when I've saved enough, I can go to school to learn about things I want to learn about."

"You mean like you said the other day? About learning to do English hair?" Katie asked.

"That's right." Hannah released her hold on Katie and stepped back. "If you could see the salon Mrs. Rothman goes to, you'd understand. It's . . . it's *wonderful.* Women come in looking tired or feeling low. They want the stylist to make them feel better. And when their hair is done and they look in the mirror, they are no longer tired or low. They feel pretty.

"I want to do that for people. I want to make them feel good."

She drank in her sister's words as she shifted her gaze to her own image — to the dull eyes, the hint of Mamm's hair she could just make out around the edges of her kapp, and a sadness that made her attempted smile not the slightest bit successful. "I want to look like you do, Hannah."

Hannah's inhale was quick and audible. "You'll let me do your hair?"

"No, I —" She lifted her gaze to Hannah's again. "I want to look happy like you do."

"Then you need to *be* happy."

"I am. Sometimes."

"Like when you're drawing?" Hannah prodded.

221

"Yah."

"Like when you've spent time with Eric?"

She looked back at herself and the sudden warmth making itself known on her cheeks. "I like to take walks, Hannah. It doesn't matter if they are in Blue Ball or here, in the city."

Hannah laughed. "Yeah . . . o-kay."

"It is true."

"Suit yourself." Hannah's attention skirted to the clock and then back to Katie. "C'mon, we need to go."

"Go where? You haven't told me."

"Because then it wouldn't be a surprise, would it?"

"Can I have at least a hint?"

Hannah considered her question for a few seconds and then crossed to the couch and her abandoned purse. "Sure, why not . . . That *happy* you want to be? You're about to be that times a billion."

Block after block, they made their way downtown, the taxi Hannah had insisted that they take alternating between fast spurts and abrupt stops. Twice, Katie asked if they could walk the rest of the way, but both times, Hannah looked up from her phone just long enough to mutter something about closing doors and special guests.

The first time, Katie protested.

The second time, she gave in and opted for the view outside her window instead — a view made up of people hurrying in different directions. "Do you ever wonder where they're going?"

"Who?"

Katie nudged her chin toward the sidewalk. "Them."

"No, why would I? I don't know them."

"*Any* of them?"

"Probably not."

"Does Travis know them?" she asked, glancing back at Hannah.

"I doubt it."

"But he's been here a long time, hasn't he?"

"His whole life."

"I have been in *Blue Ball* my whole life."

Hannah's thumbs paused just above her phone. "I know this, Katie, remember? I spent my whole life there, too . . ."

"We know *everyone* there."

"You say that like it's a good thing." Bobbing her head to the left, Hannah took in the scenery outside Katie's window and then redirected her attention to the man in the front seat. "Right here, at the end of this block." Then, after another flurry of thumb movements, Hannah tossed her phone into her purse, handed the driver thirty dollars, and grinned. "We're here."

"Here?" Katie turned back to the window and a scene that looked no different than everything else she'd seen thus far. "What is here?"

"Get out of the car and you'll see, silly girl."

Confused, she did as Hannah said only to have nothing change. "I'm out, yet I still don't see what —"

The rest of her words morphed into a gasp as her gaze fell on a series of framed paintings displayed inside a window to their left — paintings with bold colors and even bolder strokes. Mesmerized, she stepped closer, the answering thump of her heart drowning out all but Hannah's squeal.

"Ta-da!"

"What is this place?" Katie whispered.

"*This* is Mr. Rothman's art gallery. It isn't one of the big ones, but he is doing interesting things to set his apart. Like a smaller room in back where he displays new talent — unknowns he thinks need to be known."

She tried to focus on her sister's words, she really did. But at that moment, all she could think about was the swirl of colors on the other side of the window and the way they soothed her in return. She took in the varying shades of blue . . . The snippets of green that sprouted out from the darker blues . . . The —

"This is *a lake* . . . and those are *lily pads* . . . and" — she touched her fingertip to the window — "do you see those sparkles right there? That is *the sun* as it dances across the lake." Slowly, she pulled her hand back to cover her mouth. "I did not see it at first. I just saw the colors and the strokes . . . But it is a lake. I'm sure of it now."

Stepping to the left, she took in the next painting and the bright red splash of color dripping down around a soft brown.

"What on earth is that supposed to be?" Hannah stepped closer. "It looks like a red blob."

"I think it is like those popsicles that Miss Lottie would give us sometimes when we were done chasing bubbles and she wasn't ready for her quiet time with Mamm to be over." Katie held up her own fist and pointed between it and its representation in the painting. "See, it is melting around the hand."

Hannah's laugh mingled with Katie's as they moved on to the next picture. "This is a field of pumpkins or, based on the empty vines, *was* a field of pumpkins. All that is left is that one there." Katie pointed to the

225

orange object just beyond the pumpkin-less foreground before moving her finger and her focus farther into the background. "And do you see this? It is a young child, searching for a pumpkin to take home. Soon, he will find the last one."

"How are you able to see these things?" Hannah asked. "Me? I just see colors and blobs. But when you point things out, I can see things I didn't see before."

She opened her mouth to answer but closed it as she stepped in front of the fourth and final painting with its dark colors and harsh strokes. Here there was no sense of calm, no sense of peace. Instead, she found her heart twisting in a way reminiscent of pain and sorrow.

Hannah's shoulder brushed against hers as she, too, shifted to the left. "Oh good luck with this one, Katie. There's nothing —"

"It's a new burial plot." Again, Katie lifted her finger to the window, moving it to indicate each detail. "See? The brown here is lighter, older. And the white markers in this area are more faded. But that dark brown mound, there?" She pointed toward the right side of the picture. "That is fresh dirt. And these strokes here could be a winter rain or tears."

"Seriously?"

"Yah." She studied the picture for a few more moments and then stepped back just enough to be able to see all four at the same time. "They are all different things, but together, they represent the change in seasons. The lake is spring, the Popsicle is summer, the pumpkin in the field is autumn, and this" — she motioned toward the final picture — "is winter."

"If you say so . . ." Hannah took one last look at the four pictures and then looped her arm around Katie's. "Now come on, there's more to see inside. Better, more special ones."

"You mean more *paintings*?"

"Yup."

For the first time since spotting the window display, Katie looked past the four evenly spaced paintings and into a room with even more framed paintings and an occasional person milling in front of them or moving between them. "Are-are we *allowed* inside?" she whispered.

"I work for Mr. Rothman, remember?" Hannah's tug grew more firm. "Besides, you need to be here."

"But the people inside . . . They look so fancy."

"That's because it's *that*" — Hannah

redirected Katie's attention back to the paintings displayed in the window — "artist's opening. Mr. Rothman says all sorts of people come — her family, her friends, people who helped her along the way with her art, and, if she's lucky, an art critic or two who will like her stuff enough to talk it up in the newspaper and other places like that."

Katie glanced down at her aproned dress and boots, mentally compared it to the simple black dress and pretty heels Hannah wore, and then looked up as her twin continued. "I saw her binder the other day at Mr. Rothman's. They keep it up at the front desk during the showing for people to see. It has her bio, her picture, any press she's gotten, that sort of thing. She's pretty to begin with, but I imagine she'll be positively gorgeous tonight."

"Who?"

Again, Hannah pointed to the paintings in front of them. "The artist."

"You mean she will be here?" Katie asked.

"Not *will be,* Katie. *Is.*" Hannah consulted her phone again, nodding as she did. "The showing officially starts in ten minutes, so we really should get inside so you can look around before everything starts."

Then, reaching across the gap between

them, Hannah loosened the ties on Katie's kapp and then repositioned her on the sidewalk until the window became more mirror like. "Do you see your smile right now, Katie? The way it lights up your whole face? *That* is how you should be all the time — the way you say you *want* to be."

Bobbing her head until she had a clear view of her own face, Katie wasn't surprised to see the proof behind Hannah's words. The joy she felt at that moment, in that exact place, was every bit as real as her chin and her cheeks and her clothes. It was, in many ways, like that first moment when Dat's candle went out at the end of a busy day and she knew she was free to open her sketch pad and lose herself in her drawings again.

"And you know what the best part of all is?"

She smoothed the sides of her dress down and made herself turn back to Hannah. "What?"

"It's only going to get bigger and more wonderful when you see what's inside."

CHAPTER 17

The first lap around the gallery's main room had been about soaking up each and every painting — the colors, the strokes, and the picture inside the picture.

The second lap had been about trying to decide whether the artist's title for each painting was a good fit.

The start of the third lap had Hannah scurrying off in search of wine while Katie continued on, her interest moving beyond the paintings to the kind of big picture details she'd missed the first two times. Like the small red circles that were starting to show up on some of the paintings . . . Like the guests who sought out the artist to ask questions or deliver praise . . . Like the simple yet elegant cream-colored dress the artist wore . . . Like the sudden acceleration of her heartbeat as she imagined her own pictures hanging on a gallery wall and the dress she might choose to wear if —

Shaking away the impossibility, Katie wandered toward the back of the gallery and the small hallway she'd spied between her second and third laps. At the time, she'd assumed it led to a restroom, but her current reluctance over the impending end to the evening propelled her to be certain.

A murmur of voices at the other end beckoned her past a bathroom, a closet, and, finally, into a smaller version of the main gallery.

"Oh John, doesn't this make you think of our precious Suzanne when she was little?" A woman Katie guessed to be about Miss Lottie's age grabbed the hand of a gentleman standing beside her and rested the side of her head on his upper arm. "Do you remember the way they'd flock to her the moment she walked into the house and how she'd try to find a spot on her little lap for each and every one of them?"

"I do, indeed. I suspect that's when her dream of being a veterinarian was truly born."

"Standing here, looking at this picture, it's like we're being transported back fifty years, to all the peace and wonder Suzanne brought to our lives . . ."

Intrigued, Katie rose up on the toes of her boots and peeked across the woman's shoulder, her answering smile at the sight of Mary surrounded by a half dozen barn cats freezing midway across her face.

"Lovely, isn't it?" the woman asked, turning to look at her.

She tried to smile, to respond in some way, but at that moment, in that place, she could barely think let alone speak. They were looking at *her* drawing. In a frame. In a gallery. Only, she wasn't wearing a fancy cream-colored dress . . .

Confused, Katie ran out of the room, down the hallway, and across the main gallery, her eyes seeking and then finding those of her mirror image.

"Katie! Katie! You did it! You really, really did it!"

She opened her mouth to speak but closed it as Hannah shoved something long and white into her hand. A quick glance down revealed an envelope with her name scrawled across the front.

"Open it," Hannah demanded between squeals. "Open it!"

"Hannah, why is my picture of Mary —"

"Open first. Then we'll talk."

"But —"

"Open it!"

"Fine." With quick fingers, Katie ripped open the envelope, stumbling backward at the stack of money inside. "I-I don't understand . . . What is this?"

"It's money, Katie. *Your* money."

"But —"

"A woman from Connecticut just bought your picture of Luke Hochstetler and his frog! She said it made her laugh."

"My . . . my *picture*?"

"Yes! And she paid five hundred dollars for it! *Five hundred dollars,* Katie, can you believe it?" Hannah let loose a slightly louder squeal and threw her arms around Katie. "You're going to be —"

With one hard shove, Katie broke free of Hannah's embrace. "How did someone in Connecticut see my picture?"

"She lives in Connecticut, but she was just here a few minutes ago. She fell in love with the picture of Luke and the frog, and — *guess what*?" Hannah reached across the front desk, pulled a red circle off a sheet of stickers, and danced it around in front of Katie. "She. Just. Bought. It. She'll be back to get it in the morning."

"But I don't understand how she saw it."

"It's in the back room. Next to the picture of Mary and the barn cats." Hannah slipped the envelope into her pocket and pointed her sticker-adorned index finger across the main gallery. "Come on, I'll show —"

"I *saw* the picture of Mary, Hannah. But what I don't understand is how it is here . . . in a frame . . . in a gallery," she hissed.

"It's like I told you in my letter. I showed Mr. Rothman the pictures I took and he loved them."

She followed Hannah back across the main room and down the hallway toward the smaller gallery in back, her brain working hard to keep up with Hannah's mouth. "So when he told me he wanted to have them up in here in time for today's showing, I went ahead and signed your name to the release, figuring I'd tell you about it when you got here. But then I thought it would be more fun to surprise you and —"

"You signed my name?" Katie echoed.

"Yes. Because I knew you wouldn't. But this? Right here?" Hannah waved her sticker-topped finger again and then marched over to the picture of Luke that Katie had missed the first time. "Proves I made the right choice. You're good, Katie. Really, *really* good."

Reaching out, Hannah adhered the sticker to the bottom right corner of the glass-fronted sketch, and followed it up with a triumphant smile back at Katie. "*Five hundred dollars* good, in case you need reminding."

"Excuse me, miss? Do you work here?"

Katie and Hannah turned as one toward the door and the same elderly couple who had been admiring the picture of Mary not more than ten minutes earlier. Shrugging at Katie, Hannah stepped forward. "I work for Mr. Rothman, the gallery's owner . . ."

The man pointed toward the wall behind them. "That picture there? The one of the little girl with the cats? How much is it?"

Katie heard the air whoosh past her lips seconds before Hannah clapped her hands together and turned back to Katie. "Katie? How much would you like for your drawing?"

"I —"

The diminutive woman with the wire-rimmed glasses stepped past her husband and grabbed hold of Katie's hands, her eyes casting downward just long enough to take in the kapp and aproned dress. "You're Amish, dear?"

"Yes, she is," Hannah answered. "And that picture is of our little sister, Mary."

"*Our* sister? But *you*'re not Amish."

Hannah's focus moved to the man now sporting a furrowed brow. "I was. Once. But now I am English."

Releasing Katie's right hand, the woman led her toward the picture. "I see now that the head covering on your little sister isn't a bonnet, but everything else about her makes me think of my own little girl, Suzanne. When she was that age, she fell in love with animals during trips to her grandmother's home. She'd sit on the floor and my mother-in-law's cats would just flock to her from all directions, wanting her to pet them . . . cuddle them . . . play with them. And the look on her face? It was just like that — that complete sense of peace you managed to capture in your delightful picture."

Not sure what to say or do, Katie merely followed the tip of the woman's finger to the picture and Mary's sweet face, the uncomplicated joy she found there making her ache for Blue Ball and everyone she left behind.

The woman paused, sucked in an audible breath, and then continued, her voice transitioning to one choked with emotion. "Suzanne is getting ready to turn fifty-five. She owns a veterinary clinic up in New Hampshire, and we don't get to see her very often. She's had a difficult year for many reasons and her best friend is having a surprise birthday party for her next weekend. John" — she hooked her thumb in the direction of her husband — "and I have been searching high and low for just the right gift but to no avail. Little did we know we'd find it while attending a gallery showing for the daughter of one of John's coworkers."

"You-you found a present for her?" Katie stammered.

"Yes. Your picture." The woman looked back at first her husband, and then Hannah, before bringing her full attention back on Katie. "I think it would remind Suzanne of the moment her dream began and, hopefully, bring her back to what matters most — finding her happy place."

A rustle of movement was followed by a funny sound from Hannah. Her head spinning, Katie turned in time to see the man pull a stack of money from his wallet. "My wife and I discussed it and we're willing to pay a thousand dollars if we can walk out of here with it tonight."

"A *thousand* dollars?" Hannah echoed.

The man looked at his wife and, at her nod, plucked a few more bills from his wallet. "Okay, how about fifteen hundred? Would that work?"

Hannah's eyes widened as they came to rest on Katie. "Katie? What do you say? Will fifteen hundred dollars work for Mary's picture?"

Mary's picture . . .

Katie turned back to the drawing, the

memory of that long-ago summer morning tickling the senses her pencil couldn't draw. The soft mews . . . The sweet purrs . . . The occasional giggle that coincided with the peace claiming every inch of a young Mary's face —

A shame unlike any she'd ever experienced moved from her stomach, to her throat, and into her cheeks, propelling her backward and away from her sketch so fast she nearly fell over her own two feet.

"Miss? Is everything okay?"

Reaching out, she steadied herself against the wall, her gaze seeking and finding Hannah's just as Hannah stepped forward. "Katie? Is something wrong?"

"Is something *wrong*?" she half shrieked, half sobbed. "Are you really asking me that?"

"If you think it's worth more, Katie, just say so and —"

"It is worth *everything*, Hannah."

Hannah closed the gap between them only to draw back as Katie held up a hand in warning. "Don't you dare come any closer, Hannah."

"Why? What's wrong? You were fine a minute ago."

"Twenty minutes ago . . . before I came into this room . . . things were fine, as you say. Good, even. But that was before I knew what you had done — what you *always* do."

Hannah moved her hands to her hips. "And what is it that I *always* do, Katie? Care about you? Believe in you? Want the best for you? Because, yeah, I can see why that would be so upsetting . . ."

"You always try to run my life. *My* life, Hannah. *Mine.* Not yours." Katie slid her thumb underneath the front edge of her kapp, yanked it off her head, and threw it at a clearly stunned Hannah. "Only this time? You ruined *everything.*"

CHAPTER 18

She knew people were staring. She could feel it just as surely as she could the heart-pounding anger that propelled her forward, her destination the only certainty in her world at that moment. All her life she'd known Hannah to be willful, dominating, and even a little selfish, but it had never been at Katie's expense.

Until now.

And now, well, she had no idea what to do. Assuming anything could even be done . . .

"How could you, Hannah?" She hissed as she circumvented the crowd of people waiting to cross the last street. "Those were *my* pictures, *my* memories, *my* —"

"*You have both the eye and the talent to really go places, Katie.*"

Talent.

It was a word that didn't belong in her world — a world where no man was above another. Yet in the few short days she'd been in the city, she'd heard it in reference to herself and her drawings several times.

She didn't want it to feel good, didn't want it to excite her, but it did. Pretending otherwise might be what was expected of her, but it wasn't truthful. Two different people had liked her drawings enough to want to buy them, and Mr. Rothman had wanted to display the rest of her work.

That part she liked, loved even.

But it was wrong.

And now, because of Hannah, she stood to lose everything if Dat or anyone in Blue Ball found out about her —

"You know, if I didn't know any better, I'd think you had wheels on those boots with the speed you're moving."

Startled back into the moment, Katie looked over her shoulder and stopped. "Eric . . . Hello. I didn't know you were behind me."

"That's because you haven't looked up since you stepped onto the sidewalk back there." He pointed over his own shoulder toward Fifty-Ninth Street in the distance. "I called your name a few times, but you obviously didn't hear me."

"I'm sorry."

He closed the remaining gap between

241

them as his gaze left hers and traveled upward. "I wondered what your hair looked like underneath your kapp."

"My . . ." She reached up and, at the feel of her hair against her hand, gasped. "My kapp! Oh no . . ."

"Hey, I didn't say that to stress you out, I'm just not used to seeing you without it is all."

"That is because I always wear it."

His smile brought with it a single dimple in each cheek. "I won't tell."

"It does not matter because *I* know." She took in the people walking by, the sun as it peeked out at her from between the buildings bordering the park to the west, and then made herself look back at Eric. "I threw it at Hannah on the way out of the gallery."

"I take it, it wasn't a friendly throw?" he asked.

"No."

"Ahhhh, okay, so that's why you didn't hear me. You were angry."

Ashamed, she dropped her focus to her boots. "Yah."

At his answering silence, she looked up to find him studying her with an expression she couldn't quite read. "Do you want to talk about it?"

"I don't want to burden you with such things," she whispered.

"It's not a burden. Trust me." Setting his hand against her lower back, he guided her across the pathway and over to a park bench beneath a large oak tree. "So talk to me. What happened between you and Hannah?"

Katie took a deep breath and released it slowly through her lips. "She came home from work this afternoon and told me she had a surprise. I didn't know what it was about, but she promised it would make me happy."

"Okay . . ."

"At first, she was right. I didn't know such a place existed."

"What do you mean?"

She swiveled her body so that she was facing him rather than the pathway in front of them. "Mr. Rothman's gallery. It is filled with paintings."

His smile was back and so, too, were his dimples. "I see Hannah made good on her promise."

"I don't understand."

"You said she promised her surprise would make you happy, right?"

"Yah."

"Well, just now? When you mentioned the gallery and the paintings? Your eyes absolutely lit up."

"It was . . ." She stopped, swallowed, and tried again, the memory of the gallery filling her mind's eye. "You should have seen it, Eric. The whole front room was filled with one woman's paintings. They were watercolors, the book said, and many people could look at the same painting and say it was something different. But I was right many times." She plucked a blade of grass off the edge of her dress and rolled it back and forth between her fingers, the memory of the gallery exciting her all over again. "People were there to see her paintings and she wore such a pretty dress."

He, too, turned, draping his arm across the back of the bench as he did. "Did it make you wish maybe you'd let Rothman display your drawings the way he asked?"

When she didn't answer, he removed his hand from its resting spot just long enough to guide her eyes off her lap and back onto his face. "It's okay to say you thought about it, Katie."

She swallowed. "I thought about what it would be like to have people come to see my work . . . To have them ask me about the things I have drawn and why . . . To have my picture and my name in a book for people to see . . . And to wear such a dress.

But they were just thoughts."

"There's nothing wrong with that."

"I am not supposed to think such things."

"Again, I won't tell. And I'm pretty sure Hannah won't, either, if that's what you're worried about . . ."

Tossing the blade of grass onto the ground, Katie rose to her feet, the anger Eric's presence had managed to calm resurfacing in short order. "Because of Hannah I have much bigger things to worry about now."

"Meaning?"

"Two of my pictures were in that gallery. In a back room. And two people want to pay money to have them."

"Are you serious?"

"Yah."

He pushed off the bench and followed her over to the tree. "Katie! That's fantastic news! Wow! Congratulations! That has to feel incredible!"

"I didn't say they could show those pictures. Hannah did it without telling me."

His smile faltered but only a little. "Okay, so she should have asked, but look at the end result. People fell in love with your work enough to want to *buy* it, Katie. That's awesome."

"I drew my little sister's face, Eric."

"And you drew it well enough someone wanted to buy it, apparently."

She tried to nibble back her smile, but the memory of the elderly couple talking about her drawing made it difficult. "You should have heard the things they said about my picture," she whispered.

"Tell me."

And so she did. She told him about coming up behind the couple in the back room and how their excitement over the picture had made her want to see it, too. She told him about the money they offered to be able to take it home and how they hoped it would bring joy to their daughter. And she told him about the picture of Luke Hochstetler and how a different person paid money for it, too.

"I wish you could see your face right now, Katie. It's glowing."

"But it can't be."

"No, trust me, it is," he said, grinning.

She waved away his words as she leaned against the tree. "I mean, my drawings. They can't *be*."

"They already are."

"And because of that, and what Hannah did, I will be shunned if Dat or anyone in Blue Ball finds out. My family and my community will be unable to speak to me. Dat,

Samuel, Jakob, Mary, Sadie, and even baby Annie will turn their backs on me for what I have done." The smile that had been hers only moments earlier gave way to a single tear.

"But didn't you say that if you repent things will be okay?"

"I did, but . . ." She lifted her watery gaze to the dusky sky and held it there to a count of ten. "Dat would know of my drawings and I would have to throw them away to be forgiven."

"And you don't want to throw them away?"

Squeezing her eyes closed around yet another tear, she willed herself to breathe while Eric repeated his question.

"I-I'm not sure I can." Slowly, she opened her eyes to find the gap that had existed between herself and Eric gone. Instead, she found them toe-to-toe just as he reached out and gently wiped her tears away.

"Why not?" he asked, his voice hushed.

She stilled his finger against her cheek. "Because I am *me* when I draw. I am Katie."

"Then don't stop."

"Thanks to my sister, it may not be that simple."

He opened his mouth as if to respond, but closed it as he lowered his hand to hers and simply squeezed.

"It's getting late," she made herself say. "I-I should be heading back to Hannah's. I'm still angry at her, but I don't want her to worry."

"C'mon, I'll walk you back."

And so he did. For a while, he even held her hand and that was okay. There was something about his touch that she found calming. Like somehow everything would work out in the end. She wasn't sure that was the case, but at that moment, it was preferable to the images that were hovering on the outskirts of her thoughts, waiting for that moment when he wasn't there to distract them away.

"So when are you heading back to Blue Ball?" he asked as they made their way down a long set of steps and turned onto a path that had them walking alongside a small lake.

"Day after tomorrow."

"Do you have plans for your last day?"

"No."

He stopped, released his hold on her hand, and pointed toward the one lone rowboat on the water. "I'd love to take you on one of those while Hannah is at work. And when we're done, we could have lunch at the boathouse."

"Boathouse?"

"There. See?" He redirected her attention to a brick structure off to the left, just beyond a shoreline dotted with upside-down rowboats. "It's one of the most well-known places in the park and I think you'd like it."

"You want to take *me?"*

He laughed. "You sound surprised."

She looked down at her aproned dress and then back up at him. "But I am Amish."

"Okay, and that matters because why?"

Unsure of what to say, she simply looked back toward the lake and the couple now disembarking from the small boat, their laughter preceding them down the path. "I don't know."

"I like you, Katie. I like spending time with you. I like learning about your world and seeing mine through your eyes."

"But I am not special," she protested.

"That's a matter of opinion."

She saw him reach out his hand and, after a moment of uncertainty, she took it, the warmth of his skin against hers bringing a smile to her lips she couldn't completely nibble away. "Thank you for listening tonight, Eric. For turning what was a bad night into something a little better."

"You're welcome. But I think you need to reconsider the whole bad night thing at least a little, you know?"

"Reconsider?"

"Someone wanted to *buy* your work, Katie."

"Two someones," she corrected.

His laugh tickled her ears. "Ah, that's right, my mistake. *Two* someones wanted to buy your work." They rounded a corner of the path and crossed over to a different path, this one bringing them closer to the buildings Katie knew signaled the impending end to their time together. "I'd be beside myself if even *one* someone wanted to buy one of my songs."

"It could happen, yah?"

"I certainly hope so." He tightened his grip as they stepped out of the park and headed across Fifth Avenue to Hannah's street. "But really, enjoy this for what it is, Katie, even if it's only for a little while. Your work is speaking to people. And that's something you should feel pretty darn good about, if you ask me."

"But I —"

"There'll be time for buts later. There always is, unfortunately." He stopped outside Hannah's building and gave her hand one last tender squeeze. "For now though? It's okay to be a little proud of yourself. You've earned it."

CHAPTER 19

Katie was waiting in front of the building when he walked up shortly before noon, his legs and his arms tanned to perfection and his dimples on full display. For a brief moment, she wished she'd taken Hannah up on the offer to borrow some English clothes, but she shook it off for the same reason she'd declined in the first place.

Still, she glanced back at her reflection in the windowed door and quadruple checked the mascara she'd hastily applied just before walking out of the apartment. She knew it was wrong, had even taken the elevator back up to Hannah's floor two different times with the intention of washing it off, but had changed her mind at the last minute.

It wasn't that she was trying to be someone she wasn't. If she was, she'd have caved and worn the denim shorts Hannah had left on the couch for her. Instead, she'd dressed in her favorite mint-green dress and newest overlay and topped it off with the backup kapp she'd packed.

The mascara had really just been a whim. Besides, it wasn't like she'd done a second coat . . .

"Are you ready for a fun-filled last day?"

Inhaling deeply, she turned back to the man who was now no more than a step away and let loose the smile she couldn't hold back even if she'd wanted to. "I am!"

"Then shall we?" Eric motioned in the opposite direction from which he'd approached and, at Katie's nod, fell into step beside her. "I was thinking about it last night and I decided the Boathouse isn't right for us for lunch."

She stopped, mid-step, and did her best to keep the answering disappointment from her voice. "That is okay. I do not want to take too much of your day."

"I'm not trying to shorten our time together, Katie. I just thought that maybe a picnic would be nicer. You know, less distractions and all that."

"A *picnic*?"

He pulled his opposite hand into view and shook the basket she hadn't noticed until that moment. "Yup. I packed some sandwiches, a few apples, some chips, and two cookies I'm hoping Travis won't even notice are missing. I figured that gives us more time to talk before Hannah invariably calls and tells me it's time to bring you back. Which reminds me . . . how did it go last night when I dropped you off? Did you and Hannah talk about what happened at the gallery?"

"No."

"Why not?"

Together, they crossed into the park and headed in the direction of the lake he'd shown her the previous evening, her reluctance to answer catching her by surprise.

"Katie?"

"I don't know."

His pace slowed momentarily only to resume with a flick of his hand. "Hey, I'm sorry, I really shouldn't be asking such personal stuff when we've only known each other a few days."

"No. It's not that. It's just that talking to you last night made me feel better and I-I didn't want an argument with my sister to ruin that." She pinched her eyes closed for a brief second and then opened them to find she was still moving and Eric wasn't.

"Did I say something wrong?" she asked, doubling back. "I did not mean . . . wait." She gestured toward the lake she hadn't

253

noticed until that moment. "We're here, yah?"

He followed her finger toward the boats lined up along the shoreline, nodded, and then reached for her hand. "Have you ever been on a boat before?" he asked, his voice funny.

"No. But I have been an acorn person in one of Sadie's twig and leaf boats."

"Did you make it across the pond?"

"No."

His laugh floated through the air as he brought the side of his hand to the top of his forehead in a salute. "Then I'm honored to captain what I hope will be your first successful voyage."

She was still smiling nearly an hour later when, after several failed attempts, he dropped the basket on the ground not far from a maple tree and spread his arms wide. "This is it. We've got shade . . . we've got sun . . . we've got peace and quiet . . . and you" — he grinned at her — "haven't stopped smiling since you stepped into that boat."

And it was true.

Everything about being out in the middle of the lake with Eric had been special. The warm sun on her face . . . The family of ducks that seemed to hover just beyond their reach . . . The familiar croak of some neighboring bullfrogs . . . The coolness of the water as she reached over the side . . .

A faint click brought her attention back to Eric in time to see him lower his phone to his side. "I'm sorry. I know I'm not supposed to take your picture, but I couldn't let that go by. It was too perfect."

"What was too perfect?" she asked.

"Your smile. It's . . . beautiful. *You're* beautiful."

Startled, she stepped back. "I am not beautiful. I am plain."

His laughter echoed around them as he opened the basket and removed a navy blanket. "Trust me when I say there is nothing plain about you, Katie Beiler."

"My clothes are plain."

"Compared to everyone else in my universe, they're not plain. In fact, I'd go so far as to say that dress — at least the green part — is kind of pretty. On you."

She stared at him, waiting for something to indicate he was teasing. But there was nothing. "My mamm made this for me last year. Before she got sick."

"What was she like?" he asked as he snapped open the blanket and brought it down to the ground.

255

She knew she should help, but at that moment all she could really do was breathe. "You mean Mamm?"

"Yeah. Did she look like you?"

"A little, I suppose. Our hair was the same. But Hannah and I have Dat's eyes. Jakob does, too. Mary and Sadie and Samuel have pale blue eyes like Mamm's."

"I see." He moved the basket onto the blanket and then reached inside again, this time pulling out two plates, two napkins, two wrapped packages, and two bottles of water. Then, looking up, he patted the blanket next to him. "Come. Sit. Tell me more."

"What is more?"

"What was she like? Did she like to cook? Did she like to read? You know, that sort of stuff."

This time, when he patted the spot next to him, she lowered herself down to the blanket. "Mamm was a wonderful cook. Sometimes, even when my stomach was still full from lunch, the smell of dinner cooking would make my stomach growl. And her apple pie? It was always the first dessert to be gone after church on Sundays."

"Did she teach you how to make it?"

"I learned by watching and helping. But somehow, it does not taste the same to me when I make it, even though Dat and the boys say that it does."

Eric's soft laugh brought her gaze back to his. "She was special, wasn't she?"

"Oh yes . . . She was kind and smart and . . . *Mamm.* She understood that I was different than Hannah and that was okay."

"Why wouldn't it be?" He unwrapped both sandwiches and set one in front of each of them. "I took a leap of faith and picked turkey for both of us. Hope that's okay."

"It is wonderful, thank you."

He took a bite and then followed it up with a few gulps of water before reaching into the basket for the apples and chips he'd mentioned earlier. "So back to what you were saying . . . Why wouldn't it be okay to be different than Hannah?"

"Because Hannah is everything I'm not." She picked up her sandwich, tore off a sliver of turkey overhanging the roll, and slipped it between her lips. "Everything I'll never be."

"Whoa, whoa, whoa. Stop right there." Eric set his sandwich back on its wrapper and did the same with Katie's. "First up, *never* is a word no one should ever say. You don't know what tomorrow is gonna bring. No one does."

"God does."

"Okay, I'll give you that."

"He made Hannah brave, not me. And he made Hannah bold. I am not those things. It is not who I am."

"Have you always sold yourself short like this?"

She stared at him across the top of her water bottle. "I don't know what you mean."

"This whole" — he waved his newly retrieved sandwich in the space between them — "Hannah is brave and you're not stuff. Surely you see what you've done the past few months as brave, yes?"

Somehow, she managed to swallow the sip she'd taken before her mouth gaped open of its own will. "What are you talking about? What brave things have I done?"

"You mean besides caring for your mother as her health failed? And stepping in to help with your brothers and sisters in her absence even though your own heart was breaking?"

"That is not about being brave, Eric. That was Mamm . . . I wouldn't have wanted to be anywhere else but right there, next to her, soaking up every minute we had. And then . . . after . . . when she was gone . . . what I did with the children was —"

"*Do.* Present tense."

She waved off the correction. "That is my family."

He traded his sandwich for his own water but stopped shy of actually taking a drink. "As they are Hannah's."

At a loss for a suitable response, she remained silent, his words echoing in her ears.

"I may have only been eight when my mom died, but I remember how hard it was for my dad to even get out of bed in the morning after that." Eric leaned against the tree at his back, his voice taking on a hushed quality. "He was so distraught over her loss that my next-door neighbor had to step in and make sure I was eating and getting to school and talking to the right people about my grief."

She forced herself to breathe despite the lump rising up her throat. But it was hard. She could feel his pain just as surely as she could feel her own. Before she could think of something to say though, he continued. "From what you shared the other day, you didn't do that. You ran around making sure everyone else was okay even though your own heart was breaking. That's *bravery*, Katie."

The tears that always threatened when there was talk of Mamm gathered in the corners of her eyes. "I-I do not know what to say," she whispered.

"A fact doesn't really need dialogue. It is what it is."

"But Hannah? She left everything — me, Mamm, Dat, the little ones, Blue Ball, and everything she ever knew to come *here.* To the big city." Not wanting Eric to see the tremble in her hands, she shoved them under her legs. "*That* is the bravery I speak of."

"I'm not saying it didn't take courage for Hannah to come here. I'm sure it did. But you came here, too."

"For a visit that ends tomorrow," she corrected. "Hannah always just knew how to do things. When we were little, I was afraid to climb the tree by the pond. I was afraid I'd fall. But Hannah . . . she didn't care. She just climbed right up. Sometimes, when Mamm was busy with Samuel, Hannah would hang upside down from a branch and make faces at me. She wanted me to laugh up at her, but I would just cover my eyes."

Shrugging, he lowered his sandwich to his lap. "Some people aren't thrill seekers, Katie. That doesn't mean they — or you — are somehow deficient."

"But that is not all she could do that I couldn't. When we went off to school, she would shoot up her hand and answer questions I was too shy to answer."

His laughter tickled her ears and made her smile a little, too. "Okay, but did you *know* the answers?"

"Of course. But I did not say them." Feeling her smile begin to fade, she replaced it with a fast shrug. "And when we were Mary's age, and the English boys would drive by and say unkind things, I would pretend not to hear. But Hannah? She would throw rocks at their car until they would drive away."

"Okay, so she's a little tougher. But bravery wears many faces, Katie. Just because you two look alike doesn't mean the inside stuff — the stuff that makes you, *you* — is the same."

"We are different outside, too. She has always been so" — Katie looked down at her sandwich atop its wrapper and pinched her eyes closed for a few seconds — *"pretty."*

"Uh, hello . . . you're identical twins."

"But we *look* different."

"You mean because she wears makeup and you don't? Because that's just superficial stuff."

"It is not just the makeup. Because at night these past few days, when all of her makeup is off, we still look different."

"How?"

"I did not know, at first. I just knew she looked different." Katie traced her finger around the edge of the wrapper while she worked to frame the rest of her answer. "But yesterday, before we left for the gallery, I realized it was her smile. It is so big. So true. It lights up her face in a way mine does not."

He grabbed his phone and tilted it back and forth. "Trust me, your face lights up when you smile, too. I have proof."

Curious, she leaned across the food spread out between them, only to grab the phone from his hand as her eyes came to rest on her image — an image that stole her breath from her lungs.

"See?" Eric said, his voice triumphant.

"This-this is me?"

He grinned. "I'm pretty sure you're the only Amish girl I know, so, yeah, that's you."

"But I look . . . *happy.*"

"As you did when I showed you the sailboats the other day, and the whole time I was rowing you around the lake earlier, and when I snapped that picture a few minutes ago, and every time you talk about your drawings or your little sister. Your smile is there, Katie. More than you realize. It's quiet and it's discerning, but it's no less true."

It was a lot to take in, a lot to process. For now, though, she studied herself on the screen a little longer and then handed the phone back to Eric. "Thank you."

A comfortable silence filled the space between them, giving them time to eat while enjoying the peace and quiet of their spot. When the sandwiches were gone and there was nothing left of the chips but a smattering of dust, Eric pointed at the basket and grinned. "There's still two cookies in there, you know. Chocolate chip, in fact . . ."

"You mean the ones you hope Travis does not notice are missing?"

"That's right. Though, honestly, after the way your eyes sparkled just now when I mentioned them? I don't care if he *does* notice." He reached into the basket, plucked out two cookies, and handed one to Katie. "Because whatever retaliation he chooses to send my way will have been more than worth it. Trust me."

The lump was back. Only this time, it was accompanied by a flutter high up in her chest. "I have never met someone quite like you."

"Uh-oh. Is that a good thing or a bad thing?" he joked.

"It is a good thing."

And it was.

Eric made her feel . . . different. *Bigger.*

"I'm glad, because I feel the same way. About you."

Startled, she looked up just as a flicker of pain zipped across his face. "Is something wrong, Eric?"

"Yeah. You're leaving tomorrow."

CHAPTER 20

"So according to the sign, they should be starting to board your bus in about twenty minutes." Hannah dropped onto the chair next to Katie's and sighed, the burst of air sending a strand of her light brown hair up and off her face. "You still have your ticket, right?"

Katie lifted the narrow slip of paper off her lap and gave it a little wave. "It is still in my hand just as it was five minutes ago."

"I'm sorry, Katie. I guess I'm just a little scattered about you leaving. It seems like you just got here."

"It has been five days, just as it was supposed to be."

"I know that. It just went too fast is all." Hannah rummaged inside her purse and pulled out a small mirror for a not-so-quick inspection of her face. "I suppose maybe it would have been better if Travis hadn't stayed so long after dinner last night, but you still had fun, right? I mean, I did a pretty good job with the food, considering cooking was always more your thing than it was mine . . ."

"You did a fine job with the meal," Katie murmured.

"And that movie Travis picked for us to watch on the couch?" Hannah added a swipe of lipstick to her already-too-pink lips and then snapped the mirror closed. "That was funny, wasn't it? Especially the part when that one guy drove his motorcycle straight into the mud."

Katie tried to nod along, but really, she didn't remember that part, or any other part of the movie, for that matter. No, her attention had started on Hannah and Travis cuddling and giggling together on the couch and then drifted back to the park and —

"Katie? Are you even listening to me?"

She lowered her gaze to her ticket and then lifted it again to meet Hannah's. "Do you and Travis ever talk?"

"Of course we talk. We talk all the time." Hannah tossed the mirror and lipstick tube back into her purse and zipped it closed. "You know that."

"I don't mean that kind of talking. I mean . . ." her words trailed off as she visually picked her way through the crowd entering and exiting the escalators, the absence of anything resembling a familiar face sagging her shoulders into the back of the chair. "Do you ever miss it? Miss *us*?"

Hannah swiveled in her own seat so as to face Katie, instead of the crowd. "I miss you all the time, Katie. Dat and the children, too. And I-I miss Mamm every day, but now, with her passing, that would be the case even if I was still in Blue Ball."

"Do you *ever* think of coming back?" she whispered, her voice shaky.

"No."

Squeezing her eyes closed against the answering rush of pain, she willed herself to breathe slowly. "If there were no Travis, would you come back then?"

"No."

Surprise propelled her eyes open. "But I thought Travis was your boyfriend."

"He is. But I didn't know him when I left, remember?"

She did. Still, she needed to make sense of everything, to find a way to understand both her sister's actions and her own unsettled heart. "But he makes it better, yah?"

The same mischievous smile she'd known all her life raced across Hannah's face. "He does. He makes me laugh all the time. And he makes me feel . . . *special.* Like in that picture I showed you when Mamm died. The one with the rose petals on the picnic blanket."

Hannah unzipped her purse, reached inside again, and pulled out the small brown book she'd shared with Katie months earlier. When she found the picture she sought, she handed it to Katie. "I wish I could explain how special that day was. How special Travis made me feel by planning that for me."

"There is no need."

And there wasn't. Thanks to Eric, Katie *did* know how it felt. She just didn't know what to do with it, or what, if anything, it meant. Sure, she'd tried to make sense of it all in her journal after Hannah had gone to sleep, but by the time she'd finally put down the pen, her thoughts were as jumbled as ever.

"Can I ask you something, Katie?"

Surprised by the rare hesitancy in her sister's voice, Katie looked up. "Yah."

"Do you *really* like Abram? Really truly?"

She drew back at both the question and the dull roar it kicked off in her ears. "Of course I like Abram. He is a good man. A kind man. A hardworking man."

"I don't mean who he is as a person."

"I do not understand."

"I'm talking about the other stuff, Katie. Like does your heart race when you see him? Do you think about him when you are not together? Do you think of kissing him?" Hannah splayed her hands atop her lap. "You know, that sort of stuff."

"Hannah!"

"It's a normal question, Katie! You should be in love with the person you marry." Hannah leaned forward across their conjoined armrest. "Does he know that you can draw the way that you do? Does he know you stay awake for hours — drawing pictures that you hide away under your mattress?"

The roar grew silent against the pounding inside her chest. "Of course not."

"But he's going to be your husband. Don't you think he should know his wife has such a talent?"

Katie pushed Hannah back onto her own side of the armrest. "Stop it, Hannah, you know I'm not supposed to draw such things. Why would I tell Abram? So he, too, can be shunned for what I do?"

"Will you *ever* tell him?" Hannah asked.

"There will be nothing *to* tell him, Hannah."

"Uh . . . okay. Sure. So when he walks into your bedroom and sees you drawing, he's not going to ask any questions? He's just going to wait politely while you slip your sketch pad and pencils under your mattress? C'mon, Katie, you're being ridiculous. He's going to find out."

She fisted the side of her dress in her hand and worked to soften her jaw enough to speak. "He's not going to find out because there will be nothing to find out. When I get home, I will be throwing my sketch pad and pencils in the big blue trash box behind the English market."

Hannah's gasp brought more than a few unwanted glances their way. "Don't say that, Katie! You can't stop drawing. Ever. You heard what Mr. Rothman said . . . and what those people said about that picture of Mary and the barn cats they wanted for their daughter and — hold on a sec, I think I just got a text." Hannah reached inside her purse again, pulled out her phone, and consulted the screen. "I sure did. And it's from Eric. He says he's sorry he couldn't be here to say goodbye, but he got a call he had to take and now there's no way he can get here before your bus leaves. He says safe travels, thanks for everything, and brave is . . ." Hannah looked up at Katie, her brows furrowed. "Brave is *brave*? I don't get it. What does that mean, 'brave is brave'?"

Sneaking a peek at the screen, Katie read the message herself, Eric's words, coupled with his voice in her head, transporting her back to the park. She could hear the birds, see the squirrels, feel the heat in her cheeks when he listed the many ways in which he found her special —

"Oh, Katie . . ."

The sound of her name on Hannah's tongue pulled her back into the station. Hannah's fingers, digging into her arm, made her grab hold of her ticket with one hand and the handle of Miss Lottie's suitcase with the other. "Is it time for my bus?"

"He got to you, didn't he?"

She looked from Hannah to the platform doorway and back again, the lack of any sort of an official line leaving her even more confused. "*He?* He who?"

"Eric."

She bolted upright in her chair a second time, only this time, instead of grabbing her suitcase, she straightened her dress and her kapp while widening her gaze to include the area on and around the escalators. "I didn't think he had time to come."

"He doesn't." Hannah abandoned Katie's arm in favor of leaning so close their foreheads practically touched. "But what you just felt right now, Katie? When I said his

271

name? And read his text? And you thought he was here? *That*'s what I was talking about a few minutes ago when I asked you if you like Abram. *That*'s the kind of reaction you should have to someone you're going to marry, Katie."

"Stop it, Hannah, you're being silly! There is no reaction. I-I just thought you were saying he was here."

"Then why are your cheeks turning bright red and why are you looking at everything and everyone except me?"

Katie stood. "If my cheeks are red, it is because it is hot in here."

"There is a fan above our heads." Hannah pointed to the fan they'd purposely sought out when selecting their seats. "And your cheeks didn't do that until I said what I said, and you thought what you thought."

"People are lining up, Hannah. It is time for me to go home. To Dat and the children."

"And Abram — don't forget him . . ."

Katie forced her gaze back onto Hannah, the warmth in her cheeks now powered by anger. "Of course I'm going home to Abram. That goes without saying."

"But why?"

"Why what?"

"Why does it go without saying?" Hannah asked.

"Because everyone knows we are to be married, Hannah, including you!" Katie led the way over to the line as it began to move toward the platform and the bus bound for Lancaster County. "It is time for me to go. I will tell everyone you send your love."

"Yes. Please." As they neared the door, Hannah tugged Katie off the line and pulled her in for a hug. "It was wonderful having you here. You fit real good."

She held on to Hannah for a few more seconds and then, when she was pretty sure her emotions were under control, she stepped back, handed her suitcase to the driver, and side-stepped her way back into line, turning one last time at the sound of Hannah's voice.

"Remember, Katie, *are to be* and *want to be* are two very different things."

CHAPTER 21

She saw Abram's buggy the second the bus pulled into the station, his horse, Tucker, tethered to a post on the far end of the parking lot, lapping up water from a black metal bucket. Like so much of what she'd seen outside her window over the past thirty minutes, the familiar sight blanketed her in the kind of calm that had been so elusive the past few days.

Yes, there had been quiet moments in New York, but even then, she'd always been aware of the fact that she didn't belong. It wasn't that Hannah had made her feel unwelcome, because she hadn't. In fact, Hannah had done everything possible to make Katie consider staying permanently. But the world her sister had chosen to live in was so different from Katie's. There, quiet, end-of-the-day time was spent watching television rather than visiting. People passed one another on sidewalks without

274

looking up. And everything moved so fast.

Well, everything except time spent in the park with Eric.

There, and only there, did she feel truly at ease, able to dream and laugh and play in a way she'd always wanted to . . .

Swallowing over the sudden knot at the base of her throat, Katie shifted her focus from the window to the passengers now making their way toward the door, the anticipation on the faces of some counterbalanced by the relative indifference on others. She wondered, briefly, where she fell on that spectrum and then was instantly ashamed of the thought.

She was back in Blue Ball. Where she belonged. Of course she was happy . . .

Her mind made up, Katie stood, followed the aisle to the front, and exited down the stairs, the answering blast of warmth from the day's waning rays dulling the odd sense of uncertainty she couldn't explain or shake off in its entirety. She took a moment to breathe in the familiar smells of sun and earth and then stepped over to the curb, her gaze seeking and finding Abram waiting beneath a large tree, a bouquet of wildflowers in his hand.

She tried to take stock of her feelings, to quiet the Hannah-spawned questions that

275

had plagued her for most if not all of the bus ride, but before she could do much more than blink, Abram stepped to his left to reveal a smile every bit as big as his own.

"Sadie!" Katie lurched forward and spread her arms wide, her feelings at that moment no longer in doubt.

Sadie, in turn, hopped up and down, giggling, and then pulled a near perfect match of Abram's bouquet out from behind her tiny back. "Look, Katie, *look*! Abram picked *me* flowers, too!"

"I see that, sweet —"The thump of Sadie's body against her legs stole the rest of her words and sent her attention back to a still smiling Abram. She tried to blink away the tears making it difficult to see, but his answering nod and ever widening smile let her know he'd caught her nonverbal gratitude.

After several long seconds, Sadie released her grip enough for Katie to squat down to the little girl's eye level and plant a kiss on each chubby cheek. "Did you miss me while I was gone?"

Sadie's pale blue eyes shown bright as her head jerked up and down. "I missed you lots, Katie! But I only woked up Annie two times."

"You woke up Annie?"

"I *tried* to cry quiet, Katie."

Her eyes drifted upward to Abram long enough to see his answering shrug. "Why were you crying, sweet girl?"

"I was scared you wouldn't come back."

She sensed Abram closing the gap between them, but Sadie's hushed words kept her frozen in place. "I told you I'd come back, Sadie. Remember?"

"But Hannah didn't come back," Sadie whispered.

"I know that, but —"

Abram, too, squatted down, his gaze moving from Katie to Sadie and back again, his own smile suddenly . . . *uncertain*? "Katie isn't Hannah, little one. She's different."

Unsure of what to say, she looked down at the ground and waited for the normal rise and fall of her breath to return. When it did, she tapped Sadie on the nose, followed it up with another kiss, and then, taking the child's hand, stood up and waited for Abram to do the same. When he did, she accepted the bouquet.

"It's really good to see you, Katie."

She pulled the flowers to her nose and, inhaling deeply, savored their subtle fragrance. "Thank you, Abram. These are lovely."

"I saw them on my way to pick up Sadie

and they made me think of you. Especially the purple ones."

Sadie studied her own flowers and then held them up between Abram and Katie. "Which is me?"

Abram's eyes narrowed in confusion.

"She wants to know what color made you think of *her,*" Katie teased.

"Ahhh." Abram bent forward and pointed his way around the little girl's bouquet, stopping on the yellow flower. "Most definitely the yellow for you, little one. It is happy just like you."

Pulling her bouquet close, Sadie rose up on her bare toes and twirled around. "Happy, ha-ppy. I am ha-ppyyyy!"

"And you, Katie, must be tired from your trip." Abram motioned toward his horse and buggy. "Why don't you two start heading that way and I'll get your bag from the driver and meet you there. I know everyone is excited to see you."

Sadie stopped twirling to slide her hand inside Katie's. "Mary made a surprise for you! And you're gonna really, *really* like it 'cause it's apple pie!"

"Apple pie, huh?" She glanced at Abram in time to see the same smile she was trying to hold at bay envelope his face.

"So much for surprises," he whispered just

loud enough for Katie to hear.

Katie's laugh filled the space between them. "We're working on those, although it appears we must work harder . . ."

"It does, indeed." He hooked his thumb over the top of his suspender-clad shoulder. "I'll have you on your way to your secret apple pie just as soon as I get your bag."

Four hours later, her footfalls heavy with exhaustion, Katie closed her bedroom door and sank onto her bed. It had been wonderful to see Mary and baby Annie watching for them from the front porch when they came around the bend, and to have Samuel and Jakob temporarily abandon their work in the fields with Dat to say hello.

Dinner and Mary's secret apple pie had been a festive affair with the boys bringing her up to speed on the crops and the animals, Mary sharing stories about Annie, Sadie adding in her version of all, and Dat inserting an occasional nod and laugh of his own. Abram had been invited to stay and he, like everyone else, had listened quietly as she talked of the buildings and people she'd seen, and the time she'd spent with Hannah.

Once, after what had to have been her sixth or seventh story involving the park, she'd looked across the table to find Abram studying her closely, but thanks to a question from Jakob and the opportunity it provided to change topics, the moment had passed.

But even with the bits and pieces she'd been able to share, something about her time in New York suddenly felt so far away.

Too far away.

Pushing herself into a seated position, Katie reached for Miss Lottie's bag and hoisted it up and onto the bed. She peered at the gap between her door and the floor, and when she confirmed it was still dark, she retrieved her sketch pad from beneath the clothes Hannah had washed and dried in the apartment building's machines earlier that morning. For a moment, she simply looked down at the cover, its feel against her fingertips so emblazoned in her thoughts she didn't even need to touch it. Likewise, her mind's eye filled the remaining empty pages with a view of a lake from inside a rowboat, a tree-lined path stretched out in front of two sets of feet, and the look on Eric's face as he talked of her leaving.

The images were so vivid, in fact, her fingers were virtually itching to pick up one of her pencils and sketch the night away. Instead, she set the pad down, transferred her new journal from the suitcase to the drawer beside her bed, hung her freshly laundered dresses from the wall hooks, and then returned to Miss Lottie's bag to find an envelope with her name written across the front in Hannah's bold handwriting.

A peek inside revealed a thick stack of money and a folded note, the sight of both making her heart race.

Katie,
This is the money from the sale of your drawings, less the gallery's commission. Every time you look at this, remember that you earned it with your talent. And that there could be much more to follow if you came here, to New York, where you and your ability belong.

Your twin,
Hannah

With trembling hands, Katie pulled out the money and slowly counted it atop her lap. When she reached the final of sixteen bills, she sunk back against her pillow. This was the kind of money Dat made, not Katie. Her job was to look after the children in Mamm's absence and to do the things that needed to be done while Dat and the boys worked in the fields.

Yet there, on her lap, was sixteen hundred dollars . . .

Sixteen hundred dollars *she'd* earned . . .

From something she kept hidden beneath her mattress in her real life . . .

Katie looked again at the money and the sketch pad before lifting her gaze to the dresses and kapps hanging against the wall beside the door — the same kind of dresses and kapps Mamm, and her mamm before her, had worn. Good, strong women who'd lived the life she'd vowed to live when she, unlike Hannah, had chosen baptism.

To imagine a life like Hannah's was to imagine a life without the very people who had welcomed her home with open arms not more than four hours earlier. They were the ones she needed to focus on, to draw strength from, to —

Draw . . .

Blinking back tears she had no right to shed, Katie stuffed the money and Hannah's note back inside the envelope and carried it around to her hiding spot on the other side of her bed.

"Bravery wears many faces, Katie. Remember that."

Then, with little more than a single, weighted inhale, she reached across the mattress, secured her sketch pad and pencils

282

from their resting spot beside the suitcase, and slid them out of sight, once and for all.

CHAPTER 22

It wasn't hard to fall back into the day-to-day routine that was life in Blue Ball. It was as much a part of her as her mamm's soft brown hair and Dat's brown eyes. And, for the most part, that was exactly what she needed.

Each morning, the rising sun ushered in its own set of tasks — a hearty breakfast for Dat and the boys, barn and house chores for Katie and her sisters, and looking after Annie.

Evenings, of course, brought cooking, eating, cleaning up, clothes mending, and conversation. Occasionally, if there was no mending to be done, Jakob would lure them onto the front porch with a game of I-Spy.

At night, when she was alone in her bedroom, Katie did her best to go straight to sleep with thoughts of the coming day and the tasks that would require her attention. It wasn't easy as evidenced by the dark circles Sadie pointed to beneath her eyes most mornings, but at least the empty pages in her pad remained so.

Letters from Hannah arrived every Friday much to the delight of Katie's siblings. They loved to read of their big sister's adventures and then share them with everyone else after the day's work was done. After a few failed attempts at trying to keep her voice steady during the weekly ritual, Katie become proficient at letting Mary share her letter while she busied herself with whatever task she'd intentionally left unfinished.

But amid the familiar and comforting pattern of her days, she'd made a few changes, too.

Now, instead of saving a few chores for Annie's nap time, Katie made sure to have them done, the change leaving her with time to play with Sadie or, when Mary took over, walks alone. The walks, unlike the rest of her life, followed no real pattern. Sometimes, she walked east toward Miller's Pond and either wandered around it picking wildflowers, or sat in her favorite spot in the sun. Other days, like she was at that moment, she turned west, her only destination however far she could make it before needing to turn back. Regardless of the direction though, she treasured the opportunity to slow things down and *just be* as Eric had said.

Unfortunately, *just being* had a way of always leading her back to the same place whether physically or mentally. And despite her resoluteness to refrain from drawing at night, she simply couldn't bring herself to get rid of her work completely. She'd tried a few times. Even gone so far as to wrap it in one of her dresses for a naptime trek to the English market. But when it came time to leave, the thought of actually tossing it into the dumpster had her forgoing the alone time in favor of sending Mary for the needed grocery items, instead.

Still, it was something she knew she needed to do.

Soon.

She welcomed the approaching clip-clop of a neighbor's horse-drawn buggy for the distraction it was and turned to wave, the strength of the afternoon sun making it momentarily difficult to discern the identity of the driver.

"Good afternoon, Katie."

With her hand as a shield, she sought and found the voice's matching face. "Good afternoon, Abram."

"Can I give you a ride to wherever it is you're going?"

"No, I am just walking." Slowly, she lowered her hand back to her side and shifted her stance so as to let the buggy do the blocking. "Annie is napping, and Mary and Sadie are playing string with the barn cats."

"And you are just walking to walk . . ."

It wasn't an entirely accurate assessment, but in light of her reality, it would suffice. "Yah."

He loosened his grip on the reins until they were resting more atop his lap than in his hands. "I do that sometimes, too. It is a good time to think and to plan."

"You . . . *think*?"

His laughter, deep and rich, floated across the air between them. "Of course I think, Katie. It would be odd if I didn't."

"I-I didn't mean that. I-I'm sorry to sound so-so stupid." She buried her warming cheeks in her hands only to have them pried away by Abram's.

"I did not mean to make you feel stupid, Katie." He tucked the reins onto his abandoned seat and then captured her hands in his once again. "I know you are smart. I also know you are kind and creative."

"Creative?" she echoed.

"Yah. It is why purple flowers make me think of you."

She felt her mouth gape and tried her best to recover it before he noticed. "I don't understand."

"There is a sign in the English paint store that speaks of colors and their meanings. Yellow, like the sun, is happy."

"Like Sadie."

He smiled. "Yah. And blue? It is open and free, like the sky. Brown is comfort like the soil. Orange is endurance. And purple? It means creative . . . like you."

"I-I am not creative. I am just . . . Katie."

"I saw the horse you drew on a napkin at a hymn sing in the fall. It was of Tucker, here." He released her left hand so as to pat the side of his waiting horse. "You had the patch of white between his ears shaped just right. And you captured the way his eyes get big when he sees one of my sister's peppermint cookies."

"I think it is the peppermint candy *on top* of the cookie that Tucker really wants," she said, earning her an encore of a laugh that warmed her in a way that had nothing to do with the sun or any sort of embarrassment.

"I think you are right." He returned his free hand to hers and held it gently. "But that is why I picked purple for you. Because a person who can draw such a picture is creative, Katie."

She looked down at her hands inside his and then, after a beat or two of an increasingly weighted silence, extricated them to smooth wrinkles that didn't exist from her dress. "I do not know why I drew that picture."

"*I* do."

Tucker's ears perked at her gasp, necessitating a gentle word of reassurance from Abram in return. "You do? But . . . how?"

"Because I saw your smile while you were sitting on the grass drawing it."

"My smile?"

"Yah. It made you happy to draw that picture. And that is why I hope there will be more."

She knew her mouth was hanging open, she could feel it just as surely as she could hear her heart pounding inside her ears, but at that moment, in that place, she was powerless to do anything but stare back at Abram.

He, in turn, laughed. "You look surprised, Katie."

She gave thought to correcting his word choice to better reflect her shock, but settled for simply speaking, instead. "Drawing such pictures is not useful."

"You think all of *my* drawings are useful?"

"*Your* drawings?" she echoed.

"Yah. The ones I do out by the covered bridge instead of eating lunch most days."

"What do you draw?"

"The furniture I will make in my workshop one day." Reaching up, he repositioned his hat and stepped into the shade afforded by Tucker. "I will make them in the winter. When there are no crops to tend. Maybe, one day, there will be enough to have a whole shop. But even if there is not, I can still sell pieces that I make.

"I like to draw what I will build so I know how much wood I will need. Most of the time, I draw footstools and dressers and tables. But a few times, when I am finished, I am surprised to see I have drawn much more."

Intrigued, she shortened the gap between them by a few steps. "Like what?"

"One day, when I was drawing a table and chairs, I drew a whole kitchen . . . and then a hallway . . . and then a room to be used for church . . . and then a front porch . . . with two chairs — one for me, and one for you . . . and then I drew a cradle like the one my brother slept in when he was born . . . only in my head, I saw *our* child — the one I pray God gives us when we are married." He swiped a bead of sweat from his forehead with his thumb and then

290

smiled down at Katie. "I drew all those things even though I was only building a table and chairs."

It was all so much more than she could take in at the moment, but still she tried, her head reeling from their first real conversation about something other than Mamm's death or their need to wait to get married. "I knew you liked making wooden toys for your brothers and sisters, but I had no idea you wanted to make furniture."

"There was never a good time to speak of such things."

"But it's your dream," she protested.

Abram's shoulders hitched upward with a shrug. "It's just something I have wanted to do for many years. Since Dat brought me to a furniture maker when I was eight."

"Okay, but that's *a dream,* Abram, and I love hearing about that kind of thing."

He met her gaze and held it. "I want to hear about such things, too. From you. But you have been so quiet during our Sunday rides."

In lieu of an argument she couldn't make, she left her spot in the shade to nuzzle noses with Tucker. Abram followed. "I know you had much to do during your mamm's illness and now again with caring for the little ones, but maybe, now that time has passed,

291

you will be ready to share more, Katie. Because I very much want to know the things that make you happy. And I want to hear about *your* dreams, too."

No you don't, she wanted to say . . .

Because if she *did* share her dream and he said nothing to the bishop or their district, Abram, too, could be shunned.

Still, just knowing he *wanted* to know was a surprise — a pleasant surprise.

"Do you think I could see something you've made one day?" she asked, looking back at Abram.

"You will. On our wedding day. When it is finished."

"It?"

His hat moved with his nod but not enough to shield his answering grin from view completely. "It is to be a surprise."

"Does Sadie know what it is?"

"No, why?"

She gave Tucker one last nuzzle and then turned back to Abram, her mouth spreading wide with the kind of smile that hadn't been hers since —

Eric?

"Katie?"

She shook the unexpected thought from her head and forced herself back to the moment and the man standing in front of her

292

with amused curiosity. "Sorry. Anyway, don't you remember the apple pie?"

"Apple pie?"

"Specifically, Mary's *secret* apple pie . . ."

The understanding that finally dawned on Abram's face sent Katie into a fit of laughter. His subsequent "oooohhhh" only made it louder. Soon, Abram joined in, prompting Tucker to give them a more perplexed version of his infamous peppermint eye.

Eventually though, she stopped and pointed in the direction she'd come. "I better get back. Annie will be waking soon and there is much work to be done before supper."

"May I drive you back?"

The answering flutter she felt in her chest made it so her yah came before her next breath. The feel of his hand as he helped her onto his wagon seat simply made the flutter stronger.

"I am glad you were out walking today," Abram said as he joined her on the seat and guided Tucker to turn with a gentle tug of the reins. "Your laugh, it is a nice sound."

Unsure of how best to respond, she chose to let the clip-clop of Tucker's hooves, the warmth of the sun on their faces, and the comforting feel of Abram's shoulder against hers fill in the space, instead.

And it felt good.

Right, even . . .

"If I am purple for creative, what color are you?" she finally asked as they turned onto her driveway and headed toward the house.

"I am green. For hope."

She felt the buggy slow as they passed the barn and then the house. But at that moment, all she could see was the man seated beside her on the bench. "Why?"

"Because I have hope for many things, Katie Beiler. I have hope for good crops. I have hope that I will make much furniture one day. And I have hope that it will be God's will for us to share a long and happy life together. With many reasons for you to smile and laugh."

CHAPTER 23

She was just pulling a loaf of bread from the oven when the screen door banged against its frame at the front of the house, ushering in the pitter-patter of Sadie's bare feet.

"Katie! Katie!"

Grinning, she set the pan on the counter, pulled off her oven mitt, and spun around, hands on hips. "Yes, Sadie, the bread is out of the oven. And yes, I know it smells really, really good right now. But just like last time, it needs to cool a little before I can slice it and you can eat it." She squatted down next to the counter and waved the four-year-old over. "Besides, if we eat it all now, Dat and the boys will not have bread with their dinner."

"Can I sniff over it?" Sadie asked, peeking around Katie's shoulder in an attempt to see into the pan. *"Please?"*

"Since you asked nicely, yes, you can sniff

over it." Katie scooped up her sister and held her over the bread pan.

"Mmmm, that smells yummy!"

"It sure does, doesn't it? And you . . . You smell like flowers, barn cats, and" — she pulled Sadie close and sniffed — "chocolate chip cookies!"

"Miss Lottie gave me a cookie. Her gave Annie one, too!"

"She," Katie corrected. "*She* gave Annie one."

Sadie wiggled her way back to the ground and then pointed to the hallway. "She has one for you, too, Katie! And two letters!"

"Miss Lottie is *here*?"

"She's in the barn with Mary and Annie!" Sadie took a few running steps toward the front of the house and then stopped, her eyes crackling with excitement as she looked back at Katie. "Come! Come!"

"Go on, I'll be there in a few moments." Reaching behind herself, she plucked a dishcloth off the counter, gave her hands a quick wipe, and made her way onto the front porch.

"That bread smells as good as your mamm's always did . . ."

Katie turned toward the familiar voice and smiled. "Miss Lottie! Sadie said you were in the barn."

"I was. But now I'm here. Taking a wee rest on your chair."

She closed the gap between them with three long strides, her eyes skirting the rest of the porch and the yard as she did. "Where did Sadie go?"

"To help Annie find Fancy Feet."

"Ahhh." Slowly, she lowered herself onto the edge of Dat's vacant chair and released a much-needed sigh. "How are you? Would you like to come inside? The bread still needs to cool, but there is a piece of chess pie left over from last night."

"I am well, thank you, and no, it's a beautiful day to be outside. There's even a hint of fall in the air, don't you think?"

She looked across the drive to the barn and then swung her attention north toward the trees in the distance. Sure enough, the greens of summer were beginning to hint at the colors to come. "I had not noticed, but you are right. Fall is most certainly beginning to peek around summer, as Mamm would say."

"You still miss her, don't you?" Miss Lottie asked.

"Every day. I just wish Annie could have known her longer. Sadie, too."

Miss Lottie's hand closed over Katie's and squeezed. "They will know of her from the

297

stories you and Mary and the others tell, dear. Tell them when you are baking from a recipe she used. Share lessons she taught you with them. And point out things you see that made her smile. That is what will keep her alive in their hearts and minds."

"Sadies *does* like Mamm's bread."

"And the cookies I make are from her recipes, too." Miss Lottie recovered her hand and reached inside the bag at her feet. "I brought one for you, too, Katie."

She accepted the treat and set it on the armrest of her chair. "Thank you."

"I also have letters."

"I know, Sadie told me. But I'm surprised to hear there are only two. Usually Hannah sends one to each of us."

"And she did this time, as well."

"Oh. So you'd like me to read Annie's to her?"

"No, I already did that. In the barn. And now she and Sadie are sharing the contents with the cats and the chickens."

"They're fascinated, I'm sure." Katie let her laugh lapse in favor of another question. "So who didn't get theirs, then?"

"Just you."

"Ahhh, okay, so you hadn't given Annie hers when Sadie came looking for me . . . I get it."

Again, Miss Lottie reached into her bag, this time pulling out two different-shaped envelopes. "No, I had. The two letters are for *you,* Katie."

"Hannah wrote me twice?"

"Only one is from Hannah."

Katie dropped her gaze from Miss Lottie's to the envelopes in her hand. "I don't understand."

"This one is from your sister." Miss Lottie handed Katie the first of the two envelopes and then pointed to the name in the upper left corner of the second. "This, too, is from New York, but it's from an E. Morgan."

"E. Morgan?" Katie echoed. "I don't know an E. Mor—"

She bit down over the rest of her sentence as the face that coincided with the sender's name claimed center stage in her thoughts.

"I take it this is someone you met while visiting Hannah?" Miss Lottie asked.

"Yah."

"What does E stand for?"

She tried to cool her cheeks with her hands, but it was no use. Instead, she took the letter from Miss Lottie's outstretched hand and ran her fingers across her name. "Eric," she whispered. "He-he is a friend of Hannah's."

"And of you, too, from what I can see."

Miss Lottie's gaze was heavy on the side of her face, but try as she might, Katie couldn't take her eyes off Eric's name long enough to meet it. Instead, she swallowed and tried to nod the best she could. "I-I suppose."

Seconds turned into minutes as she slid her fingertips across his name, her head filling in possible reasons he would write . . .

She left something behind that he found . . .

He —

No, there was no reason that she could imagine that would have him reaching out to her via a letter. It made no sense.

"The only way to know is to open it, child."

She glanced up. "Know? Know what, Miss Lottie?"

"What the letter says." Miss Lottie nudged the bag away from the front of her chair with her foot and leaned back. "So, while I rest here for a little while longer before I head back home, why don't you take those two letters down to the pond and see what Hannah and your friend, Eric, have to say."

Pulling the letters to her chest, she tried to steady her voice enough to protest, but she couldn't. All she could do was think about the envelope on her lap and the fact that Eric had written a letter. To her . . .

"It's okay, dear. Mary is in the barn with the girls, and I'll see that they start setting the table for supper if you're not back in the next thirty minutes."

She rose up onto shaky legs, the gratitude she felt making her lips quiver along with her voice. "Are you sure?"

"Yes, child."

"Thank you, Miss Lottie. I-I won't be long."

First, on slow feet, and then with gathering speed, Katie made her way across the porch and down the driveway to the main road; her need to know what Eric wanted no longer encumbered by have-to's and shouldn'ts. The fact that Eric had written, rather than simply ask Hannah to pass something along, pointed to one simple and pulse-racing fact: Eric had *wanted* to reach out. To her.

It was a realization that guided her steps east to a trail she'd traveled often in life. There, just beyond a grove of trees, was Miller's Pond, the stretch of earth at the base of the old climbing tree calling to her with the same pull it had held all her life.

Lowering herself to the ground, Katie set Hannah's envelope on her lap and carefully opened Eric's. Inside, she found a tri-folded piece of white lined paper that she promptly unfolded and smoothed across her legs.

Dear Katie,

It's been a month since you were here, and my walks in the park are no longer the same as they were before your visit.

Now, when I cut through the park to get to the west side, I find myself stopping to watch squirrels and birds for far longer than I ever did before. And while I can imagine you smiling and telling me, "that's good," I've been as much as ten minutes late to three different meetings because of that.

Her answering laugh quieted a pair of birds standing watch atop the branch of a neighboring tree. Leaning her head against the trunk at her back, she tried to imagine the reaction of the city squirrel or bird as Eric ran off, muttering about lateness.

"You must learn to look and talk at the same time, silly," she whispered before turning her attention back to the letter.

One of those meetings was actually with the agent of a pretty well-known singer. They like one of the songs I sent them and wanted to talk to me about it.

It was cool, sure, but it was also incredibly unnerving. Needless to say, while I'm not sure it was the same squirrel who'd made me late, I found myself talking to one from a bench not far from our picnic spot when I was done. The people walking by must have thought I was a crazy person, talking to myself like that.

Come to think of it, the squirrel probably thought that, too.

Anyway, I just wanted you to know that I think about you a lot, that I look at that picture I shouldn't have taken (but am so glad I did) at some point every day, and that I often wonder how things are going for you. I imagine your family was really happy to see you when you got home from here. Abram, too.

She ignored the heat resurrecting itself in her cheeks and, instead, moved on to the final line.

I miss you, Katie.

Your friend,
Eric

Eric . . .

Closing her eyes, she let herself travel back

to the moment, in the bus station, when he'd tapped her on the shoulder and introduced himself. At the time, she'd been so overwhelmed and frightened, the only other emotion she'd felt was hurt. She'd been so sure Hannah was going to be there when she stepped off the bus.

Instead, it had been Eric.

Eric with the dark brown hair that had glistened in the overhead light, the green eyes that had hitched her breath, and the kind of genuine smile that had dulled her fear and somehow let her know that everything, while daunting, would be okay. And it had been.

Because of Eric . . .

Startled by the unexpected realization, she tried to shake it off, to remember all the things she'd done with Hannah during the same visit. But every encounter with Hannah had ended in anger and frustration, while every encounter with Eric had ended in laughter and a quiet, yet determined confidence she'd never felt with Hannah.

She blinked hard against the tears she knew were building and, instead, carefully folded Eric's letter and slipped it back into the envelope. For a few moments she simply sat there, looking down at it, trying to absorb everything about his handwriting, his choice of pen, and the tiny crease she imagined him making while carrying it to the mailbox. Eventually though, she shifted it to the bottom of the two-envelope pile and opened the pale blue, slightly thicker than normal one from her twin sister.

Tucked inside her sister's familiar notepaper was another folded page that, at first glance, appeared as if it had come from the Amish newspaper Dat read each week. Confused, she set it down atop Eric's envelope and focused her attention on Hannah's letter.

Dear Katie,

It is almost bedtime and it has been a busy day. I took Jack to the zoo to watch the sea lion feeding. He loves to watch them do tricks to get fish. I wish Sadie and Annie could see them, too. I bet they would just stare and stare.

I saw Eric on my way home from work the other day and he asked me for your address. When I asked why, he said he wanted to write you a letter! I hope that he does.

Now, about the article I have sent. Mr. Rothman received this in the mail from the woman who bought your drawing of Mary for her daughter. Remember her?

Anyway, from what Mr. Rothman explained to me, the local paper in the town where the daughter lives did this story on her and her veterinary practice as part of a who's-who in town kind of thing. Her story is nice as it's about childhood dreams and making them come true. But it is the picture that goes with the story that made her mother send it to Mr. Rothman. Look closely at the wall behind the daughter and be sure to read the caption underneath! I hope that seeing it here, in print, will remind you of your own dream and help you to see that New York City is where you should be. With me. And with Eric.

Your sister,

Hannah

Swapping the letter for the still-folded piece of paper in her lap, Katie opened it a fourth at a time, the color photograph it revealed sucking the air from her lungs.

CHAPTER 24

Katie did her best to act as normal as possible when she returned to the house, the pile of potatoes waiting to be peeled providing the opportunity she needed to focus on something other than her stupidity. But it didn't last long.

Looking back, she should have demanded Hannah remove her drawings from the gallery the second she saw them. If she had, she wouldn't have an envelope of cash stuffed under her mattress and a ticket to her own shunning tucked between her boot and her ankle bone. Instead, she'd stood by, in sinful pride, listening to strangers elevate her and her ability. And now, because of her sins and her stupidity, her little sister's face looked out at people in places it should not be, and Katie's name and ongoing sin were written in black and white for all to see.

Slowly, she peeled her way through each and every potato and then transferred them to the pot of boiling water. Mamm's recipe for Dat's favorite chicken dish was next and while rounding up the ingredients certainly helped occupy her thoughts in quick bursts, it, too, led her back to her sin.

Mamm had been so good. So thoughtful. So focused on making sure their family was okay before she took her last breath. Even on those days when she'd been unable to keep the pain hidden, Mamm had mustered up enough energy to write directions on how to make each child's favorite meal.

That was the way she'd promised Mamm she would be — making sure to look after Dat and the children. Yet, in reality, she'd taken care of no one but herself, giving in to the sinful urge to draw the things she drew, and then to cover it up with lies. And now, because of her choices, good people — people she loved — stood to be harmed by shame and disappointment.

"Is something wrong, Katie?"

She looked up from the assembled ingredients that sat, untouched, in front of her to find Mary looking at her with worried eyes. "No, I am fine. Why?"

Hooking her thumb in the direction of the hallway and the voices they could hear through the open screen windows, Mary crossed to the cabinet of dishes and removed a stack of seven. "Many hands make light work. But yet, for some reason, you do not let me help with dinner tonight."

"I don't know, Mary. I guess I just thought I'd take care of it this time." She turned back to the counter, added the ingredients to the bowl in front of her, and gave it a quick, yet thorough mix. "It won't be long before you must do all of this on your own."

"Sadie said you took two letters to the pond before Miss Lottie left. Hannah has not sent you two letters before."

"Only one was from Hannah." She wiped the sudden dampness from her hands onto a nearby dishcloth and hoped its originating case of nerves didn't manifest itself in her voice. "The other was from a friend I made when I visited."

"That is nice. What is her name?"

She pulled a baking dish from the cabinet above her head, filled it with chicken, and then poured the contents of the bowl across the top, the desire to be more like Mamm mandating the truth. "Eric."

"Eric? But isn't that a boy's name?"

Katie took advantage of her back being to Mary for a few seconds to draw in a much needed and fortifying breath. "Yah."

"An English *boy* wrote to you?"

"Yah."

"What did he say?" Mary asked, surprise pushing her eyebrows toward her kapp.

She hoped her shrug was casual as she grabbed hold of the baking dish, slid it into the oven, and mentally picked through the letter for parts she could share. "He talked about the park by Hannah's house and a job he might get."

"Why did such a letter make you mad and sad?"

"Who said I was mad and sad?"

"I saw you, Katie." Mary carried the dishes over to the table and set one in front of everyone's spot. "I saw you walk right past Sadie and into the house when you got back from the pond with your letters."

"I-I must not have seen her . . ."

"I'm not sure how you couldn't. She was hopping up and down in front of you, telling you how the baby goat drank all of its milk, and you looked down at her, gave her a half smile like this" — Mary demonstrated, using the left side of her mouth — "and then walked right around her and up the front steps without saying a word."

Katie sank back against the edge of the counter. "Oh no . . ."

"I told her you were busy with thoughts of supper, but I still see worry in her eyes, Katie. It is the same worry *I* feel looking at

310

you now."

"Oh Mary . . . I-I don't know what to do. I have made a mess of everything with my —" She jerked her gaze up to Mary's as her words circled around to her ears, the horror of what she'd been seconds away from saying pulling her from her spot at the counter and sending her running for the back door.

"Katie? Katie? Are you okay?"

Tightening her hand around the knob, she opted to answer with a lie rather than a far worse truth. "Please take over for me with dinner and everything else . . . I-I think I am going to be sick."

No matter how many times she looked at the photograph, or how many times she read the caption underneath it, Katie still couldn't believe it was true.

Sure, she'd drawn the picture of Mary and the cats that hung on the wall behind the woman in the photograph, and, yes, Katie Beiler was her name. But to have all of that end up in a newspaper for people to read and see? It was beyond her comprehension. Especially when Hannah knew as well as she did what would happen if Dat or anyone else in the district found out.

She fell back against the pillow and stared up at the ceiling, the memory of Josiah

311

Fisher's shunning emblazoned in her brain. Josiah had been caught using electricity inside his home. Although he'd been the one to do it, his wife and his one baptized child had been shunned, too, for knowing about it and not going to the bishop to report the sin. For weeks, Katie and the rest of their district had to sit with their backs to Josiah, his wife, and his son, Isaiah, a boy Katie had gone to school with and often socialized with at hymn sings. And while they'd repented and things had since returned to normal, Katie couldn't forget the shame Isaiah had worn. Or the sadness that had hung heavy across the rest of Josiah's children, even the little ones.

Now, because of Katie, that shame and that sadness could be Dat's and the children's if they found out about the picture in the paper and did not tell the bishop of her sins.

She wanted to be angry at Hannah, and in many ways, she was. But Hannah hadn't told her to buy a sketch pad during Rumspringa, and Hannah hadn't told her to keep drawing in it even after baptism. That had been all Katie.

And while Hannah was the reason Katie's secret was no longer a secret, it still came back to Katie and her choice to do wrong in the first place.

"Oh, Mamm," she whispered. "I have let you down. I have made such a mess of things and I am so very, very —"

A soft tap at her bedroom door bolted her upright so fast the article with its accompanying photograph skittered off the edge of her bed and sailed onto the ground. Before she could grab it, the door inched open.

"Are you feeling better?" Sadie padded into the room on bare feet, her focus solely on Katie.

She tried to nod, to offer the closest thing to a reassuring smile she could, but all she could really think about at that moment was the article that was no more than two feet from Sadie's toes and the sound of Mary nearing the door with baby Annie in tow . . .

Dropping her own feet onto the floor, she reached down, grabbed the article, and balled it inside her hand. "I'm doing much better, sweet girl."

"What's that?" Sadie asked, pointing at Katie's hand.

"Oh Katie, you're up!" Mary strode into the room with a thumb-sucking Annie in her arms and stopped behind Sadie. "Does that mean you're feeling better?"

"She is!" Sadie lunged forward, wrapping

her arms around Katie. "And she made a ball with the paper from the ground!"

Mary surveyed the floor and then cast a quizzical eye in their direction. "I do not see paper on the floor."

Sadie squeezed Katie hard and then stepped back to point at her closed hand. "It's in her hand!"

She knew her face was red. She could feel it just as surely as she could the two sets of eyes trained on her hand while the third remained on her face. Slowly, she looked up, her gaze meeting Mary's with what she hoped was a silent plea to let it go.

After several long beats of silence, Mary reached down, took Sadie by the hand, and retraced their steps back to the door. When she reached it, she set Annie on the ground alongside Sadie, directed them toward their room, and then turned to Katie one last time.

"I know it has only been a few months, but sometimes I am afraid I will forget many things about Mamm — the way she smiled when we brought her flowers, the sound of her laugh when Jakob did something silly, the way she'd walk out to the field with water for Dat when it was hot.

"For now, I remember those things. I see them in my head, and I am glad for that.

But they are not the only things I see when I think of her, Katie."

Intrigue laced with pain accompanied her onto the bed, her thoughts no longer on her hand but, rather, on Mary. "What else?"

"I see Miss Lottie coming for visits just as she does now."

"Miss Lottie?" she repeated, confused. "I don't understand. You were speaking of Mamm."

"Yah. I am. I see the cookies Miss Lottie would bring for us to eat while we wandered the garden and they sat on the porch and talked."

"They, meaning Mamm and Miss Lottie, yah?"

Mary nodded. "I also remember times when Mamm would take us to Miss Lottie's house. Sometimes she would give us jars of bubbles to play with, remember?"

She smiled at the memory. "I do."

"Miss Lottie would tell us to take Digger into the yard and blow bubbles for him to chase."

Her smile morphed into a laugh. "That old dog sure did love to jump for the high ones, didn't he?"

Again, Mary nodded, her eyes never leaving Katie's. "Sometimes, when we would walk to Miss Lottie's house, Mamm would

315

be quiet and her shoulders would be low with worry. But when we were done with our bubbles and our cookies and it was time to leave, she would be Mamm again, talking and laughing with us as we headed down the street and across the fields toward home.

"We did not know what they talked about, but I think we all knew the time with Miss Lottie had been good for Mamm."

Katie looked down at her hand and then back up at Mary, her heart rate accelerating once again. Only this time, instead of being powered by fear and shame, it was propelled by . . . *hope*? "Thank you, Mary. I think tomorrow, when Annie is napping and you are working on your quilt, I will take Sadie to play with bubbles. Maybe Digger still has some jumps left inside him."

CHAPTER 25

Katie sat on the top porch step and watched as Sadie blew bubble after bubble, the little girl's uncomplicated pleasure temporarily easing the stress that had accompanied her all the way to Miss Lottie's front door. Sadie, of course, had jumped at the opportunity to have special time with her big sister, and Katie, in return, had savored the feel of Sadie's small and trusting hand inside hers as they made the three-quarter-mile trip.

More than once, Katie had almost doubled back, the thought of sharing her sins with Miss Lottie churning her stomach in a way that promised to make good on her previous night's purported ailment. Yet every time she stopped and opened her mouth to tell Sadie they needed to turn around, she found herself flashing back to all the same memories that had prompted her to come in the first place.

Mary was right. Miss Lottie had been a steady pair of ears for Mamm for as long as Katie could remember. And while she often wondered what they spoke about, she knew the time had been good for Mamm.

Casting her eyes down at the cookie in her hands, she sucked in a breath and then addressed the woman seated just over her shoulder. "I hope it's okay Sadie and I just stopped by. I don't want to impose if you have something else you need to do."

"Hush, child, you are never an imposition. In fact, seeing you and Sadie walking up my driveway was just what I needed to make a sunny day even brighter. Though, I do wish you'd tell me what's been troubling you since you got back from your visit with Hannah." Pushing the big toe of her right-sandaled foot against the porch floor, Miss Lottie adjusted the pace of her rocking chair and lowered her chin so as to allow a clear view of Katie across the top of the reading glasses she wore whether she was reading or not.

"I guess I'm still trying to get use to Mamm being gone."

"While I'm sure there is some measure of truth to that, you have done a wonderful job, Katie. Yes, you were sad at times before your trip, but it has been different since you came back." Miss Lottie smiled out at Sadie, but her focus, her attention was on Katie. "I see you going for walks you didn't take before your trip. And Mary talks of you pacing in your room at night."

She, too, looked out at Sadie, the little girl's squeals of delight every time Digger caught a bubble helping to steady Katie's breath and quiet her fears enough to speak. "I did things I should not have done, Miss Lottie. Bad things, sinful things. Things that would bring my family shame."

The soft beat of the rocking chair ceased and Katie waited for the scolding she knew was next. But it didn't come. Instead, the woman stood, dragged the chair closer to the steps and Katie, and then sat back down. "Did you drink, Katie?"

She drew back, startled by the question. "No!"

"Were you with a man? Perhaps this Eric who wrote that letter to you?"

Her cheeks flamed hot as she made herself look at Mamm's special friend. "No, n-not in the way you mean."

"Why did he write to you, Katie?"

Pivoting her body to the side, she leaned against the upright so as to afford a view of both Sadie and Miss Lottie. "He is just nice. He came to get me when I arrived in the city and when I asked to walk instead of ride in the yellow car, we did so."

She watched Digger bound after a bubble and then gave words to the memory she'd revisited in her thoughts at least once a day since she'd been back in Blue Ball. "I was so scared, Miss Lottie. There were so many people . . . *Everywhere.* They walked one way and another way, passing by so close they practically touched. Yet they didn't look or speak to one another. They just walked. And the buildings — they were so big, so tall. And there was so much noise. It was all so scary. Yet . . ."

"Go on, dear."

"He made it fun, Miss Lottie. He answered my silly questions without making me *feel* silly. He told me things about some of the buildings I could not know. And he made me try New York pizza."

Miss Lottie's laugh, both hearty and familiar, helped lighten the atmosphere temporarily and Katie was grateful. Even Sadie paused in her playtime to wave at them.

"So? Did you like the pizza?" Miss Lottie asked.

"It was so very, very good. I think it is something Samuel and Jakob would love."

"You say that as if your brothers do not

like to eat everything in sight.'"

It was Katie's turn to laugh, making Sadie pause even longer. She waved out at the little girl to let her know it was still okay to play and then continued with the kind of things she'd wanted to share with someone, *anyone* since the moment they happened. "Later, on another day, Eric knew I was missing home, so he took me to Central Park where there is grass . . . and trees . . . and squirrels . . . and birds . . . and little toy sailboats that share a pond with ducks who do not seem to care they are there."

"Yes, it is a beautiful park."

She stared at Miss Lottie. "You have been there?"

"I have."

Feeling suddenly foolish for asking an Englisher such a question, Katie moved her hand from her lap to the porch floor and began to trace the outer rim of a knot in a nearby board. "The day before I was to leave, Eric took me to the park for a picnic. He packed sandwiches and chips and cookies. I felt" — she rescinded her hand as her voice dipped to something resembling more of a whisper — *"special."*

"Because of the picnic?"

"That was some, yah. But it was more the way he listens."

Miss Lottie leaned forward, grabbed hold of Katie's hand, and held it until Katie looked up at her. "I have seen Abram with you. He cares very much for you, Katie. And I know he listens, too."

She returned Miss Lottie's squeeze and then, pulling her hand back, rested her head against the upright, as well. They'd come full circle, back to the reason she was there in the first place — a reason that churned her stomach with dread.

"Katie?"

"You're right, Miss Lottie, Abram does listen. But there are things he cannot know."

"Tell me, child."

She looked from the wooden-beamed ceiling above her head, to Sadie and Digger, and then back again, all the while praying silently for the same peace Mamm always seemed to have after a talk with Miss Lottie. "I draw things I should not draw."

When she heard nothing but silence in response, she peeked out. Miss Lottie was simply sitting there, watching her, with an odd expression on her gently lined face.

"They are things I should not draw, Miss Lottie."

"Is that what is wrapped inside?" Miss Lottie asked, directing Katie's attention back to the folded quilt she'd set aside upon

322

her arrival.

"Yah."

"May I see it?"

Wordlessly, she stood, crossed to the table on the other side of the porch, and slowly unwrapped her sketch pad, her shoulders heavy.

"Bring it here, child."

She did as she was told, but it wasn't easy. The knowledge that she would soon see disappointment on the elderly woman's face was almost more than she could stand.

Miss Lottie set the sketch pad on her lap and flipped the cover over her knees. Page by page, she made her way through the book —

Mamm gardening.

Samuel chasing the chicken with Mary looking on and laughing.

Mary and Sadie walking across the pasture, hand in hand.

Hannah dangling upside down from a tree.

Dat guiding the team back to the barn after a long day in the fields.

Annie looking up from her crib, her thumb unable to hide her joy at seeing Mamm looking back.

Jakob playing leapfrog with Sadie in the front yard.

Fancy Feet licking herself in the center of a sunspot.

A bedridden Mamm during her final weeks of life —

"Oh, Katie . . ."

"I'm so sorry, Miss Lottie. I know I should not draw such things. I-I know —"

"It is like looking at a photograph," Miss Lottie said, her voice husky.

She swallowed, but it did nothing to dislodge the lump that had suddenly affixed itself midway up the inside of her throat. Instead, she cast her eyes down at her feet and waited for the reprimand she deserved.

"How did you learn to draw like this, Katie?"

Snapping her head up, she stared at Miss Lottie, the disappointment she expected nowhere to be found. "I-I just try. I make lots of mistakes and erase many times, but I try until it looks the way it does in my memory."

"When do you draw these?"

"At night. After Mamm —" She shifted her weight across her feet and tried again. "After Dat blows out his candle."

"Do you draw by lantern?"

"I draw by moonlight when I can. When there is no moon, I wait until I am sure Dat is asleep and then, yah, I light a candle."

Miss Lottie paused her fingertips on the side of Mamm's face and peered up at Katie. "And the pacing Mary spoke of yesterday?"

"I didn't know she could hear me. I will find another way to keep from drawing. But it is just that it . . . well, it's . . ." At a loss for how best to explain her feelings, she looked out at Sadie.

"It's become a part of you, hasn't it?"

She turned her watery gaze back on Miss Lottie. "Yah."

"Oh, Katie . . ."

Lowering herself to the floor, she stared out over the carefully tended lawn she could see through the slats of the railing. "I know I should not draw such things. I know I am making graven images I should not make. But the memories I draw are so vivid in my head, and it is something that is *just me*. It is not something Hannah taught me or helped me do or did for me because I was too afraid. It is something only *I* do. On my own. As Katie, instead of Hannah's sister."

Miss Lottie stopped, mid page-flip, and stared at Katie. "You have always been Katie. Do you look like Hannah? Of course. That is what twins do. But you and Hannah have always been different."

"But Hannah is better."

"Katie!"

She felt the lump rising still farther, the effort to speak becoming greater. "She is funny and strong and . . . *brave.*"

"Bravery comes in all shapes and sizes, Katie."

"Eric says brave is brave."

"And he is right. Yes, bravery is climbing high in a tree. And, yes, it is following what you know to be right in your heart. But, Katie, it is also things like helping your mother when she is dying, finding your own way through unimaginable grief, and establishing a new normal for your siblings in an effort to ease their sadness, as well."

A pair of tears escaped down her cheeks and she rushed to wipe them away before they could multiply. "People, in New York, think I have talent, Miss Lottie. That my pictures are good."

"You do. And they are."

"Mr. Rothman, Hannah's boss, owns an art gallery. It is this wonderful place with paintings that people come to see. The artist wears a pretty dress and everyone wants to speak to her and ask about her work."

Miss Lottie turned the page, her eyes guiding Katie's across the nuances of another memory her pencil could not ignore. "Keep going."

"In the back, in another, smaller room, Mr. Rothman has started to show things that different people have done. Things he fears will never be seen any other way."

"I take it he wants to show your work?"

Somehow, she made herself answer despite the quiver in her lips. "He already did. When Hannah came home for Mamm's service, she took two pictures without asking."

"I was wondering about these jagged edges." Miss Lottie pointed upward toward the pad's binding and then settled her gaze on Katie once again, waiting.

"She showed them to Mr. Rothman." A soft tisking from Miss Lottie simply hurried her words until they were pouring from her mouth. "When I met Mr. Rothman during my visit with Hannah, he saw the rest of the drawings in my sketch pad and asked if he could display those, too, but I told him no. I didn't know Hannah had already given him permission to display the two she took."

"And he did?"

Hunching forward, mid-nod, she gave in to the tears she was no longer fast enough to wipe away. For a while, Miss Lottie let her cry, her quiet hand on Katie's back a comfort. When the tears finally slowed to a more manageable pace, Katie looked up. "I walked into the room to see what was inside and I saw a man and woman standing in front of a picture I could not see. They said such nice things about it I wanted to see it, too. But when I stepped closer to see, I saw that they were looking at one of my pictures — the one of Mary with the barn cats that Hannah had taken from my sketch pad after Mamm's funeral.

"I yelled at Hannah for letting that happen but" — she pinched her eyes closed, trying to slow her breath and her words — "I liked what those people said about my drawing. I liked that it made them happy and that it made them think of their daughter when she was young. And I liked them saying they wanted to buy it."

Miss Lottie's quiet gasp ushered in the part of Katie's story she still couldn't believe. "After I ran out, they must have bought it. Because when I got home here, to Blue Ball, and unpacked the suitcase you let me borrow, there was an envelope inside with money — lots of money."

"Where is the money now, child?"

"It is under my mattress, where I keep my pencils and" — she pointed at Miss Lottie's lap — "my sketch pad. It is wrong to have such things. I know this. But it is even more wrong that a graven image of Mary now hangs in someone's house in New Hampshire!"

The tears were back. Only this time, when she dropped her head forward, Miss Lottie's arms were there to pull her close. "Katie, Katie, please don't cry. It will be okay . . ."

She pulled back in horror. "If Dat finds out . . . if anyone in the district finds out . . . I will be shunned."

"You've stopped, haven't you?"

"Yah. But now, with the newspaper story, I —"

"What newspaper story?" Miss Lottie asked.

"The people who said such wonderful things about my drawing of Mary bought it for their daughter. The newspaper in the town where she lives did a story on her. She is a veterinarian who has loved animals since she was Sadie's age. There is a picture with the story — a picture of this woman and one of her dogs. Behind her, on the wall, is the framed picture of Mary and the barn cats. Underneath the picture, it says my name as the artist who drew the picture!"

Miss Lottie noticeably stiffened. "How did you find this out?"

"Hannah sent it to me in her letter yesterday."

"Where is the article and the picture now, Katie?"

"I scrunched it into a ball and hid it under the mattress with the money and my pencils."

The sound of Digger's paws on the steps stole their attention and redirected it toward the four-year-old bounding toward them with an empty bubble jar in one hand and a wand in the other. "Me and Digger blew all the bubbles, Miss Lottie!"

Katie wiped all remaining tears from her cheeks with her dress sleeve and stood. "That's okay, sweet girl. Annie is probably awake by now and we need to be getting back to help Mary."

Sliding forward on her rocker, Miss Lottie took advantage of her goodbye hug with Sadie to address Katie. "I'll be sure to have a brand-new bubble jar come nap time tomorrow."

CHAPTER 26

This time, thanks to a little coaxing via a scrap of cheese and a bowl of milk, Sadie and Digger were joined by a trio of cats. Digger jumped, the cats ran this way and that, and Sadie sat on the grass, blowing bubble after bubble for her animal friends. For a while, Katie watched while quietly working through the sounds happening on the other side of the screen door.

Miss Lottie opening the refrigerator . . .

Miss Lottie setting something on the table . . .

Miss Lottie's approaching footsteps . . .

And, finally, the smack of the door as it closed behind Mamm's dearest friend.

"I brought out a bowl of apples instead of cookies. Sadie seems a bit tired today."

She looked out at her little sister and mentally compared the view to the previous day's — a view that had had Sadie jumping alongside Digger, again and again. "Perhaps she is afraid she will hurt one of the cats."

"Maybe you are right." Miss Lottie set her tray with the bowl of apples and glasses of lemonade onto the small table and then lowered herself onto her rocking chair. "How did you sleep yourself, dear?"

"If I could quiet my thoughts, I would sleep better."

"I spoke with Hannah yesterday. After you left. And I'm glad I did because you have one less thing to worry about now."

She pushed off the steps and, instead, perched herself against the railing, her back to Sadie. "I do?"

Miss Lottie nodded.

"But how?" she asked, glancing back at Mamm's friend. "If someone from Blue Ball were to see —"

"The picture came from a very small town paper in New Hampshire. I did a search after our call and found the circulation is quite minimal."

Snapping her focus back to the rocking chair, she stared at the elderly woman. "But Hannah got it in New York!"

"Because the couple who bought the drawing of Mary sent it to Mr. Rothman in a thank-you note. Mr. Rothman, in turn, gave it to Hannah."

"But why would it be in that picture?"

"Because the piece resonated with the couple's daughter so much, she hung it in her veterinary office. When the local paper did an article on her, as per the note to Mr. Rothman, the woman insisted her picture be taken in front of your drawing. She even walked the reporter through its background, which included you as the artist. Hannah sent it on to you as a memory of your work and why it resonates with people."

"I don't need to be reminded of why I draw." Katie stepped away from the railing and headed back toward the stairs, her footsteps heavy against the wood boards. "And I know how it makes me feel when I do it."

"Then tell me."

She sat on the top step and rested her chin atop her knees. "Drawing my memories makes me happy. It is like I am reliving them all over again . . . Like whatever it is I am drawing at that moment is happening in front of my eyes right then and there. And then, when I am done, and I really look at the paper and the memory my pencil has recorded, I smile even more."

"I can see why. But I think there is more to it than that, Katie."

She wanted to argue, to insist it was all about the memories, but she couldn't. Being there, with Miss Lottie, was about owning up to her sins. "When we were on Rumspringa, Hannah would buy these English magazines at the store. She liked to try to make herself look like the girls she saw on the covers. But that is not what I liked about them. I liked to read the stories about girls our same age who did such interesting things. One was a rock climber, one helped care for pets who didn't have homes, one designed clothes, and another took beautiful pictures of people on bridges and paths. Samantha was the one who took pictures. She was sixteen, just like I was. She talked about how photography made her happy.

"I read her story many times those first few weeks. And I looked at the pictures she took that they included in the story, too. I tried to imagine *my* family being photographed in such poses — next to the barn, or seated on our porch chairs, or looking out from Dat's buggy. But instead of seeing everyone looking at me, I began to see different things — Jakob's frustration as he chased the chicken, Mary's joy as the barn cats begged for attention, and so many more memories. I wanted to *see* them again, Miss Lottie."

"So you bought a sketch pad and drew them."

Her chin bobbed against her hands. "Yah. I made so many mistakes at first, I almost stopped. But I didn't. I erased and erased and erased. Each time I erased and tried again, it got better, closer. When I got it right, I felt . . . *proud.* On nights when there was a moon, I would wait until Hannah was asleep. Then, I would sit on the floor by the window and draw.

"But when Rumspringa was over, I could not stop. I liked the way the pencils felt, I liked trying to get better, and I liked the feeling I had when I was done and I could see the memory in front of me." Now that she was talking, she couldn't stop. "When Hannah left, it gave me something to do besides cry. Then, when Mamm was so sick, I felt better knowing I was awake and nearby in case she needed something. And when she was gone, I just had to keep going so I could . . . *breathe.*"

"And now that you've stopped?"

"I-I feel lost." When Miss Lottie said nothing, Katie sagged against the upright. "You think I'm awful, don't you?"

"No. I understand more than you realize, dear." Miss Lottie stilled her rocker long enough to offer a glass of lemonade to

335

Katie. When Katie declined, the elderly woman took a sip and set the glass back down. "In fact, your pull toward art isn't really all that surprising."

"It's not?"

"Your great uncle, Leroy, was a gifted painter. Until he became sick, anyway."

"That is not a name I know."

"Leroy left after baptism."

She parted company with the upright. "So he was banned?"

"Yes."

"If Mamm didn't speak of Leroy to *us*, why would she tell you?"

"She didn't need to. Leroy was my brother."

All movement in the yard ceased at Katie's answering gasp. "Your brother? But that would make you —"

"Your mother's aunt," Miss Lottie interjected. "And *your* great aunt."

The air around her grew so still she was almost certain she could hear the grass moving in the afternoon breeze. Yet despite the sudden quiet, her thoughts were anything but as she tried to make sense of what she was hearing. "But you are . . . *English*. And your name is Jenkins."

"Now, it is. But long ago, when I was not much younger than you are now, I, too, was

Amish just like you. But like your sister, I left before baptism. So that is why your mamm and I could talk."

"But why didn't she tell us you were *family*?"

"Because she didn't know. Your grandmother — *my sister* — was only six when I left. Since I moved so far away, I never saw her again. I didn't know the woman she grew to be or the man she grew up to marry."

"My grandfather."

"Yes. And, therefore, I didn't know her children — which included your mamm — either." Miss Lottie sighed and leaned back in her rocker, her eyes, her focus somewhere far from the porch on which they sat. "When I came here to live just after you and Hannah were born, I didn't make the connection at first. I knew only that she walked by my home each day with the two of you, holding your little hands. In the beginning, I would just wave. Sometimes we would speak of the weather or the crops that were coming to harvest around us, but that was all. In time, there was more chatter, and finally actual visits. I loved watching you and Hannah, and soon, the others grow. And it wasn't until years later, while telling me about Hannah's choice, that I began to put two and two together."

"I don't understand. How could you not have known?"

"I was a Miller, like my siblings. When your grandmother married, she became a Fisher and moved into another district. When your mamm married, she became a Beiler and moved here, to Lancaster."

"Why didn't you tell Mamm when you realized the truth?"

"Because she needed an ear, child."

"Okay, but what about *after*? When Hannah had already made her decision?"

"That's when she got sick and needed a friend."

"Couldn't you have been both?" Katie asked.

"I couldn't chance one for the other. Not when we had such little time left."

"But you left before baptism," Katie reminded, her voice breathless. "That means it would have been okay . . ."

"In theory, yes. But the more I strayed from who I'd been, the more unfamiliar this life became. In hindsight, I realize I didn't want your mamm to look at me differently, and I didn't want to have it change the bond we'd built because we *wanted* to."

"You are good, Miss Lottie. You are kind. Mamm loved you."

"And I loved her, too, Katie. But sometimes fear is the biggest liar of all. It tells you things that aren't true. It makes you doubt yourself, and your worth."

She looked down at her hands and then shoved them under her legs in an effort to stop their trembling. "I feel as if I do that all the time."

"You mean, doubt yourself?" The chair creaked as Miss Lottie rocked forward and stopped. "You shouldn't. Your mamm never doubted you. I don't doubt you. Your family and Abram don't doubt you."

Abram . . .

"When you doubt yourself, child, step back and into the shoes of those who love you and see with *their* eyes. Very often that will bring clarity to your own vision."

Unsure of what to make of Miss Lottie's words, she looked out at the yard and Sadie, the little girl no longer blowing bubbles but, rather, just lying in the grass, her head atop Digger's back. "What became of your brother's art?"

"I have a few pieces in my home. As for the rest, I can't answer that. He got busy, I got busy, and then, one day, it was too late."

Katie watched Sadie for a few moments. "Did he at least have a happy life?"

"I have done some searches, even found

some articles about him. But those speak of his work more, not his life outside of his brushes."

She turned Miss Lottie's answer around in her thoughts until the only question still remaining found its way past her lips. "Why did *you* leave?" she whispered.

"In the beginning, I think it was because I didn't want to lose my brother. But then, once I was out, I got swept up in the English world and, just like a sheep who is too busy eating to notice what's happening around him, I lost my way." Miss Lottie took a sip of her lemonade and then pulled the glass close against her chest.

"But you came back. To a place where Amish live."

"You're right, Katie. I did."

"Why?"

"Because eventually, when I looked up and saw all that I had lost, I realized what I really wanted and needed was the peace this area and its people bring to my life. Even if it's from the outside looking in, now."

"Did you make the wrong choice back then, Miss Lottie?"

"You mean when I chose to leave?" At Katie's nod, Miss Lottie shrugged. "I made my choice. And it was a choice that came with ups and downs along the way. Do I

340

have regrets? Certainly. But all of it — the good, the bad, and everything in between — led me to where I am now — a place of contentment and wisdom."

It was a lot to take in, a lot to digest. Lifting her hand to her brow, she shielded some of the sun's rays in an attempt to see whether Sadie was talking to Digger or, perhaps, napping. "It is different for me than it was for you and for Hannah."

"How so, child?"

"You both had choices," she said, dropping her hand back down to her lap. "I do not."

Miss Lottie returned her glass to the table. *"Choices?"*

"Yah. You could choose to leave and not have it change things unless you wanted it to. Hannah could choose to leave and still be a part of our family. But I do not have those choices."

"You have choices, Katie. And you have made many."

Katie turned and stared at Miss Lottie. "What choices have I made?"

"First and foremost, you chose to stay when Hannah left."

"I couldn't leave Mamm the way Hannah did," she protested. "Especially when she was so sick."

"Your mamm was not sick when Hannah left."

She didn't know what to say, so she said nothing.

"You also chose to keep drawing after your Rumspringa was over." Miss Lottie took an apple from the bowl, polished it with the hem of her colorful skirt, and then placed it back in the bowl.

"But that was wrong."

"And you knew that when you were doing it. Yet you chose to do it anyway, yes?" Miss Lottie slid forward and off the rocking chair, her attention still on Katie even though her gaze had her in the yard with Sadie and Digger. "And most importantly, you chose to get back on the bus at the end of your visit in the city with Hannah."

"Of course I got back on the bus! Sadie made me promise I would come back — that I wouldn't leave her like Hannah did! I couldn't tell her that and then do the opposite . . ."

"Of course you could have, Katie. But you chose not to. You chose to come back."

"I have to take care of them, Miss Lottie."

"Maybe that was the case at first. But Mary can do it now. She is ready."

"But —"

"You have made choices, Katie. All that is

342

left for you to do now is to decide if they're the right ones for you."

CHAPTER 27

She rolled onto her side and stared at the swath of moonlight illuminating the floor between her bed and the window. Before Hannah left, Katie would have been sitting on that same stretch of floor, transferring whatever memory she was desperate to record onto paper. On those nights, when Hannah rolled, Katie had frozen. When Hannah had coughed or uttered something in her sleep, Katie had pushed the sketch pad under the bed and prayed for the moment to pass.

Back then, a single picture could take months to complete thanks to the stage of the moon, Hannah's need to talk into the wee hours of the morning, or Katie's own need to get every detail right.

When Hannah left and Katie no longer had to rely on the moon and someone else's ability to sleep, she could complete a picture in a matter of weeks, instead of months.

But regardless of whether it had been pre- or post-Hannah, it was this exact time of day that had been her favorite of all.

Had been.

Past tense.

Now, the time between Dat's candle going out and being able to fall asleep stretched out in front of Katie like a country road with no visible end. It didn't help, of course, that the pencils she ached to hold were housed mere inches beneath her body. But every time she gave serious thought to throwing them away, she'd found something else to do, instead — a pie that needed to be baked, a floor that needed to be swept, or a stall that needed to be mucked. At. That. Exact. Moment.

"You have made choices, Katie. All that is left for you to do now is to decide if they are the right choices."

She flipped onto her back and stared up at the ceiling. Maybe drawing had been a choice, but stopping wasn't. She *had* to stop. For Dat. For her siblings. For —

A soft knock, followed by Mary's hushed voice, propelled Katie up and off her bed. Padding across the wood floor on bare feet, Katie opened her door, the worry in Mary's eyes igniting a rush of panic up her spine.

She peeked around the corner toward

Dat's still closed and darkened door and then pulled the thirteen-year-old all the way into her room. "Mary? What's wrong? Why are you awake?"

"I am sorry to wake you but something is wrong."

"Wrong? Wrong how?"

"With Sadie. She was making funny noises. I tried to shush her before she woke up Annie, but she did not stop," Mary whispered. "So I went to her bed to check. She was shivering all over, but her face was hot like fire."

Katie grabbed the cloth hanging next to her washbowl and dumped it inside the pitcher of water she used to clean her face each morning. When she was sure it was good and wet, she pulled it out, wrung the excess off, and ran into the hall, looking back at Mary as she did. "Find a blanket somewhere and bring it to me right away."

"But she's hot, Katie!"

"Her face may be, but the rest of her will be cold."

She continued down the hall and into the room shared by her three sisters. A peek at Annie's crib showed no sign of movement from the toddler. Next came Mary's bed, her covers still turned back from her unexpected exit. At the far end of the room, closest to the window, was Sadie, her little body shaking from head to toe.

Perching on the edge of the narrow bed, she brought her lips to Sadie's temple as Mamm had always done when she suspected someone was ill. Sure enough, Mary's description fit.

"I'm here, sweet girl. You're going to be okay. Mary has gone to fetch an extra blanket for you, and I'm going to try to cool your head down a little." She folded the wet cloth in half and gently laid it on Sadie's forehead. Sadie, in turn, barely flinched, her lashes fluttering against her pudgy cheeks without ever fully parting. "Does anything hurt? Like maybe your tummy?"

She ran through a mental list of everything Sadie had eaten that day but came up with nothing different or out of the ordinary. Certainly not anything Katie, herself, hadn't eaten, too. Realizing Sadie hadn't answered, she brought her ears in line with the little girl's mouth just in case she'd missed something.

"Sadie? Does anything hurt?"

Again, Sadie didn't answer — not in words, anyway. Instead, a series of heartbreaking moans made their way past her clattering teeth. Katie glanced over her shoulder at the sound of Mary's approaching feet, the sight of her newly completed quilt tucked underneath the teenager's arm sagging her shoulders in relief.

"Bring it here, Mary."

"The blanket is in Mamm's chest and I didn't want to wake Dat. So I took the quilt you finished last week. I didn't know what else to do."

"No, this is fine. We just need to keep her warm." Katie stood, took the colorful quilt from Mary's arms, and spread it out across the four-year-old. "Shhh, sweet girl . . . this should make you feel better."

The shivering continued.

So, too, did the moaning.

Mary lowered herself down onto the bed next to Sadie's blanket-clad feet and looked up at Katie, her eyes wide. "What's wrong with her, Katie?"

"I don't know. She walked kind of slow on the way to Miss Lottie's this afternoon, but she didn't complain and I just figured she was enjoying the sunshine. Then, when we got there, she didn't run and jump with Digger like she did yesterday, but she still seemed happy."

"She did not eat all of her dinner," Mary offered. "She gave most of it to Samuel, remember?"

Katie did. She also remembered Sadie sitting quietly on the porch while the rest of the family played one of Jakob's silly guessing games. Looking back, she'd seen them all as separate things. But now, in light of the shivers and the fever, they came together in a way that made perfect sense.

"Mamm would have known," she said, her voice barely audible to her own ears.

Mary looked up. "Mamm would have known what?"

"That Sadie was getting sick." Katie checked Sadie's cheeks with the back of her hand, and then flipped the cloth onto its other side. "Mamm was good at being Mamm."

"Yah. But, Katie, you have done a good job since she has passed. You take good care of the little ones and you take good care of all of us. Dat says so, too."

She held her hand to Sadie's forehead and stared at Mary. "He does?"

"Yah. To Miss Lottie."

"Maybe, if I'd noticed sooner, Sadie would not be so sick." Katie turned back to Sadie and gently cupped the little girl's cheek. "Oh, sweet girl, I'm sorry you're not feeling —"

"Ka . . . tie?" Sadie's eyelids fluttered open, her eyes unfocused.

Dropping onto the edge of the bed next

to Sadie, she leaned in close. "I'm here, sweet girl. So is Mary. Would you like a sip of water or —"

"Keep . . . with . . . me . . . here."

"Of course, I'll keep with you here, Sadie. I'm right here. And we're going to get you all better, you just wait and see. You and Annie will be chasing after Fancy Feet and Mr. Nosey the Second in no time."

Sadie released a small moan and then closed her eyes again. Terrified, Katie lowered her hand to the little girl's chest, and when she felt a tiny breath, released one of her own.

"Katie?"

She heard the worry in Mary's voice and tried her best to counteract it with the kind of reassurance Mamm had always given. "She'll be okay, Mary."

"Should we wake Dat?"

Katie thought back over the times she and her siblings had been sick. Never could she recall Mamm summoning Dat from his sleep . . . "No. I'll sleep in here with the little ones. You take my bed. We'll tell him when he wakes in the morning. Hopefully, by then, her fever will have broken and she'll be back to her smiley, happy self."

The English doctor came just after breakfast

the next morning. He walked into Sadie's room, set his black bag on the floor beside her bed, and proceeded to check her head, her ears, her throat, and finally her chest, his brow furrowing at her labored breaths.

"How long has she been breathing like this?" he asked.

Stepping around Dat, she looked down at Sadie, the midmorning light making the skin around the little girl's mouth appear almost blue. "She started making that funny sound just before dawn. That is when I woke Dat and he sent Jakob to get Miss Lottie."

"And before that? What was she doing?"

"Her fever started sometime last night. I wanted to give her a bath, but she didn't have the strength to sit up. Instead, I kept cold cloths on her head throughout the night." Katie stopped, took a breath, and tried to slow her words. "The few times she woke, I made sure to give her sips of water."

He nodded, his eyes never leaving Sadie. "How about during the day yesterday? Any wheezing? Coughing?"

Katie was shaking her head before the doctor was even done talking. "No, nothing like that. She was a little quiet, a little less chatty, but that was it."

"I see." He pulled the stethoscope from

around his neck and popped it into his bag. "Sadie is a very sick little girl, I'm afraid. She needs to be hospitalized."

She tried to hold back her answering gasp, but based on the feel of Miss Lottie's hand on her shoulder, she knew she'd failed. "Why? What's wrong with her?"

"Normally, I'd want an X-ray to confirm my diagnosis, but in this case, there is no need. Sadie has pneumonia. For it to come on this hard, this fast, is worrisome and she needs around-the-clock care."

Nodding, Dat stepped back from the bed. "I'll get the buggy —"

"Wait!" Katie pleaded. "Please. I-I can do it. I can take care of Sadie."

"That's honorable, Katie, but it's not wise. With as hard and fast as this has come on, I'm afraid it will continue to move from the serious case it is now to, potentially, something much more life threatening."

"L-life *threatening*?" Looking back at first Dat, and then Miss Lottie, Katie knew the shock she saw on their faces was surely a mirror of her own. "But she's only four."

"Yes. And that just means there's even less of her to fight with."

She grabbed for the wall and used it to steady herself. "Please! Just tell me what to do to take care of her and I will do it."

"But she's a very sick little girl . . ."

Katie closed her hand over Dat's arm. "Please, Dat. Don't send her away. I-I told Sadie that I would stay with her. Here. Please. I-I know I can do this, Dat. *Please.*"

When Dat looked at the doctor, Katie moved on to Miss Lottie, her growing desperation making it difficult to breathe. "Miss Lottie . . . please. I-I want to do this. I *can* do this. Just let me try."

"Katie, dear, I —"

She met Miss Lottie's gaze and held it steady. "Please," she whispered. "I need to try. For Sadie . . . and for Mamm. I promised I would."

"Doctor?"

Holding her breath, Katie, too, glanced back at the doctor. "Tell me everything I need to do, and everything I need to watch for. If something goes wrong, I will put her in Dat's buggy myself and bring her straight to you."

"Straight to me with no delay." He reached down, retrieved his bag from the floor, and beckoned them to follow him into the hall. "I'm going to call in a prescription for an antibiotic she needs to take twice a day, every day, until it's all gone. Beyond that, just let her sleep. Make sure she's drinking. And if her breathing grows even more difficult or you find anything even the slightest bit alarming, you skip the buggy and use that phone booth between Fisher and Yoder to call for an ambulance, do you understand?"

"Yah."

"Don't make me regret this, Katie."

"I won't. I promise. Thank you, Doctor."

CHAPTER 28

The sun was just beginning its descent when Mary poked her head into Sadie's room, the lack of sleep, coupled with a day spent running up and down the stairs checking on both Sadie and Katie, beginning to show in the thirteen-year-old's stance.

"Katie?" she whispered.

Slipping off the chair she'd inhabited for coming up on eight hours, Katie crossed to the door, glancing back at Sadie every few steps. "Is Annie settled in next to my bed?"

"Yah. Samuel helped me make up a spot on the floor so she can't fall, and I'll be right next to her in your bed if she wakes up and gets scared."

"That is good. Thank you. And please thank Samuel for me, too."

"I will." Mary's worried gaze drove her own back to Sadie. "Has she woken at all since she had her first medicine?"

"No. But I will have to wake her in about an hour to take more."

"She . . ." Mary stopped, took what sounded like a gulp, and then continued, her voice shaky at best. "She's going to be okay, right —"

A sudden rush of footsteps pulled their collective attention from the room and fixed it, instead, on the fourteen-year-old bounding up the staircase. Instinctively, Katie held her fingers to her lips until Jakob's steps became quieter.

"Is something wrong, Jakob?" Katie asked.

Rising onto his toes, he took a quick peek at Sadie, and then lowered himself back down, his gaze seeking Katie's as he did. "Abram is downstairs. He'd like to see you for a few minutes."

"Abram? Abram is here?"

"Yah."

"Why?"

"He heard about Sadie and wanted to see how she is."

"Dat can tell him," she whispered even as she smoothed her hands down the sides of the dress she'd changed into before the doctor's arrival. "I-I can't leave Sadie."

"Dat says Mary is to sit with Sadie while you speak with Abram on the porch."

She started to protest but stopped as

Mary's hand closed over hers. "Katie, it will only be for a few minutes. If Sadie wakes, I will send Jakob for you right away."

"But —"

"You're not leaving, Katie," Mary insisted. "You're just stepping downstairs for a few moments."

Looking back at Sadie, Katie noted the little girl's still-closed eyes and the rise and fall of her chest beneath the blanket. "You are to sit right next to her, and you are to watch her every second."

"I will," Mary promised. "I will even keep Jakob here with me so I can send him to get you if she wakes up or does anything you need to know."

Katie pulled Jakob in for a quick hug and then released him to follow Mary into the room. "I'll just be downstairs. On the porch."

She took the stairs down to the kitchen and then, at Dat's quiet nod in the direction of the hallway, made her way out to the porch and Abram.

"Katie!" Abram stepped from the railing to the doorway with two long strides. "How is Sadie?"

Unsure of whether she could answer without crying, she took a moment to breathe in the night air and to lift her chin

357

to the same gentle breeze that had made it difficult for Mary to clip the laundry to the clothesline earlier in the day. She'd watched Mary fighting with the boys' pants from the chair beside Sadie's bed and had felt bad she couldn't help. But until Sadie was better, there was no other choice.

She jumped at the feel of Abram's fingers beneath her chin as he redirected her focus from the fields she wasn't really seeing to the bright blue eyes looking back at her. "Tell me, Katie."

And so she did. She told him how Sadie had been quiet yet still cheerful the previous day. She told him how Sadie had given Samuel most of her dinner yet never complained about not feeling well. She told him about Mary summoning her during the night and how Sadie had been burning hot with a fever. She told him about sitting beside Sadie throughout the night and changing the cloth on the little girl's head every thirty minutes. She told him how Sadie had woken just once during the night and how she had begged Katie to stay with her. And she told him about the moment when she knew the doctor needed to be called.

"He wanted to put Sadie in the hospital, but I begged him to let me keep her here.

That way I can be the one taking care of her just like I promised Mamm *and* Sadie." She shivered as she stepped away from Abram's touch. "Dat agreed and the doctor told me what to do and what to watch for."

Abram followed her over to the railing and looked out at the fields. "And?"

"She woke once. After the doctor had come and gone. I was able to get her first dose of medicine into her, but she has been asleep ever since. It is difficult for her to breathe. The doctor . . . he says the next few days are critical. And" — her voice faltered — "I . . . I am scared, Abram. She is so very, very sick and . . ."

He turned her to him, his hand finding hers and holding it tight. "And?"

"I cannot lose Sadie." She tried to be strong the way Mamm had always been, but if the tears she felt building behind her eyes were any indication, she was failing, miserably. "She is such a happy girl. She makes me laugh in a way I do not normally laugh. She is gentle with Annie, and kind with the animals. She is so like Mamm. I can't think of life without her."

Katie balled her hands at her sides and willed herself to calm down, to get her emotions under control. But it wasn't until Abram pulled her into his arms and held her close that she was truly able to breathe.

"It will be okay, Katie. This thing that Sadie has may be strong, but Sadie is even stronger. Like you."

Katie listened for any sound of life in the darkened hallway, and when she was sure there was none, she closed the door and headed back toward the window and the lone sliver of moonlight that stopped just shy of Sadie's bed. Beside it, on the floor, was the quilt-wrapped sketch pad she'd commandeered from her room in the wake of Abram's visit.

She'd tried to tell herself that she'd removed it from beneath her mattress as a way to eliminate any chance Mary would find it, but she knew it was more than that. Yes, she'd grown to love the feel of the pencil inside her hand and the sound it made against the paper in an otherwise silent room. And, yes, she loved being good at something all on her own. But more than that, more than all the other reasons she loved to draw, the biggest of all was the opportunity it afforded to record those moments in life that made her truly happy — moments that gave her the strength Abram seemed to already think she had.

Abram . . .

She wasn't sure what had surprised her more, that he'd held her while she cried, or that being in his arms had managed to quiet her fears and give her a much-needed energy boost to see her through until everyone else was fast asleep. Now that they were, she wanted nothing more than to lose herself in a happy Sadie memory.

Closing her eyes for just a moment, she allowed herself to drift back to that first day at Miss Lottie's, when Sadie was matching Digger's every jump as the bubbles she blew sailed high into the air above their heads. In her ears, she could still hear Sadie's happy squeals and Digger's excited barks. With her nose, she could still smell the soapy bubble scent mingling with the chocolate chip cookie Sadie had waited to eat until the bottle of bubbles was dry. And in her mind's eye, she could see Sadie's smile and the way it had transformed her pale blue eyes into something that resembled a bright blue summer sky . . .

After a quick check on Sadie, she pulled the oddly folded quilt onto her lap and slowly unwrapped her sketch pad and pencils from its center. For weeks she'd laid in bed, mentally looking at each picture, seeing them as clearly as if they'd been in front of her. Yet now that the pad was in her hands once again, she flipped past all of them to the first empty page, her fingers seeking and closing around the sharpest of her pencils.

She started with Digger — his body leaping into the air for what would eventually be a big bubble. She drew his hind legs, his arching body, his floppy ears, and his opened mouth. Then she moved on to Sadie — her legs, her torso, her neck, her face, her cheeks, and her eyes coming quickly. It was as if she were back on Miss Lottie's front porch, sitting on the top step, looking out at the scene unfolding on her paper. Twice, Sadie's laughter in her ear was so clear, so real, she'd actually popped her head up over the edge of the bed to see if Sadie had woken.

Never, with any of her previous drawings, had it all come so fast, so right the very first time. She even managed to capture the way the breeze lifted the wisps of hair that had escaped the kapp Sadie always insisted on wearing *just like Katie.*

She added the grass as it swayed in the breeze . . .

She added Digger's collar and the heart-shaped tag that dangled from its side . . .

She added the wand in Sadie's tiny hand . . .

She added the bottle of bubbles in the grass not far from Sadie's bare ankle . . .

She added the bubble responsible for Digger's leap and the laugh that made her look, again, at a still sleeping Sadie . . .

She added a second bubble, just beyond the main one, and somehow managed to capture it just as it was popping on its own.

She added the line of trees in the background, separating Miss Lottie's land from the Amish farm to the east . . .

She added Miss Lottie's fattest cat, as it kept a sleepy yet still-watchful eye on the grand adventures taking place only a few yards away.

She even managed to set the uneaten cookie in the lone bare spot in the yard where Sadie had tucked it for safe-keeping . . .

And, finally, she added the smile she needed to see more than any of it — the smile that endeared the four-year-old to everyone who crossed her path in much the same way Mamm's always had. Its impact reached into Katie's chest and calmed her in much the same way Abram's arms had.

By the time she was done, night was giving way to dawn. Soon, Dat and the others would be opening the door to check on Sadie . . .

Taking one last look at the picture, she made herself close the sketch pad and tuck it, along with her pencils, back inside the quilt. Then, rising to her knees, she pushed it underneath Sadie's bed until she was fairly certain it couldn't be seen by anyone standing in the doorway. If Mary noticed it at some point and asked why it was there, she'd come up with something then.

A strange noise from the top of the mattress redirected her attention back to Sadie in time to see the child struggling to catch her breath.

"I'm here, Sadie. I'm right here. I'm not leaving you, sweet girl."

Sadie's eyelashes fluttered open, her pale blue eyes, dull and tired, stared up at the ceiling in a way that suggested she wasn't really seeing it at all.

"Why . . . is . . . it . . . God's will?"

"Why is *what* God's will?" Katie whispered past the fear working its way up her throat.

"That . . . people . . . die."

CHAPTER 29

Day after day, she sat by Sadie's side, ready with sips of water, the next dose of medicine, and the removal or addition of another blanket. Occasionally, she'd leave her chair to stand at the window and stretch her legs, but even when she did, she spent more time looking back at Sadie than anything outside. When Annie napped and Mary could sit by Sadie's bed, Katie slept. It wasn't adequate sleep but it was better than the nothing she was getting at night when everyone else in the house was asleep and the only sound she could hear was Sadie's labored breath.

She tried to draw at least part of the night away, but other than the picture of Sadie that had been almost effortless from start to finish, Katie had no interest in making anything other than an occasional tweak in some of her other work.

Miss Lottie stopped by every afternoon, her questions always the same; how is she, do you want to take her to the hospital, how are you?

Likewise, Katie's answers followed a pattern, as well; no change, no, and I'll be fine once Sadie is.

The questions and subsequent answers were always followed by the offer to watch over Sadie so Katie could take a break. But it was an offer Katie always turned down. Somehow, the thought of missing even a second of the kind of lucidness she hadn't seen since the whole God's will question was more than she could bear.

So she sat.

She watched.

She listened.

And she tried to quiet her fears long enough to pray.

The lone bright spot in her days came at night, after the post-dinner cleanup sounds had ceased. There would be a knock at the front door, footsteps in the hall below, and then Abram's deep voice would float up the stairs as he inquired about her and Sadie. Each time Dat would offer to have Katie come down, but Abram would always decline, saying she was where she needed to be — by Sadie's side.

Still, he found ways to let her know he was thinking about her — a freshly picked bouquet of flowers, a cookie his sister had made, a bookmark he'd found in an English shop, and a book of poems he thought she'd like. His effort and his kindness always gave her a much-needed burst of happy even if it was short-lived.

It had been five days. Five days since Mary came into her room and told her Sadie was sick. Five days since she'd seen Sadie smile. Five days Sadie had literally slept away . . .

Rising to her feet, Katie made the two-step trek to the window and looked out over her father's fields, her gaze coming to rest on her brothers' black hats as they walked beside Dat surveying the crops they would soon harvest. She tried to imagine what she, herself, would be doing at that moment if Sadie were well.

Maybe a little canning?

Or some gardening?

Or, better yet, baking cookies . . .

Sudden movement from the fields redirected her focus back to her brothers in time to see first Jakob, and then Samuel, take off in a run toward a section of the driveway she couldn't see from Sadie's window. She waited a few seconds to see if they'd return, but when Dat, too, headed in the same direction, she merely returned to her chair.

Leaning forward, she captured Sadie's

hand inside her own and brought it to her lips. "Soon, when you are well, you will help me bake a cake for Dat's birthday. Perhaps Miss Lottie will know a recipe for cherry frosting. Dat would love that, don't you think? And later, the next month, it will be your birthday and you will be five! You are getting so big. This time, next year, you will be going off to school and learning all sorts of fun things like . . ."

A series of footsteps, all far heavier than either Mary or Annie could make, stole the rest of her sentence and sent her attention toward the door. The telltale creak of the second step from the top brought her to her feet.

"Mary?" She started toward the door only to stop as a second and third creak on the same step struck a note of fear where before there had been only curiosity. "Who's there?" she called.

The question was no sooner past her lips when Hannah peeked around the corner, her normally mischievous smile somewhat subdued. "Hello, Katie."

"Hannah?" she sputtered. "What are you doing here?"

"Miss Lottie called and told me what's been going on. I couldn't stand waiting around for word, so we got on the next bus, instead."

"*We?*"

Hannah's eyes moved past hers to Sadie just as Travis stepped into view. Before Katie could fully process their dual presence, another familiar face stepped around the corner.

"*Eric?*" she echoed from behind her hand. "What . . . What are you doing here?"

"Uh, hello? He's worried about you, Katie . . ."

She heard Hannah's words, even registered the playful sarcasm that had ushered them in, but at that moment, in that spot, all she could do was hold her breath and stare.

Eric was *there* . . .

In Blue Ball . . .

Standing less than two feet away from her at that very moment . . .

"Travis told me what was going on with Sadie and I wanted to make sure you're okay." He stepped closer, pulled her in for a quick hug she neither expected nor fully processed, and then released her back to her original position. "How is she? How is Sadie?"

Before she could answer or even fully shake off the sudden and strange fog brought on by his embrace, Hannah made a beeline for Sadie's bed. "Did she just fall asleep? Because I was kinda hoping that seeing me might be just the perk she needs —"

"She's been asleep for the past five days."

Hannah paused, mid-step, and turned to stare at Katie. "Seriously?"

"Yah." Katie trailed Hannah across the room and then stepped around her to check Sadie's breathing and skin color. When she was sure there was no change, she pulled the blanket over the little girl's shoulders. "I can wake her just enough to get a swallow or two of her special drink into her every hour or so, but she does not really see me. And as soon as I lower her head back to her pillow she is asleep again."

"So Miss Lottie was right? She's really that sick?"

"Yah. She is very sick."

"Then why is she here?" Hannah demanded, her voice rising to something outside the whisper category. "Why is she not in a hospital with doctors and nurses who can take care of her properly?"

Katie drew back, Hannah's words hitting her like a slap across the face. "Because *I* am taking care of her. Here. At home. Where she belongs."

"If she's this sick, Katie, she belongs in a hospital!"

"She wants *me*!" Katie thundered back. "*Me,* not a stranger."

"But a doctor —"

"The doctor has told me everything I am to do. And I am doing it." She swept her hand toward first Sadie, and then the chair. "I sit here, next to her, all day and all night. If she moves, I am here. If she doesn't move, I am here. I will take care of Sadie just like I told Mamm I would."

Hannah held up her hands and took a step back, her eyes open nearly as wide as her mouth. "Okay, okay, Katie, relax. I have a right to ask."

"But you don't *ask,* Hannah. You *tell.*" Now that the words were flowing, she couldn't really stop them. "*I* am the one who is here, not you. *I* am the one looking after Sadie, not you. I am the one —"

"Are we back to that again?" Hannah hissed while simultaneously waving Travis and Eric over. "Come on you two, come closer. This is the part where little miss perfect, here, reminds me — for the *bazillionth* time — that I am a horrible person for wanting to have my own life."

Eric stepped between them and quietly cleared his throat. "Hannah, I'm pretty sure that's not what's going on here. So, rather than add more stress where there is already plenty, how about we let Katie tell us what we can do to help. *Katie?*"

She looked from Eric to Hannah and back again, the anger draining from her body along with most of her energy. "There is nothing, unless . . ."

"Unless?" Hannah prodded.

"Unless you would want to sit with me for a while and keep me company? Maybe tell me things you have done since my visit. It has been a very quiet five days."

"Done." Eric motioned Hannah and Travis to take the edge of Mary's bed while he claimed the spot on the floor beneath the window for himself. "So, let's see . . . Oh, I know! Hannah, tell your sister about that award Jack just got — the one you told me about on the bus ride here."

So Hannah told her about Jack and the umbrella stand he knocked over learning to do a cartwheel in gymnastics class. That story morphed into one about the gym Hannah and Travis had just joined and how everyone's umbrellas tended to slicken the floor in the entry foyer. Soon, she was quietly laughing along as Travis pretended to fall backward, his arms spinning wildly in the air above Mary's bed.

"There it is."

She pulled her attention off Hannah and

Travis and fixed it, instead, on the English man looking up at her with the dimples she'd almost forgotten on full display. "There *what* is?"

"Your smile just now. It's as beautiful as I remember it being."

"That's the smile Mamm wanted you to find again, Katie." Hannah interjected. "Because when you smile like that, it means you are truly happy. Like when you saw those paintings in the window of Mr. Rothman's gallery that first time, and when you walked into my apartment after your picnic with Eric."

Katie's gaze flew to the open doorway and the hallway beyond before settling, once again, on Hannah. "Shhhh . . . Please."

"Sorry. I forgot. But you know I'm right."

Keenly aware of three sets of eyes bearing witness to her reddening face, she stood, held her ear to within inches of Sadie's lips, and then lowered herself to the section of the bed most conducive to hand-holding.

"I took Sadie over to Miss Lottie's the day before she got sick." She reached under the blanket and closed her hand over Sadie's. "She and Digger chased bubbles together for close to an hour. She laughed and ran just like we did when we were little, Hannah."

"Who's Digger?" Travis asked.

"That's Miss Lottie's dog." Hannah pushed off Mary's bed and came to stand beside Katie. "He's got to be pretty old by now, doesn't he?"

Katie moved her thumb back and forth across Sadie's skin while watching for any sign of awareness on the little girl's part. "He is. But that day, Sadie had him barking and jumping just like a little puppy.

"And the next day, when we went back, he was out in the middle of Miss Lottie's yard, waiting for another round of bubble play before Sadie even stepped off the porch, isn't that right, sweet girl?"

She waited through Sadie's imaginary response and then transitioned her thumb rub to a whole hand pat. "You'll be running and jumping with Digger again in no time, Sadie. And next time, I want you to blow some of them for me, too. That way I can try to jump as high as you and Digger can."

A silence, unlike any other over the past five days, met her ramblings and forced her line of vision up and onto Hannah, her twin's elevated eyebrow catching her by surprise. "Do you not remember blowing bubbles with Digger when we were a few years older than Sadie? He was just a puppy back then, but you got him so worked up he jumped *over* your biggest jump to catch one of the bubbles I made . . ."

"Of course I remember. How could I not? I also remember you getting excited every time I made one bubble land on another bubble without either of them popping."

Katie dropped her gaze back to Sadie. "Oooh, I will try to show you how to make a double bubble, too, sweet girl . . . just as soon as you're up and about and feeling better again."

She lowered Sadie's sleepy head back down to the pillow, set the glass of water on the floor beside the bed, and tried her best to stifle a yawn. "I would have understood if you'd wanted to stay at Miss Lottie's with Travis and Eric, you know."

"I know. But I wanted to stay here. With you." Hannah patted the other side of Mary's bed. "So we can talk."

"We've chatted — with Travis and Eric, remember?"

"We talked about Sadie and the bubbles, but I want to hear the rest."

She looked up from the wisps of hair she was pushing off Sadie's face and gave permission to the smile she felt building in the corner of her mouth. "If you are wondering if there were cookies to go with the bubbles, there were. Chocolate chip."

"While that's a fun detail, I'm talking about the reason behind the whole bubble visit in the first place."

Casting her eyes back to Sadie, Katie busied herself with a few necessary blanket adjustments. "I thought it would be good. For Sadie."

"I know there is more, Katie."

"You know no such thing."

"I know Miss Lottie called me and that she was upset about what I sent you in my letter. So I know you were talking about me, and New York, and" — Hannah scooted forward across the bed until her head was hanging off — "your sketch pad that you have wrapped in that quilt over there."

"That is not . . ." She let the rest of the denial go and, instead, sank onto her chair.

Hannah sat up, grabbing her hairbrush from beside the pillow. "Don't worry, Katie. I only knew that's what it was *because* I know you. To anyone else, it's just a blanket you stuck under there in the event you need another one."

"Unless they have seen that picture you sent from that paper. The one that could get me shunned if it is seen."

"Who is going to see it, Katie?"

"I don't know, Hannah . . . Maybe someone Amish, maybe someone who knows Amish . . . It could happen." She clamped her mouth over the *because of you* that would serve no purpose. What was done, was done.

"The caption under the picture says only your name and that you are Amish. It doesn't say where you're from or your age or anything." Gathering her hair into a single handful, Hannah pulled it across her left shoulder and began to brush. "Just so you know, there are hundreds of Katie Beilers in America. Even if someone from right here in Blue Ball were to see that picture, it doesn't mean it was you who drew it."

"But the picture is of Mary!" she whispered.

"Who is now six years older."

She wanted to believe Hannah was right but really, the only thing she knew at that moment was that her head was starting to hurt and her eyes were getting very heavy —

"Katie, why don't you come to bed. You need to sleep."

"I sleep when Annie naps. That way, with Mary right here" — she pointed to her chair — "I know I'll be called right away if Sadie wakes up."

"But that's only what? An hour of sleep if you're lucky?"

"Yah."

"Katie, if you don't get more sleep than that you're going to get sick, too."

"She is very weak, Hannah. I have to be able to hear her."

"And you will." Hannah patted the bed again, mid-yawn. "We . . . are . . . just a few feet away. If she moves, one of us will hear her."

"I can't. I —"

"You need to be strong. For when Sadie is well."

Katie looked from her sleeping sister to Mary's bed and knew Hannah was right. If Sadie stirred, one of them would know . . .

"I will try." She made one last check of Sadie, assured the sleeping child she was still there in the room, and then climbed into bed beside Hannah, her eyes heavy with the promise of sleep.

"Katie?"

"Yah?"

"How come you only wrote about the picnic in your journal?"

She stared at Hannah. "What are you talking about?"

"The book the little ones gave you. I found it in your drawer when I was helping Mary put away the wash earlier. You told me when you came to visit that you were to

378

use it to write about your adventures in the city. But all you wrote about was the picnic and —"

"How much did you read?" Katie whispered.

"I don't know, maybe a paragraph or two. I wanted to read more, but I heard the buggy out on the driveway, and I went downstairs to see who was here, instead."

She closed her eyes against the memory of her written ramblings and willed herself to breathe, to sound unaffected. "Hannah, you said yourself, I need to sleep."

"But we did so much those five days. You met Jack, we went to the gallery, we —"

"I don't know, Hannah, I guess I'm just better with pictures than words."

"I guess, but —"

"Please, Hannah, let's get some sleep."

"Okay, but one more question first?"

More than anything, she wanted to close her eyes on the day just as surely as she did her sister's questions, but she knew sleep would come faster if she simply gave in this one last time. "Yah."

"With you talking to Miss Lottie and all, I have to know . . . Have you made your choice?"

"My choice?" she murmured.

"Are you going to stay because you *have*

to or leave because you *want* to?"

Katie rolled onto her side, her back to Hannah.

"Katie? Did you hear me?"

Opening her eyes to the window, she made her breath rise and fall with a sleep that was no longer hers for the taking.

CHAPTER 30

She didn't need Mary or Annie to announce Eric's pending arrival. His footsteps on the staircase were just different. Where Hannah clacked with a seemingly unending supply of fancy shoes, Eric's simple pair of sneakers never changed. Where Travis's steps were heavy with an almost oblivion, Eric's were quiet and respectful, as if Sadie's plight was uppermost in his mind at all times.

So she wasn't really surprised when, glancing over her shoulder toward the open doorway, she saw Eric standing there, studying her with the same concern he'd worn since arriving nearly forty-eight hours earlier.

"Knock, knock," he said, his voice hushed. "Is it okay if I come in?"

"Yah."

Quietly, he stepped into the room, his eyes traveling across a still-sleeping Sadie before landing on Katie and her temporary spot at the window. "No change?"

"No." She turned back to the window and leaned her forehead against the glass pane. "I don't know if I am doing the right thing any longer."

"Meaning?"

"I am doing everything the doctor said. I am giving her sips of water and that special food drink Miss Lottie brought. I am making sure she gets her medicine. I am holding her hand and talking to her about the things we will do when she gets well. But still, she sleeps."

Eric stepped in beside her, his gaze soaking up the same fields she'd stopped seeing days earlier. "Sleep is the body's way of healing, Katie."

Oh, how she wanted to believe he was right. To believe that Sadie was getting stronger somehow. But the hope and conviction that had made her fight to keep the four-year-old at home was starting to wane. "She needs to be outside, Eric. Running with Annie, chasing the barn cats, picking me wildflowers on the edge of the woods."

"In other words, she needs to *just be.*"

Parting company with the window, she made her way back to Sadie's bed, his words and the memories they stirred only adding to her restlessness. "I can't lose her, Eric. I just can't."

"I know."

She sank down onto the edge of the bed and turned the uppermost part of the blanket down along Sadie's chest. "I don't know what to do anymore. I really don't."

The same footsteps that had alerted her to his presence in the doorway let her know he'd left the window and was closing the gap between them. "Come for a walk with me, Katie. The fresh air will do you some good and maybe it'll help clear your head a little."

"I can't leave her," she whispered, looking up. "She might need a sip of water or —"

"Mary can do all of those things. When I was downstairs, she was talking about getting Annie ready for a nap and then coming in here to relieve you so *you* can nap."

"But a walk would mean not being in the house," she protested. "At least if I nap, I'm just at the other end of the hall."

"True. But Hannah said you slept last night and —"

The bed squeaked as she pulled her hands into her lap. "I only pretended to sleep. So she would stop asking me things I do not want to talk about."

"Katie, you can't keep doing this. You're going to get sick!"

"I-I promised Sadie I would stay with her."

"And you have. But you need sleep and you need a change of scenery, too. You've been in this room for six days."

"I told you, I nap with Annie in my own room sometimes."

Shaking his head, he squatted down beside Katie, the concern in his eyes making hers mist. "Katie, you need to get out for a little while. It'll be good for you *and* for Sadie. Besides, I'd love for you to show me some of the places you told me about."

"Places?" she asked.

"Yeah like Miller's Pond, and the place where you stashed your sketch pad when you first started drawing, and the spot where you sat with your mother while Hannah was swinging from trees like a lunatic. You know, *those* places."

Sadie's bed shook with Katie's answering giggle. "Hannah did not *swing* from trees. She just climbed them. And sometimes hung upside down from them."

"There we go. There's that smile." He stilled her restless hand with his own and squeezed. "Come on. Let's go for that walk."

She glanced down at Sadie and then back up at Eric. "But what happens if she wakes up and I'm not here?"

"Someone will come and find us."

"They must promise to come and get me right away or I will not go."

"You got it." He reached for her hand again, this time holding on long enough to pull her up and onto her feet. "Come on. Let's get Mary and be on our way."

Closing her eyes, she lifted her face to the afternoon sun and breathed in through her nose.

"I wish you could see yourself right now."

She stopped walking to check her kapp strings and then her dress. When she found nothing amiss, she looked up at Eric. "What is wrong?"

"Nothing's wrong. You just look so . . . peaceful, I guess."

"But I'm not at peace. I am worried sick about Sadie."

"I know." He gestured in the direction they'd been walking. When she began to move again, he fell into step beside her, his hands finding their usual spot inside the front pockets of his jeans. "Still drawing?"

She listened to the crunch of the graveled road beneath her boots for a half dozen or so steps and then shrugged. "I drew one picture about three or four nights ago but that's it."

"I imagine worry and sleep deprivation would make it hard to draw." He slowed to check out a cow on the other side of the fence and then flashed her one of his dimpled grins. "Though, I suspect, even with all this stuff with Sadie, you'd still draw better than most."

"No, I've only drawn once since I've been back. In Blue Ball."

"I didn't know you went somewhere else."

She motioned toward a path just beyond the fence to their right. "I didn't."

"Whoa." He veered off the edge of the road and onto the grass. "Are you telling me you've only drawn *one* picture since you left New York?"

"Yah."

"But it's been like five weeks since you left."

"Six." She pointed again at the path and continued walking, looking back at him when he didn't budge. "If you want to see the pond and the tree, we cannot keep standing in the middle of the road. I don't want to be gone too long."

He jogged away the gap between them, reaching her just as she left the road in favor of the three-person-wide trail that would take them to Miller's Pond. "Why only one in all that time?"

"I have told you why. The Bible says, 'you shall not make for yourself an idol, or any likeness of what is in heaven above or on the earth beneath or in the water under the earth.' That is what I have been doing. And because of me, Mary's face — Mary's *graven image* — now hangs in someone's office."

"Actually, that was Hannah's doing, not yours," he reminded.

"If I had not drawn Mary's face, it could not hang somewhere." She hurried her pace as they rounded the final corner, her hand sweeping outward as the pond came into view. "This is Miller's Pond. The bench and that picnic table on the other side were added by Englishers as was that sign right there telling people to swim at their own risk. Other than those three things, nothing else has really changed since I was a little girl."

He broke ahead several feet and then turned around. "And the tree?"

"It is right there." She directed his attention back toward the pond and the stump not far from the edge. "It came down in a storm a few years ago."

"I didn't know that."

"The stories I told you were from back

387

when it was still standing. It was bigger than that tree right there" — she pointed to a different maple tree tucked farther back from the pond — "and it had one big long branch that spread out over the water."

"I'm surprised Hannah didn't use it to swing her way into the pond," Eric mused.

"She did. Once. But that is when she cut her chin open."

"Ahhh."

Stepping around him, she headed toward the stump and the patch of dirt between it and the pond. "This is where I would sit with Mamm when Hannah would climb."

"Not always. You climbed sometimes, too, you said."

"Only when Hannah insisted and Mamm encouraged. I liked sitting right here with Mamm more."

"Why?"

"It was safe for one thing." She wandered over to the shoreline and toed at an odd-shaped rock. "I could not fall if I were already on the ground."

Eric's laugh tickled her ears as she looked out over the same pond she'd visited nearly every day since she was a little girl. "Sounds like you've got yourself a meme right there."

"Meme?" she asked, looking back.

"It's like an expression or a thought that

people share on social media that speaks to people on some level. Anyway, I'm babbling." He sat on the stump and rested his forearms atop his thighs. "So go on, why else did you prefer sitting with your mom instead of chasing after Hannah?"

It was a good question. One she'd never really stopped to answer until that moment. But even now, with the passage of time, it wasn't hard to figure out why her younger version had loved coming to this same pond. "With Hannah busy, I could talk."

"You mean about things you didn't want her to hear?"

"No." She took one last look at the water and then made her way back to what was left of Hannah's climbing tree. "For Hannah, the pond was a place to swim or throw rocks . . . The butterflies were to chase . . . The leaves in the fall were to be gathered into a pile and jumped into."

He patted the open piece of stump next to him. When she didn't take it, he rested his chin on his palms to study her. "And what were those same things for you?"

"Look at it." She pointed to the far side of the pond. "Look at the way the sun makes those sparkles shimmer and dance across the top."

Katie skimmed the grass and trees to her

right and to her left before finding and pointing to a butterfly darting from wild-flower to wildflower just beyond the next reasonably sized tree. "And the butterflies? They are all so very different, yet beautiful. Sometimes, when I was little, if I sat perfectly still, one would land on my arm and I could see the pretty designs on its wings — swirls and dots and so many colors."

Bracing his hands on the stump behind him, Eric stretched his legs across the dirt and looked up at the sky. "That's the way I was with songs when I was little. I liked the music, but when a new song came on the radio, I was always yelling at my friends to be quiet so I could hear the words. I guess that stuff was the start of our respective passions in life."

She turned her back on the butterfly to stare at Eric. "I'm not sure I understand what you are saying. What stuff? What passions?"

"Your artwork, my songwriting. I liked song lyrics as a kid, and you saw your surroundings in a way few your age did — with the eye of a budding artist."

Intrigued, she looked around for a patch of leaves on which to sit, but when she found nothing suitable, she eased herself onto the stump beside him. "I'm listening . . ."

"It makes sense, Katie. An artist needs to *see* in order to create pieces that *speak*." He swept his hand toward the pond and then brought it back to his forehead to help filter the sunlight enough to see her face. "And that's what you do. Or, rather . . . *did*. Before you stopped."

She cast her eyes down at the ground and tried to think of something to say, but she was at a loss.

"So tell me, what was the one picture you *did* let yourself draw when you got back?"

"It was the other night. While Sadie was sleeping. I kept thinking about her laughing and playing with the bubbles at Miss Lottie's house. And" — she rose to her feet — "I needed to see her like that again even if it was just on paper."

"Makes sense." He, too, stood, only instead of remaining by the stump, he found a flat rock and carried it down to the water's edge. "But I know from all our talks in the park that you have lots of special memories with Sadie. Why don't you draw those, too?"

"I don't know . . . It didn't take my worry away."

"But seeing her happy had to be a boost, didn't it?"

"For a moment, maybe. But that is all."

Eric cocked back his hand and then flicked his wrist, the motion sending his carefully selected rock skipping across the surface of the pond. "So I officially sold my first song last week. To a fairly well-known singer."

"You sold a song?" At his slow nod, she clapped her hands just below her chin. "Why didn't you tell me this sooner?"

"Because it's not exactly important compared to what you're going through with Sadie right now, you know?"

"But it's your dream!" she protested.

"It's an *accomplishment,* Katie. Is it something that's kinda cool? Sure. But I'm really the only one who's even going to know."

She watched him search the area around his sneakers for another rock before sending it skipping across the water in almost exactly the same spots as the first. "*I* know . . . *Hannah* and *Travis* will know . . . *Your father* will know . . ."

Dropping his elbow back down to his side, he maneuvered the uneven ground between them until he was standing no more than two feet away. "Here's the thing with what I do, Katie. I write what I think is a good song. If I'm lucky — as I was in this case — a singer buys it and combines it with their talent. If all goes well, maybe it'll become a song that you'll hear people singing on the street or in a car or on a beach somewhere. And I'll get a kick out of that, don't get me wrong. But I'm smart enough to know that it'll be the *song* people know, not me."

"I don't understand."

"People hear music and they either like it or they don't. If they like it, they'll listen to it again and again, even learn the lyrics so they can sing along. But they won't remember the name of the person who wrote it, if they even bother to find out that information in the first place."

Resting her hands on her hips, she shook her head at him. "Don't say that!"

"I'm not saying it to sound like a martyr or to be whiney or whatever, because I'm not. I'm just telling it like it is so you don't put more on this whole thing than it really deserves, you know? Dreams are great, they give you something to walk toward. I just don't want to discount the squirrels anymore."

"Did you just say *squirrels*?"

His smile was followed, in short order, by the dimples she loved. "Don't look at me like I just grew a second head, Katie. Before you, I saw the park as an easy way to get from point A to point B most days. The people I passed, the paths I took, and the squirrels that scurried across my path were essentially background noise."

"The paths are noisy?"

"No. It's an expression. The people, the paths, the squirrels were all there, but I didn't see them. I was always focused on the end goal — to get to this meeting or that restaurant or that friend's apartment. But with you it was different. Suddenly it wasn't about getting somewhere, it was about *being.*"

"But that is what you said to me, remember?" She plucked a leaf off a low-lying branch and slowly spun it between her fingers. "You said *just be.*"

"Funny thing is, before your visit, that was just something I said, you know? It sounded good, maybe even a little deep." He backed himself up against a nearby maple tree and tucked his hands back inside his front pockets. "But now, because of you, so much is different, better."

"It is nice, what you say. It really is. But I don't know how someone like *me*" — she scrunched her nose — "can change something for someone like *you.*"

Crossing his arms in front of his chest, he met and held her gaze with his own. "Remember those people in the park I referred to as background noise a few minutes ago?

I actually see them most days now. And all those offshoot paths I'd never bothered to check out because I didn't have the time? I've made a point of trying a new one every week or so."

"Where do they lead?"

"Usually to the same exact place as the next closest path. But definitely still worth checking out."

"That is good, yah?"

"Absolutely. And that brings us to the squirrels . . . They're actually fun to watch if you take the time. And let me tell you, when one of them doesn't want to give up an acorn to the next guy, they sure can move faaaast —"

A strange sound from the direction of the path made her turn in time to see a familiar horse rounding the bend. Before she could even begin to recognize the animal, the buggy it was pulling came into view with Abram at the reins.

"Abram?" she rasped, stepping forward. "What are you . . . ?"

The rest of her question faded away as the reality of the last six days returned to the forefront of her thoughts. "Oh no, oh no, oh no . . ." She ran toward the path with Eric close on her heels, her mind's eye noting everything from Abram's widened eyes to the way his hands looked unusually white around the reins. "Abram? Abram, what's wrong? Is it Sadie? Has-has something happened to her?"

"I stopped at your Dat's farm to check on you again and while I was there, talking to Hannah, Mary called down to say that Sadie is waking up. When Hannah said you went for a walk, I said that I would find you. Come, Katie, come, I will get you there quickly."

Katie ran around the front of Abram's horse to the opposite side of the buggy, reaching up for his hand as she stopped. But as he helped her up and onto the seat, she looked back to find Eric still standing in the same spot. "Please, Eric, come, quick! There is room for you if we all squeeze close. But we must hurry! I want to be there when Sadie opens her eyes!"

He waved her offer away before returning Abram's nod of acknowledgment. "No. Go. Be with Sadie. I can find my way back."

CHAPTER 31

She'd watched Hannah take the stairs two and three at a time throughout most of their childhood, but until that moment, Katie had always been the one lagging behind, taking it slow — making sure not to fall, get hurt, or be too loud. Knowing Sadie was starting to come to just beyond the top step, though, changed everything. In fact, now that she thought about it, she wasn't entirely sure Abram's buggy had come to a complete stop before she was off the seat and running for the front door.

"I'm here! I'm here!" she called as she crested the last step and turned left toward Mary's room, her heart seemingly vacillating between rapid, staccato beats and no beats at all.

More than anything, she wanted to believe Sadie was truly waking. But the other part of her — the part that had been sitting by her little sister's side nearly nonstop for six days — was afraid it was nothing more than the periodic semiconscious state that enabled medicine and liquid nutrition to be ingested.

Stopping just outside the open doorway, she made herself breathe — in, out, in, out. "Please, Sadie," she whispered. "Please . . ."

Hannah popped her head through the doorway, grabbed Katie by the forearm, and pulled her inside. "She's awake, Katie!"

She looked past her twin to the little girl stretched across the bed no different than she'd been when Katie left. Her heart sank. "No, Hannah, she does this. She opens her eyes but she doesn't really look at anything. It's enough for me to get her medicine and a few sips of her special drink into her, though, so it's better than nothing."

Steady footsteps just over her shoulder pulled her attention off Sadie and fixed it, instead, on the top of the staircase from which she'd just come. Abram stepped into full view, his gaze seeking and holding Katie's long enough to offer a nod of encouragement and a smile that belied the emotion she saw in everything from the way he swallowed, to the way he clutched and unclutched the top post. "It is a shame to waste such speed now, Katie."

"I-I'm sorry, I didn't mean to jump from

the buggy like that," Katie said, glancing back at Sadie in her bed. "I thought she was really waking up. But I just need to give her that special drink the doctor wants her to have."

Squaring her shoulders, she stepped into the room, made her way past Hannah, Travis, and finally Mary, and claimed her spot beside the narrow bed. With a practiced hand, she felt Sadie's forehead, cheeks, and —

A gasp from the general direction of Mary's bed made her look up long enough to follow the teenager's pointed finger right back to a now wide-eyed Sadie. Grabbing the edge of the bed for support, Katie leaned into the little girl's sight line.

"Ka . . . tie!"

She heard her answering intake of air, even felt the sway of the bed as Abram lunged forward to keep her from falling off the open side, but really, all that mattered at that moment was the clear-eyed little girl smiling — *smiling!* — back up at her with the kind of love Katie felt all the way down to her toes. "I'm here, sweet girl, just like I promised."

"We're here, too, Sadie!" Hannah said, moving in beside Katie and gesturing toward Travis and Mary.

Sadie turned her head just long enough to smile at the other faces in the room before they scattered to share the news, and then brought her undivided attention back on Katie. "I feel better!"

"I am so very, *very* glad to hear that, Sadie." And she was. In fact, there was no amount of lip nibbling, cheek biting, or rhythmic breathing that could hold back the tears of joy now running down her cheeks.

Sadie, in turn, yawned and rolled onto her side, her pale white hand instantly moving in to pillow her soft cheek. "I love you, Katie. Abram, too."

Abram . . .

Katie watched Sadie's eyes drift closed and then turned to find Abram smiling at the two of them with so much love in his eyes it literally took her breath away. Like the chair that had provided her weary body shelter during the nearly weeklong string of sleepless nights, her faith and Abram's quiet yet steadfast support over the past six days had given her what she needed most — strength. And hope. "She-she's going to be okay, Abram," she whispered in a voice choked with so many different emotions it was a wonder she could talk at all.

"Yah."

"Thank you, Abram. Thank you for understanding my need to stay by Sadie's side, and for coming to get me when she began to wake. I-I don't know what I would have done without your support these past six —"

Something resembling pain faltered his smile a split second before he waved off the rest of her sentence. "Sadie is well again. That is all that matters."

And then he was gone, the fading sound of his footsteps enveloping her in an all too familiar sadness.

She was waiting alongside the covered bridge on Route 15 when Abram slowed his buggy to a stop beneath the large maple tree that shielded the oft-dry creek bed from the view of passing cars. With three easy motions, he jumped down from his seat, tethered Tucker to the trunk of the tree, and pulled his drawing pad off his seat, the anticipation she would have expected to see noticeably absent.

"I was hoping I'd find you here," Katie called out as she stepped out from the side of the bridge to meet him. "And . . . here you are."

The sparkle her unexpected presence ignited in his eyes was just as real as it was short-lived. "Katie? Is everything okay? Did

401

something happen with Sadie?"

"No. No. Sadie is fine. She even ate all of her own scrapple and some of mine this morning. Miss Lottie says that is a sure sign she is feeling better."

"That is good to hear." He peeked over his shoulder at the road. "I don't see your Dat's buggy . . ."

Dropping her hands to the sides of her lavender dress, she shrugged. "That is because I walked."

"Alone?" he asked, looking around again. "Yah."

"But Miller's Pond is" — he pointed in the direction from which they'd both come — "that way."

She made a face as she met and held his gaze. "I know that, Abram. I'm here to see *you*."

"*Me?*"

"You sound surprised."

He studied her for a second before stepping around toward the large rock she'd suspected he used. When he reached it, he lowered himself to its relatively flat surface and repositioned his flat-brimmed hat to lessen the glare of the noonday sun. "I guess I am. Surprised, that is."

"About what?" she asked, shifting her weight from foot to foot.

"That you found me here, for starters."

"It's lunchtime. And you said this is where you like to come to plan out the next piece of furniture you will make."

"You remember that?"

"Of course." She held her breath as a butterfly fluttered to a stop on the sleeve of her dress, and then redirected her focus back to Abram as it flew off. "And the other reason you're surprised I'm here?"

"Because of the Englisher at your Dat's farm."

"You mean Eric?"

Pain propelled his attention off her face and down toward the pad of paper in his hand. "Yah."

"Eric left this morning. Travis and Hannah leave tomorrow."

"I imagine that makes you sad?" he asked, glancing back at her.

"I'll miss our talks, but that is where he belongs."

"Will you follow?" he asked. "When Sadie is stronger?"

She drew back, startled by the question. "Follow Eric to New York? No, of course not. *This* is my home."

"But I saw your face when you were together. He made you happy at a time I could not."

She tried to make sense of what he was saying, but just as she started to ask for clarification, the memory of Abram and Tucker rounding the corner near Miller's Pond the previous day brought everything into focus. "I was happy *for* Eric yesterday. But I was not happy. Sadie was still sick."

He shifted the pad in his left hand to the rock. "After that first night, you did not leave Sadie's side when I stopped by. But yesterday, you went to the pond. With the Englisher."

"Annie was napping and Mary sat with Sadie." But even as she said it, she knew her answer sounded hollow. Abram was smart, observant, and thoughtful — all qualities that had led them to this place.

Harnessing every ounce of courage she could muster into a single inhale, Katie closed the gap between them, sweeping her hand toward the vacant section of rock to the left of the pad. "May I?"

At his nod, she sat down, pulled the pad onto her lap, and flipped back the cover, the detailed drawing of a corner cabinet sucking the air from her lungs. "Oh, Abram, this is . . . this is *beautiful.*"

"I sold it last week. At the furniture store in Goodville. The person who bought it has asked me to build a chest with the same edging as this." He pointed toward the cabinet, his finger brushing across the piece's top and side edges. "And this morning? I got an order from the person's neighbor, who wants me to make a new table for their kitchen."

Her answering squeal echoed through the air. "That's wonderful! Before long, you will have that furniture shop you spoke of!"

"If it is God's will."

"You don't sound as happy as I would have expected," she said, looking between Abram and his picture and back again. "Isn't this what you said you wanted?"

"With you, yah. But without you, it is just a different kind of work."

Flipping the cover back into place, she set the pad to her left and scooted closer to Abram. "Mary was wonderful with Annie and the boys these past few days."

"I'm glad."

"I am, too, for it means she is ready to take over for me."

"Take over for —" He stopped, pulled up his shoulders, and sighed. "You really think you will be okay with not seeing them again?"

She pivoted her body atop the rock so she was facing Abram directly. After a beat or two of silence, she covered his hand with her own. "I'm hoping we can find a home here in Blue Ball. Dat says there's one with a small field not more than a mile or two from Miss Lottie's place. Even has a workshop behind the barn that would be perfect for you."

"But —"

"*This* is what I want, Abram. *You* are what I want." Slowly, hesitantly, he lifted his gaze to hers. "But the Englisher is the one who makes you smile."

"He does, yes. And I'm thankful to him for that. The sadness I felt after losing Hannah made it so I couldn't think straight. All my life I was Hannah's sister and then, one day, she left. I wasn't sure how to be me without her. Or even if there *was* a me without her. And then Mamm got sick and went to the Lord and I was needed here. To be . . . *Mamm*."

She tried to breathe, to slow the words in the event Abram couldn't keep up, but it was no use. Now that she was talking, she couldn't stop. All she could do was pray that somehow, someway he would understand. "And my pictures . . . They were mine. I-I thought that stopping them would mean I'd just keep on being Hannah's sister and Mamm's stand-in. But then, this week, when Sadie got so sick, I didn't want to draw anymore. I could have . . . I had plenty of time . . . But when she was lying there, so sick, I realized it's *all of you* that make me whole. It's the laughter and joy I get from watching Samuel chase down a chicken. It's the peace I feel when I look out the window and see Mary and Sadie walking hand in hand. It's the contentment I felt watching Mamm working in her garden, and it's the strength and love I felt from you these past few days."

"I did not do anything, Katie. I wanted to . . . I really did. But I couldn't."

"Oh, Abram, even when I did not see you, I felt your hand in mine every time you stopped by to check on us. You knew that I needed to be with Sadie, and you honored that. Thank you, Abram. Thank you for being there for me and for Sadie in all the ways that mattered most."

This time, when he looked at her, there was only joy — the same joy she felt clear down to the soles of her feet. "There is nowhere I would rather be, Katie."

She was halfway through her fourth yawn in a row when the light from Dat's candle disappeared beneath her closed door. "I guess it is time to say good night."

"Not when it's our last night together, it's

not." Hannah swung her legs over the side of the bed and stood. "We've got less than twelve hours until Travis and I head back to the city."

"Hannah, it has been a very long day on top of many long days and I haven't slept for more than an hour or two at a time since the night Sadie got sick. Even last night, with Sadie doing better, I was still too restless to sleep. Afraid, I guess, that it was all just a dream."

"I know, and I know I should probably let you sleep . . . but I just want a little time together first. Please?"

She wanted to protest, but she was too tired. So, instead, she mustered up enough energy to pull off something between a groan and a frustrated sigh. Hannah, of course, ignored both, dropped into a squat next to her side of the bed, and retrieved the sketch pad Katie had recovered from Sadie's room during a lull in activity.

"Hannah, no. Please. I'm too tired to talk about that stuff right now."

"I just want to look, that's all. I want to see what you've done since you left."

Somehow, she managed to push herself up to a seated position despite the overwhelming urge to roll onto her side and pull the covers over her head. "I've only drawn one picture you haven't seen. It's of Sadie and Digger."

"Playing bubbles?" At Katie's nod, Hannah set the sketch pad on the center of the bed, climbed into place next to Katie, and flipped back the cover. "You've been home for six weeks, Katie. Surely you could've drawn more than one picture in all that time, yes?"

"Maybe. But I do not want to be shunned."

"Then why the picture of Sadie?"

Katie nestled back against the pillow and stared up at the ceiling, her words coming faster than she would have expected considering how badly she wanted to sleep. "I *needed* to draw that picture. For me. Besides, it helped make that particular night pass much more quickly."

"I would have thought, with you being awake all night anyway, that you'd have been drawing like crazy."

"I made a few tweaks in some of my earlier pictures, but really that was just about changing the curve of a mouth or an eye, that sort of thing."

Picture by picture, Hannah made her way through the book. Picture by picture, Katie studied her sister's reactions — joy, quiet laughter, sadness, back to joy, and, finally, to the surprise she both expected and welcomed.

"Um, Katie?"

She closed her eyes. "Yah?"

"This Central Park picture? The one of Travis and me on the bridge that you did from the picture I gave you?"

A variety of possible replies flitted through her thoughts but when she could barely make her eyelashes part enough to even look at her sister, the notion of speaking probably wasn't smart. Besides, if there were any truth to the whole notion that she had God-given talent when it came to drawing, she really just needed to wait . . .

"You added a scar just like mine," Hannah said, tapping her finger atop the sketch.

Katie fought through another yawn. "Yah."

"But why? You don't have a scar."

"I know. But you do."

When Hannah said nothing, Katie forced her eyes open and onto her sister. "The picture you left is of you . . . With Travis. The whole reason I drew it in the first place was to see if I could do it. That's all."

"But in the beginning you drew *you* instead of me."

"Yah. But that's because I wasn't sure of my place anymore. All these things were happening to make my world look different and it scared me. When we were little and you came across something new, you always wanted to do and *then* think."

"If I thought at all," Hannah quipped.

"But *I* wanted to think first. I needed time to step back and look at it through my own eyes rather than yours. And now that I've had that time, I see that *you*'re the one who belongs on that bridge. It's your world, Hannah, not mine."

Hannah pushed the sketch pad farther into the center of the bed and then spun around to face Katie. "Don't you see? That world can be yours, too, Katie. I mean, I know you'd miss Dat and the children terribly — especially Sadie. But you would still have me. And you'd have Travis . . . And Eric . . . And Mr. Rothman . . . And Jack . . . And all sorts of people you're still yet to meet."

Reaching back for the sketch pad, Hannah wiggled it at Katie. "And best of all? You could *draw* there, Katie! You could have a real art desk! And you could put your pencils in a drawer instead of wrapping them in a paper towel! You could draw in the middle of the day and leave your work on your desk! You could give more to Mr. Rothman for that special room in his gallery! And you wouldn't ever have to worry

411

that you're doing something wrong or that someone is going to find out and make you repent *for drawing a picture!*"

On the surface, Hannah was right. Moving to New York City would make it so all those things she'd just said would be true. But as wonderful as some of those things sounded, their cost was simply too great . . .

"Did you know that colors have meanings?" Katie asked, pulling her pillow around to her chest. "That yellow is happiness, and green is nature and hope, and purple is creative?"

"No, I didn't know that. But I guess that means you probably should change your favorite color to purple."

"Actually, I think blue fits me better than ever now."

Hannah lowered the sketch pad back down to her lap and sighed. "Why?"

"Because blue is open and free. Like the sky. And like choices."

"Choices?" Hannah echoed. "Does this mean you've decided?"

She released her hold on her pillow long enough to point at the still-open sketch pad. "Keep turning."

"Why?"

"You will see."

Hannah held her gaze for several beats

and then did as Katie asked, her fingers flipping to the next picture in the pad — the one of the toy sailboats and the ducks in the pond. "I love this one. I feel like I'm you, Katie. Like I'm looking out at all of this through your eyes."

"Good. That is what I had hoped."

"So when are you going to add yourself in?" Hannah asked, looking up.

"I'm not. *You* are."

Hannah's brows furrowed. "I don't understand. How am *I* going to add you in? I don't draw, remember? That's your thing."

"Your view into that scene is through my eyes. *That's* how I'm there." She reached across the sketch pad and flipped ahead to the picture she'd made in one sitting, yet adjusted in bits and pieces over each of the nights that followed.

Hannah laughed the moment her gaze fell on the bubbles flying in the air, just out of reach of Digger's paws and Sadie's outstretched hand. "Oh my gosh, Katie, this is great! The way we see just her hand . . . It's as if *I'm* her and *I'm* the one reaching for the bubble."

"Yah. But that is not how I drew it at first."

"Oh?"

"See that?" She moved her finger around the page, stopping again and again to point

413

out the numerous yet faint erase marks throughout the foreground of the drawing. "And that right there? That was Sadie, chasing the bubble."

"Meaning?"

"You could see her face, her smile."

Hannah studied the picture for a few moments, her mouth contorting in different shapes and positions. When she was done, she shrugged, dramatically. "I actually think what you changed it to is even cooler. I can feel her excitement as if *I'm* her . . . As if *I'm* the one reaching for the bubble . . ."

"Don't you see?" Katie scooted up next to her sister, pointing at the drawing as she did. "I *can* draw here, Hannah! *In Blue Ball.*"

"How?"

"I don't draw the faces."

Hannah scrunched up her nose. "I don't understand."

"I don't draw the faces. I mean, I don't really need to. I'm already here *with* my loved ones — with Dat, with Samuel, with Jakob, with Mary, with baby Annie, with Sadie, and with Abram. I don't need to draw their faces. I can see them every day."

"I'm not here . . ." Hannah reminded, her shoulders drooping.

"I know, but you are only a letter and a bus ride away, remember? And as for my

414

memories, I still have them right here." She pointed at her head and then her heart. "But now, when I take out my pencils, I get to use them to help me see those same memories in a different way. I can see what it was like for Mary to have those cats climbing all over her . . . I can see what it was like for Samuel to try and catch that chicken . . . Or what it was like for Mary to watch him try . . . Or what it was like to look down, into that lunch pail, and find the frog that Luke Hochstetler put inside . . . Or to see the garden that Mamm so loved from inside *her* eyes rather than my own . . . Don't you see? I can still do all the things Mr. Rothman loved about my drawings. But instead of making someone *want* to see their life in a different way, I can help them to actually *see* it. Instead of showing them an innocence as he said, I can let them *feel* it. If you are Samuel and you're chasing the chicken, you will feel his panic or his urgency. But if you are Mary and you're watching him chase the chicken, you will feel her joy and her laughter."

"I guess." Hannah leaned back against the plain headboard and sighed. "But are you sure? Because I think you'd like it in the city, I really do."

"For too long, I have seen myself next to

you. I didn't climb like you did. I didn't run like you did. I wasn't daring like you were. I didn't make bold decisions like you did. I saw only what I did compared to you. But just because we look alike, doesn't mean we are the same. It is like these memories." She ran her hand across the drawing of Sadie and Digger. "For me, I saw *Sadie* jumping and laughing as she chased the bubbles. For Sadie, it was all about *the bubbles* and *Digger.* For you, when we were little and at the pond, you saw trees as things to climb. For me, I saw them as places to sit and talk with Mamm about all the pretty things around me. For you, leaving Blue Ball was a fresh start. For me, leaving and then coming home was a reminder of what makes *me* happy.

"I am not you, Hannah. I am me. New York is your choice — for you. Being here, in Blue Ball, is my choice — for me."

"What about Eric? He made you happy. I saw the way you smiled every single time you got back from spending time with him."

"Yah. He is a good man. He has taught me much."

"But . . ."

"I love Abram."

Hannah drew back. "Are you sure? I mean, *really* sure?"

"Mamm said that when I was little I loved to look at the sky but that she never knew why. She just knew that there were times when I was upset or worried or scared about something and then, when I would look up, I would smile."

"You *still* do that, silly."

"Well, I think I've finally figured out why. Only I didn't figure it out looking at the sky. I figured it out looking into Abram's eyes. I see hope in his eyes, just like I do when I look up at the sky. Hope is faith, Hannah. And I can't imagine living my life without faith."

Dropping her head onto Katie's shoulder, Hannah sighed. "I get it, I really do, but I'd be lying if I didn't say I was a little disappointed. For me. I've spent a lot of time imagining you coming to live with me in the city."

"But that's not all you've pictured about your life there, right?"

Hannah sat up, grabbed the sketch pad, and swung her legs over the bed once again. "I take it you're talking about the whole hairstyling thing?" At Katie's nod, she shrugged and then gestured toward the pad. "Should I put this back in its spot?"

"For now, yah. Soon, I will show it to Abram so he can see what it is I would like to do. Perhaps, one day, one of my pictures can be sold in a store in town, or even in the special room in the back of Mr. Rothman's gallery."

"I don't think there will be any *perhaps* about it, Katie. You're good. Really, really good."

"And if that is true, that is nice. But I do not need people to buy my pictures to be happy. I do not even need to draw to be happy. I enjoy it, and I will continue to do it without faces, but it is really the people I have made my memories with that make me happiest of all."

Hannah's soft laugh filled the space between them with something other than joy. "Wow. I don't know what to say other than I am happy for you."

"And I will be happy for you when you are able to do hair the way you want."

"Thank you, Katie, but it will be a long time before I can take classes to learn what I must learn. I am fine to live and to eat, but there is not extra money for such things."

"That is not so." Swinging her own legs onto the floor, Katie got out of bed, reached underneath her side of the mattress, and extracted the same white envelope Hannah had hidden in the bottom of Katie's suitcase at the end of her trip. "Remember this?" Katie asked, holding it up.

Hannah's eyes darted from Katie, to the envelope, and back again. "Is that the money you got for your drawings?"

"It is." Locking eyes with her twin, Katie extended the envelope in her direction. "It took me a while to see it, but I'm where I want to be, where I *choose* to be. So I don't need this. Instead, I want you to take it and use it to figure out where *you* want to be. Take classes, go on a trip — it's up to you. I just hope that one day you, too, will find whatever it is that gives you hope and brings you peace."

■ ■ ■ ■

READING GROUP GUIDE: PORTRAIT OF A SISTER

LAURA BRADFORD

■ ■ ■ ■

ABOUT THIS GUIDE

The suggested questions are included to enhance your group's reading of Laura Bradford's *Portrait of a Sister*.

DISCUSSION QUESTIONS

1. When Katie steps off the bus in New York City, she's more than a little overwhelmed. In many ways, it's like she's landed on a new planet. Have you ever gone somewhere that is so utterly different from everything you've ever known? Did you like the change — why or why not?

2. All her life, Katie has been a rule follower. She's done what was expected of her, when it was expected of her. It's the way she is, and the way she's seen by everyone else — even herself. Do you feel as if you're seen a certain way, and do you find that you maintain that because it's the way you are, or because it's the way people expect you to be?

3. Katie keeps her drawings to herself because she knows it's something she's

not supposed to do. But she also keeps it to herself because it's something that is hers, alone. So much of her life has been about following a certain path and acting a certain way, yet in this one area, she allows herself to be different. Do you have a hobby or a passion that you either indulge in now or hope to at some point? What is it? And what about it speaks to you?

4. While there was the potential for Eric to become a love interest for Katie, the friendship was richer in many ways. Through his eyes, Katie was able to see herself as something other than just a daughter and a twin sister. Do you have a close friend of the opposite gender? Is that friendship different than ones you have with people of the same gender? How so?

5. If someone you loved had an extraordinary talent and you had an opportunity to help them go somewhere with that talent, would you? Why or why not? Do you think Hannah acted selfishly in showing Katie's pictures to her boss?

6. What do you see as the turning point for Katie — the moment when she realized

the path she'd been walking was, indeed, the right path for her?

7. If you were Katie, what would you have chosen? For bonus questions and/or to find out how the author might be able to Skype or call in during your group's discussion of the book, visit her website at www.laurabradford.com.

For bonus questions and/or to find out how the author might be able to Skype or call in during your group's discussion of the book, visit her website at www.laurabrad ford.com.

ABOUT THE AUTHOR

Laura Bradford is also the author of several bestselling mystery series, including the Amish Mysteries. She lives in Mohegan Lake, New York, with her husband and their blended brood. Visit her website at laura bradford.com.

The employees of Thorndike Press hope you have enjoyed this Large Print book. All our Thorndike, Wheeler, and Kennebec Large Print titles are designed for easy reading, and all our books are made to last. Other Thorndike Press Large Print books are available at your library, through selected bookstores, or directly from us.

For information about titles, please call:
  (800) 223-1244

or visit our website at:
  gale.com/thorndike

To share your comments, please write:
  Publisher
  Thorndike Press
  10 Water St., Suite 310
  Waterville, ME 04901